Inheriting Murder

Jerry Evanoff

Seven Four Press

Inheriting Murder

(Sam Norris Murder Mystery Series, Book 2)

Contents

Please consider joining my Facebook Author Page.
https://www.facebook.com/jerryevanoffauthor

I sprinkle in pictures of my dog, my food, some random true crime and info about my latest books.

Chapter One

Carey Layne had said goodbye at the hospital, cried at the grave and sat down tonight to hear his father's words one last time.

"I, Emmitt Layne, a resident of the state of Georgia, in the United States of America, being of sound mind and body, declare this to be my last will and testament, dismissing any and all wills and codicils previously made by me."

The longtime Layne family attorney, Allen Bryce Foster, peeked over his glasses, making sure everyone was ready for what came next. Then, using two fingers, he pushed them to the bridge of his nose and continued reading.

"To Kristie Breckenridge. You were the daughter I had always wanted but never had, and I'm glad I found you when I did. You've meant more for Savannah Palms than anyone else. The day I hired you was the day this place turned the corner and became what it is now. I can't thank you enough for what you've done."

Brock Layne, the second oldest of Emmitt's four boys, spun his head around to Kristie, who stood near the kitchen door with three of Emmitt's most trusted course employees working the event by making dinner and serving drinks. The plastic water bottle Kristie held crackled as she squeezed it, a tear running down her face. Emmitt had told her not to work while his will was being read. She would attend the event as a member of his family, but even standing in the back, looking more put together than in her normal work clothes, she still kept an eye on her kitchen.

"To you, I leave the sum of twenty-five thousand dollars."

Kristie ducked her head and offered a small, bittersweet smile, acknowledging Emmitt's kind words along with his generous gift.

Next to Carey, his girlfriend, Madison York, also turned toward Kristie while whispering in Carey's ear. "That was sweet of Emmitt. I don't think she expected anything."

Brock turned around, facing Allen while his foot tapped against the floor. At another table, Dexter Layne, the third oldest, moved closer to Emily, his wife of fourteen years.

Carey followed Allen's eyes as he checked the room, wondering what his brothers had been expecting from the will. He shook his head slightly. "Four brothers sitting at four different tables," he whispered to Madison. "Dad wouldn't have wanted it this way."

It was the first time Carey had seen Brock and Dexter in the same room at the same time in a long while. It had already led to one argument. Carey hoped to get out before round two.

He glanced toward Peyton, the oldest and most successful of the four brothers, once a promising quarterback prospect for the Atlanta Falcons. A shoulder injury had ended his career before it started, but while he was playing, he wrote down names and friended the right people. After his career was over, he built the Layne Sports Group, a sports-marketing agency that landed endorsements and appearance deals for athletes who weren't yet household names. Carey saw so much of his father in Peyton, not only in his look but in his ability to create something successful from nothing more than an idea.

Next to Peyton sat his one mistake in life: his fiancée, Maryanne Preston. Her hair was big, the kind of big that could easily survive a Georgia hurricane, and her face was made up like a piece of artwork by a painter who had used all his paint. Jewelry covered her neck and ears. In front of her sat her favorite drink, an Aperol Spritz. That drink—its bright orange color, the oversized glass and the orange slice hanging on to the rim—represented a microcosm of who she was. Everything about her was bigger, way too flashy and certainly more than what was called for on a night like this.

"Typical," Carey muttered under his breath as Maryanne very delicately took the orange slice off the glass and set it on a cocktail napkin without taking a sip.

"To Brock and Dexter. I leave the sum of ten thousand dollars each."

Brock's eyebrows shot up, and his foot-tapping ceased. He blinked twice and scowled at Dexter, who had let out a chuckle as the number was being read.

"To Carey, my youngest—"

"Wait," Brock said. "Ten thousand? That's all I get? No explanation? No kind words?"

"That's what it says," Allen said as he once again adjusted his glasses, moving them a little further down the bridge of his nose.

Brock pushed back from the table, his chair screeching against the tiled floor. "You can keep your shitty ten grand. I didn't want any of the old man's money anyway."

It was another lie of the many Brock had told. He had spent most of his adult life moving from one "big thing" to the next, usually with big ideas that came with big speeches and big promises that led to someone else paying the bill. Sometimes he was forced to take jobs, but after a few months, he would grow bored and quit. When money was tight, he would show up at family functions, usually leaving quickly with a check from Emmitt.

"I'll take it if you don't want it," Dexter said.

Brock stood and shouldered past a cart, knocking a water glass to the floor. Kristie's eyes narrowed, and she exhaled through her nose. She held out her hand to one of the employees, stopping them from cleaning up the spill. The last thing she needed was another employee quitting because of Brock Layne. She grabbed a towel from a tray, and while keeping her gaze on him, she approached to clean it up herself.

"Old man dies and turns me into a fucking punch line," Brock muttered.

"Mr. Layne," Allen said, his voice holding the authority that had been missing from the golf course since Emmitt died. "Sit down and be quiet."

"Save it, Allen," Brock said. He took one last drink from his glass and dropped it on the floor next to the towel. "Clean that, too," he said to Kristie. "Use some of your newfound cash." He hurried toward the door and left the room, sending all eyes to Dexter.

Dexter didn't say much. Only eighteen months younger than Brock, he shared many facial characteristics with his brother: a narrow face, close-set eyes, and a cleft in his chin. But time, along with Brock's smoking and drinking, had changed him. He and Dexter were no longer mistaken for twins.

The chuckle Dexter had let out wasn't at the paltriness of his inheritance. He had received his money while Emmitt was still alive. His house had been paid for, his debt had been erased, and Ethan, his teenage son, wouldn't have to worry about college. Dexter had bragged more than once about how he had used the old man's money correctly, while Brock kept "pissing it away." His chuckle was of amusement at another ten thousand he hadn't expected.

The room quickly settled, allowing Allen to continue. "To Carey, my youngest."

Carey sat up, holding his breath as feelings of dread flooded into him. Madison put her hand on his.

"I leave the sum of one hundred and fifty thousand dollars."

But then Allen stopped talking. He was at the end of the sentence. He didn't add "and full control of Savannah Palms Golf Course" as Carey had been hoping, as the others had been expecting. Emily looked his way, her face showing sadness as if she were giving Carey a mirror of his own expression.

Allen continued reading. "I know what we talked about this summer, son, but you're not ready to run a business. Not yet. You have big dreams, but the little details, the things we do each day to keep the customers coming back, still escape you. If you really want to take over, use this money, and get yourself educated. Finish your MBA. Get involved in the day-to-day, and when you are ready, you'll be like your old man, even reaching as high as your oldest brother and possibly higher."

Carey exhaled, absorbing the words as Allen spoke. He had known this was a possibility. His father had told him more than once during the summer that he wasn't sure if Carey was ready to take full ownership of the course. He had turned thirty-four a few days earlier, and though he was technically an adult, his father had not always treated him that way. Now that the decision was final, Carey couldn't find the words to express his disappointment.

He pulled his hand away from Madison's and went back to fiddling with the cuff of his shirt. It felt too large. He ought to have worn a cufflink as Madison had suggested, but the only one he had, a silver one with two golden crossed golf clubs, had seemed more adequate for a happier day. Unwilling to give in to feeling like a child who didn't belong at the big table, he ignored everyone else and kept his eyes on Allen.

"Are you all right?" Madison whispered.

"It's fine," Carey said. He wasn't in the mood for sympathy. He had thought about following Brock through the double doors, picking up a golf club and hitting balls until the anger was gone, but that would have validated his father's thoughts of him still being a child, and he wasn't about to do that.

Allen continued. "To Peyton, my oldest, I leave the remaining sum of my estate, including the houses in Savannah and Fort Myers. I also leave to you Savannah Palms Golf Course. Take care of it as I did, son."

Next to Peyton, Maryanne let out a soft, involuntary gasp. She leaned closer to him and put her hand on his. Carey glanced at her, his brain still trying to understand why his father had decided against him owning the course. He had been doing the job for months by himself, including the day-to-day, as his father lay dying in the hospital. He had done a great job at it, and he knew the course better than anyone, especially Peyton, but now any hope of it becoming his had disappeared. In the end, he was still another employee working for someone else in the Layne family.

Allen read, "Work with Carey, teach him how to run a business. Show him how you made yours so successful. If he decides to go back to school, work with him. If you think he's ready, then let him take it over. Make him an offer. If you don't, keep it or sell it, it's up to you."

Carey looked back at his oldest brother, surprised by the conditions his father had put on him. How could his future hinge entirely on a brother he barely knew? Peyton was twenty years older than Carey. They rarely spent any quality time together. Why would it be his decision?

Allen cleared his throat and finished reading the will, continuing his father's instructions to Peyton. "Take good care of the employees, especially Kristie. Do not let her take an offer from anyone else. Without her, without them, the course would still be the money pit it was when I bought it."

Emily stood. "Peyton gets everything? Just like that?"

"You're surprised?" Dexter asked as he raised both hands in the air. "He was always Dad's favorite."

Emily glared at him. "Stop that," she said. She waved her arm toward his, her hand catching his glass of water. She lunged for it, but it toppled off the table, most of its contents filling Dexter's lap.

Dexter shook his head and stood, his lips pressed together. "I need to go clean up." He pushed his chair back and walked out, tugging the tucked-in wet shirt out of his pants as he left through the same set of doors Brock had used.

Allen adjusted his glasses. He held Emmitt's will in the air. "That's what it says."

"But there are four boys." Emily looked back at Carey. "How is that fair? Why should it all go to him?"

Maryanne let out a high squeak while Peyton cleared his throat the way people do before they're about to make a speech. He grabbed Maryanne's drink; the seltzer water in front of him was not strong enough to help him face down the rest of the family during dinner. He downed his wife's drink in one gulp. Heads turned their way, but Peyton said nothing, and the awkwardness in the room grew. It was how the brothers had always reacted when an emotional elephant was in the room – all except Brock, who had left kicking furniture aside.

Allen gathered the paperwork and stuffed it into a manila folder. "That's it for me tonight. If anyone has any questions, stop in and see me bright and early tomorrow morning."

"Won't you stay for dinner?" Maryanne asked.

"Oh, no, thank you," Allen said as he hurried past the head table toward the kitchen's swinging double doors. "I'll grab something from the cook for the ride home."

"Thanks, Allen," Peyton said.

"Yes, thanks, Allen," Maryanne said. "We appreciate everything you've done."

Carey stared at the attorney, watching him disappear into the kitchen. He tried to breathe. Madison touched his arm again, but he pulled away.

"I'm going to call my mom."

Carey saw the hurt in her eyes, but said nothing. Instead, he watched her leave. He had considered reaching for her, but she meant well. They had been together for eight years. She knew he needed a few minutes to himself and was always willing to give them before comforting him.

***

Kristie spent the next ten to fifteen minutes refilling drinks, putting together the dinner plates and bringing them out to each table one at a time. The earlier outbursts had given way to a quiet room, with a few of the family members forcing smiles to hide the anger they held inside. She started with Peyton and Maryanne, serving the head table first, as she would at any banquet. Emily had left the room a few minutes after Allen to gather Dexter, both returning as their dinner was being put down in front of them, while Brock had also come back. One thing about Brock, he never passed up a free meal.

Serving Carey last, she approached him carrying two plates, one in the palm of her hand, the other resting on her forearm. Carey turned again but found no sign of Madison.

"Is she coming back?" Kristie asked him. "Should I leave both of these with you?"

Carey nodded without looking up.

"Are you okay? I know you thought—"

"I will be," he snapped, a little more anger in his voice than he had wanted. He took a breath and looked up at her. "I didn't want to believe it could happen, but deep down I always knew it was a possibility."

"I'm sure it will work out," she said as she put her hand on his back, rubbing soft circles.

Madison returned to her seat next to him. Before sitting, she smoothed her dress and leaned in closer.

"Mom says hi," she whispered.

Carey stabbed at his baked potato. "How is she doing?"

"She's already planning Christmas. She asked if we're coming down."

"I'm not sure if—"

"I told her we didn't know," she said, nodding toward his plate. "Eat something. You're going to get a headache."

"We're already past that."

Kristie had started to enter the kitchen, but she stopped mid-step, and her shoulders tightened. Carey followed her eyes.

"Something's wrong," he whispered to Madison.

A man stood in the doorway, half in the hall, half in the room. He appeared to have wandered into the wrong banquet hall but decided to stay anyway. Kristie walked toward him fast, not the way someone moved when they were trying to be polite.

"I saw him in the pro shop," Madison said. "He didn't look like he was interested in buying anything."

The man lifted his hands toward Kristie, his palms out, as he was signaling that he hadn't done anything wrong. Kristie pointed to the hall, her mouth moving, but she was whispering, and Carey couldn't make out her words. The man answered, his chin tipping forward. Kristie stepped closer, putting herself into the man's space. She jabbed a finger toward the hall again, holding it there. After a beat, his shoulders slumped, he muttered something, and backed into the hall. Kristie stayed in the doorway for an extra second, watching the man go. When she turned, her eyes found Carey's. He froze, his fork halfway to his mouth, but her face didn't change.

She held his eyes longer than he found comfortable, then looked away, heading back into the kitchen, saying nothing.

"What was that about?" Madison said.

"I don't know." Carey pushed his potato around his plate, turning his attention back to Peyton and Maryanne. They were the only two people in the room who seemed happy.

"We could move to Tampa," Maryanne whispered.

Her whispers were a normal volume for everyone else, although in this case, Carey sensed she was speaking loudly on purpose. She didn't like the rest of the family, and they weren't exactly fond of her. She had come out of nowhere, romancing Peyton, convincing him to get engaged, all in less than a year. They were troubled by her, but she never seemed to care.

"And we can get that big boat we talked about."

"I thought you wanted to go to Europe," Peyton said.

"We'll do that first," she said, her voice a little louder.

A sharp clink cut through the air as Emily's fork hit her plate, metal against porcelain, not by accident. Heads turned, including Maryanne's.

"We could have a place in both," Maryanne said as she turned her head enough to glance at the rest of the family. The corner of her mouth curled up slightly. "Maybe somewhere in Spain near the coast. You know how much better that Spanish sun is for my complexion."

"Oh, Jesus Christ," Emily mumbled.

Maryanne pulled a tissue from her purse, rose, and headed toward the women's restroom. As she disappeared through the door, Emily got up and began walking toward Peyton. Dexter grabbed her arm, stopping her.

"What are you doing?"

Emily didn't answer. Instead, she fixed her gaze on Peyton, shook free of Dexter and clenched her fists. She approached him, the four-foot width of the table the only thing separating them. She leaned forward and rested the palms of her hands near his empty plate.

"You're going to sit and tell us with a straight face you didn't know what was going to happen?" Emily asked.

"I'm as surprised as the rest of you."

"In that case, how about you do what's right and give Savannah Palms to Carey? Sign it over to him right now. I'm sure we can catch Allen and make it legal."

Peyton looked up at her as if she had asked him to donate a kidney. "You heard his instructions. I get to decide after a year what I want to do."

Emily's voice rose. "And now the golddigger gets to squeeze every dime out of this place before you eventually sell it? You do realize she's not going to let you keep it."

Flattening his hands on the table, Peyton countered, "Say whatever you want about me, but leave her out of it."

Dexter stood. "Come on, Peyton, we all know it's true. Why can't you see it?"

Now Peyton stood. "Look at you. At all of you. Brock throws a fit like he always does when he doesn't get what he wants. Dexter shrugs it off, but you"—he stared at Emily—"you always want more." He glanced past her at Carey. "And you sulk as if—"

"I'm not sulking!" Carey cried out. His voice had come out in a squeak.

Peyton smiled, a stifled laugh escaping his lips. "You want to know why Dad gave me the course? I'll tell you why. He gave it to me because I understand what it takes on a daily basis to manage people, manage customers and manage everything that keeps a business going. You're still young, you have a vision, nothing more. You can see in your head what you want this course to be, but you have no idea how to get it there. That's why—"

A fit of coughing interrupted him, allowing Carey to say, "I've been working every day! I know more about this place than you'll ever know."

Peyton reached for his water again and took another sip. "Knowing where to hit the fairway on the third hole isn't knowing the golf course. It's keeping the kitchen stocked, the pro shop profitable, and the maintenance budget from bleeding out every time some idiot drives a golf cart into the pond."

"You're a jerk," Carey said.

Sitting down again, Peyton took another sip of water. His expression softened. "I'm sorry it worked out this way. I really am, but this is a huge deal for Maryanne and me." He looked at Emily, his face tightening. "I've already decided I'm going to sell this place after that year is up, along with both of Dad's houses."

"Everything?" Carey asked.

"I'm really sorry, Carey," Peyton said, pausing again to cough. "But this is the chance for Maryanne and me to live the life we've been dreaming of."

"You mean the life Maryanne's been dreaming of," Dexter said.

"What are you talking about?" Peyton asked, his calm demeanor wearing away.

"You know exactly what he's talking about," Brock said.

Peyton's cough was more violent than the last. He tugged at his collar, pulling it away from his neck. "Dad gave it to me and—"

He stopped talking as the color drained from his face. His eyes widened. A single bead of sweat rolled down his forehead.

Emily stepped away from the table. "What's happening?"

"I...I... can't...breathe," he gasped, grabbing at his neck. His chest heaved with every forced breath.

"Someone call a doctor," Emily said, her voice trembling. Her eyes darted around, seeking help, but no one moved.

Peyton began to rise, but his hand slipped on the chair's edge, and he fell to the floor. He rolled onto his back and tried to speak, but nothing came out. Maryanne appeared in the restroom entrance, paused to see what was happening, then rushed across the room. She dropped to her knees next to Peyton.

"He's choking," Emily said.

"On what?" Maryanne screamed. "What did you give him?"

"Nothing. We were talking."

"Nuts," Peyton managed to choke out.

Maryanne sprang from the floor and grabbed her purse. "How the fuck did he get nuts?" She pushed her dinner plate to the side and flipped her purse, dumping the contents on the table. Her drink crashed to the floor, most of the liquid splashing Emily. Maryanne rummaged through the pile, tossing items to the side.

"What are you looking for?" Emily asked.

"EpiPen."

"Did it fall to the floor?" Carey asked, scanning the area around Emily.

"Got it!"

Maryanne lifted the EpiPen. She turned it once but paused and stared at the label. Something was clearly wrong. She touched the tip where the cap should be, but it wasn't there. Her eyebrows squeezed together, and she squinted, a slight twitch in her hand.

Peyton wheezed, and Maryanne spun around. She drove the pen into his thigh through his pants. The click cracked through the entire room. Peyton's body went stiff. His back arched, and his jaw clamped shut. His eyes widened, then shut, and his body curled. He came to rest on his side. A gasp escaped from Maryanne's lips as she waited for him to open his eyes. She leaned closer, grabbing him and rolling him onto his back again.

"Did it work?" Dexter asked, breaking the silence.

Carey hurried around the table, stopping a few feet from his brother's limp body. Dizziness overtook him, and he fell into an empty chair.

"No, no, no!" Maryanne's scream pierced the air. "Wake up, damn it! Wake up!" She sobbed and clutched Peyton's inert body, pulling it close to hers, but his glassy eyes, staring beyond Carey, said he was gone.

Chapter Two

Early the next morning, Sam Norris sat at his desk for the first time since returning from South Plainfield a couple of weeks ago. Dani had come for a few days from Wyoming, and after what they had gone through, they both decided to take another week off from work after she had left to go back home.

He pulled his keyboard forward, fired up his laptop and opened his email. It showed over one hundred emails that he had missed while out. They were a mix of meeting invites, email chains he had nothing to do with, and junk mail. Without thinking about the consequences, he highlighted the entire list and pressed delete.

"If it's that important, they'll reach out again," he mumbled as he ran a hand through his short brown hair.

Behind him, one row over, he could hear footsteps. A chair rolled, then bumped into a desk. Another chair followed, the wheels rattling, a groan as someone took their seat.

Linus's voice came first. He sounded quiet but cheerful. "Look who decided to come back to work."

Another one of the web developers, Scott Lancaster, spoke next. "Welcome back, Sam."

Sam didn't look. He lifted one hand, offering a small wave and moved his mouse to the company's chat app, which gave him access to everyone in the entire company, including those at the manufacturing plants worldwide. He double-clicked the list of names he had saved into his favorites. Slowly, he removed everyone, then looked for one name. He found it and added it to his empty list.

She was green.

He double-clicked, opening the chat window. There was no history. It struck him they had never chatted one-on-one with each other. They had only met a few weeks earlier. He had been in Wyoming, then she had come to Savannah. She had only left a week earlier, and he already missed her more than he had expected. He tapped out a message.

Sam: Morning. You're still there?

He waited. Three dots. They disappeared but then reappeared again.

Dani: Morning to you. I'm still here, but I'm leaving soon. You at your desk?

Sam: I am. Feels strange being back, but at least it's a short week. How's the plant doing?

Dani: Feels strange here, too, but we're not shipping much this week with us being closed on Thursday and Friday. How was it last night?

Sam's fingers paused, hovering over the keyboard. Linus's chair squeaked. Papers rustled on his desk as he set a bag down with a thud. Sam knew what it was. Linus stopped every Monday morning at a donut shop on his way in and brought a breakfast sandwich and a donut. Sometimes he brought donuts for everyone, although he hadn't come by Sam's cube yet to give him his.

Sam: It was long. Carey didn't want to be alone. He hung out until after two. I'm not on much sleep right now and could use a nap.

Dani: He doing okay?

Sam: He's trying to act like he is, but he's not.

Another email hit his inbox, a meeting invite forwarded from Carly, this one starting in a few minutes.

Dani: I missed you last night.

Sam moved his hand to his desk, feeling for the bumps of the dried super glue he had left there years back when he tried to stick a rubber foot back onto the bottom of his keyboard and made a mess instead.

Sam: I missed you too.

Dani: Did he say what happened?

Sam glanced over his shoulder at Linus and Scott, who were standing, chatting over their shared cubicle wall. Scott pointed at his watch and held it up, showing it to Sam.

Sam: I can't get into the details right now. Carly scheduled a meeting. I'll call you on your lunch.

Dani: Promise?

Sam: Count on it.

The small dot beside her name switched from green to yellow, signaling she had stepped away from her computer. Sam rolled his chair back, staring at her last message before clicking the window closed.

"Are you coming?" Scott yelled to Sam, his voice carrying across the IT area. It was a small section in the back half of the building, seven desks with four-foot cubicle walls separating them from each other and six-foot cubicle walls around the outside, keeping the rest of the building from seeing inside the IT area unless they walked into it.

Linus grabbed his bag and stepped into the aisle behind Scott. Sam grabbed his notebook and stuck a pen behind his ear. He stood. The office looked the same way as it always did. Gray, bland cubicle walls, fluorescent lights overhead and the low hum of printers. He kept his eyes forward, not interested in talking with anyone who wanted to hear all about what had happened in South Plainfield. He had already talked to the local news and newspaper more times than he had wanted. He'd told the story over and over and had no desire to tell it again.

The Mini Main was the smallest of the two conference rooms in Morello's headquarters. It seated eight to ten people around an oval table and had a television monitor built into the wall that could easily be accessed by plugging any laptop into an HDMI port built into the table.

Linus was the first through the door, taking his usual seat, the last chair near the end, his back to the door. He set down his laptop, opened it, took his sandwich from the bag and set it in front of him. Lastly, he took out three donuts and set one each in front of himself, Scott and Sam.

"You remembered," Scott said.

"Of course," Linus said as he wiped the crumbs from his beard.

Sam took a bite of his donut, nothing flashy, a simple glazed, and ran his forearm across his mouth, wiping the sticky sugar from his lips. Carly was the next one through the door. She was the trio's manager, having started at the division around the same time as Sam. She was well-liked throughout the building, including by the three web developers she oversaw, and most thought she would be the successor to Gil Graham, her boss, who had been talking about retirement. She stood tall, taller than either Sam or Linus, although Scott had a few inches on her.

"Did you tell them?" she asked Scott.

Scott's eyes widened as he looked up at her, chewing the last bit of his donut. He looked toward Sam and Linus, then shook his head.

"Tell us what?" Sam asked.

Carly put down her laptop and plugged it into the projector. The wall glowed white until it caught up with her laptop and mirrored her computer screen. "We have two things to talk about and a half hour to do it, so no dilly-dally."

"Two things?" Linus asked. He took a donut from his bag and set it in front of her; a smile appeared on her face. Like Scott, she liked the chocolate-covered ones. "But there was only one thing in the meeting invite."

"While we were in South Plainfield, the company was hacked," Carly said as she pulled the donut closer.

Sam and Linus exchanged looks.

Carly continued. "Someone in one of the overseas offices clicked a link they shouldn't have, and it took us down, but only briefly."

"We were down?" Sam asked.

"Okay, you talk now," Carly told Scott. "I'm going to eat my breakfast."

"We were down about an hour," Scott said. "It was while you guys were on the jet. I flipped us to the secondary network pretty quickly. Once you landed, you wouldn't have noticed a difference."

Scott Lancaster had turned thirty-one while Sam and Linus were in South Plainfield. Originally from Las Vegas, he had spent the first four years of his programming career working in the basements of several casinos along the Vegas Strip.

"They get anything?" Sam asked.

"They weren't out to take anything. It was one of those 'give us money, or we delete your stuff' type situations. Gil told me to pay them."

"That's like letting the terrorists win," Linus said.

"I said the same thing," Carly said.

"Gil didn't care. He told me to do whatever it took to get back up and running. We needed to do it and do it fast."

Sam wasn't surprised he had gone to Scott for this. Scott was a good programmer, a great networking guy and a better database analyst, a skill needed in the department as both Sam and Linus considered it their weak spot.

"How much did we pay?" Sam asked.

"Four and a half Bitcoin."

Sam did some quick math in his head, his eyes widening. "Isn't Bitcoin like nineteen thousand dollars each?"

"Last time I checked," Scott said, "it was nineteen thousand, three hundred, forty-six dollars and twenty-nine cents."

"You know that to the penny?"

Scott shrugged. "I like to dabble. I may not play poker anymore, but I still like to mess around with my money."

Sam and Linus glanced at each other. It wasn't exactly breaking news that someone living in Vegas played poker, but they hadn't been able to learn much about Scott since he'd started. He rarely talked about his life in Sin City, and he had no social media at all for Sam to stalk. He was tall, thin and had a scar near his right eye that Sam and Linus had speculated about multiple times, but they hadn't yet asked how he got it.

"The grand total was a little over eighty-seven thousand dollars. Gil told me to take care of it." He paused before continuing and looked around, making sure the coast was clear. "I'm not supposed to say anything, so keep it to yourself. I don't know how good it would look to our customers if they found out we were hacked. We may be a manufacturing company, but we send apps to our customers for them to use. We should be better than that."

"Why did we pay in the first place? We have backups. We could have shut everything down, spun up a few new servers, pulled the data from the backup, and we're back where we were."

"Gil said the development time we would lose was far more valuable than a few bucks."

"We're keeping this to ourselves for now," Carly said. "We're still trying to assess the damage and determine what we can do to keep them from hitting us again." She turned and punched a few keys on her browser. "As for meeting topic number two, we're going to talk about a new corporate time-saving app that Gil wants us to use for project management."

"We already have something for that," Linus said.

"This is called TNT."

"TNT? Seriously?" Sam asked.

"It stands for Top Notch Teamwork."

"An explosion of teamwork!" Scott said, holding his arms in the air as if he were signaling a touchdown.

"Something like that." Carly pulled up her browser and began to type the URL of the new app, but a headline across the top caught everyone's eye. It was about the death of Peyton Layne.

"How's Carey doing?" Linus asked.

"He was at my house last night for a while, hanging out, chatting for most of the night."

"What's going to happen to the course now?"

"No idea," Sam said. "But I'm hoping Carey will be at the course tomorrow night. Maybe he'll have more details."

"Guys," Carly said. "Focus. We have twenty-three minutes left to talk about TNT, then I'm off to another meeting."

She moved her presentation to page one. It showed a cartoon-like piece of dynamite exploding a host of numbers onto the people gathered around it. The numbers showed percentage increases in efficiency inside the company's different departments.

"That's really awful," Sam said.

"I know it is," she said. "But we all know this won't last long. A higher-up was hired, and they need to leave their mark. For now, that mark is TNT and its triangles. I need the three of you to smile and nod so I can tell Gil we talked about it." She spun back in her chair and looked up at the screen.

As Carly began explaining how TNT used a triangle structure to handle its project management, Sam opened an app on his laptop that allowed him to send a text from his phone. To everyone else in the room, he was following along and taking notes, but in fact, he'd sent a text to Carey, asking how he was doing and if he would be at the golf course tomorrow night.

"And Gil wants us to use this going forward," Carly said.

"But what about what we currently use?" Linus asked. "Do we have to transfer everything to this? That's gonna take hours."

Sam turned his attention back to Carly, but a response came through quickly from Carey, saying he'd be there. Sam replied he'd go early so they could hang out before his round started.

He had already learned what it was like to lose his parents, and Carey would need someone to lean on for the next few days, probably months, as he worked through it. Carey had been there for him. He would return the favor.

Chapter Three

Sam sat in a golf cart next to the thirteenth tee at Savannah Palms Golf Course watching Linus go through his pre-shot routine. Next to him sat Madison York, with the fourth in their group, Libby Price, sitting in her cart ahead of them.

"I was hoping Carey would be here tonight before we started," Sam said to Madison.

"He was a little late getting out of the house, but I texted him a few holes ago, and he's here now."

"Do you mind if I ask what happened Sunday night?"

"He didn't tell you?"

"Not much," Sam said. "We talked about the past, lots of reminiscing, trying to remember the good times."

"After the will reading, I knew Carey would want a little time to himself, so I left the banquet room and went outside to call my mom. I talked to her for maybe fifteen minutes, and when I came back, dinner was being served."

"He didn't leave the room with you?"

"I don't think he left the room all night," she said. "Although I can't be sure. I do remember Emily yelling at Peyton in front of everyone, which surprised me. She's always so quiet. Then Peyton began choking."

"In front of the entire family," Sam said. "How awful it must have been for them."

"Kristie was there, too. He must have thought of her as family because he left her twenty-five thousand dollars. She got more than Dexter and that fuck-up, Brock. It pissed off Brock enough to make him leave, but he did come back for dinner."

Sam turned his head and leaned back a little, surprised to hear those words come out of her mouth.

"Sorry," she said. "As Carey and I were walking in that night, him and Dexter were fighting about something. The words that came out of Brock's mouth at the reading of his father's will were awful. He's trash."

"What did they argue about?"

"Same thing Brock always worries about, how to get more money from that family." She shook her head and turned to Sam. "Sorry. I really can't stand him."

"I see that."

"You know, there was one guy there briefly who I don't think belonged there. He looked homeless, standing in the doorway. I thought he had wandered in off the street, but when Kristie saw him, she hurried over and made him leave."

"Any idea who he was?"

She shook her head. "I'm still surprised Emmitt didn't leave Carey the golf course, but he'll take the money his father left him, make good decisions, and I bet he eventually buys this place from whoever ends up owning it."

"Doesn't the course go to Maryanne?" Sam asked.

"I don't know how the law works, but they were only engaged, so I assume it stays in the family."

Madison pulled the scorecard from her pocket, and Sam watched as she counted the number of holes she had won so far.

"Through the first three, I'm up two to nothing," she yelled to Linus, who had stopped with his pre-shot routine and stood over his ball, staring at it as if he could will it to go straight, something he rarely did on the thirteenth. It was teed up and ready to be struck, but Madison didn't care. "You were lucky on twelve, so you only owe me fifty cents."

Linus backed away from his ball, clenched his jaw and shifted his weight from one foot to the other, taking short practice swings as he moved. He looked over his shoulder at Madison.

"Thanks," he said, his voice flat. "I really needed the update after three holes."

"No problem," she said with a smile. "Make sure you're careful here. I know you love the trees."

Sam leaned closer to Madison and whispered, "Why do you do that to him? You do realize that we're all on the same team, right?"

"I love messing with the little runt," she said.

Sam hopped off the cart and walked over to Linus. He put his hand on his friend's back and kept his voice low to avoid Madison hearing his pep talk.

"Pretend we're back on ten, and you're getting ready to hit your first ball of the day. You always hit that one straight."

Linus nodded, although Sam knew exactly what was going through his head. For Sam, it was the sixth hole, a long par five with a sand trap in the middle of the fairway that always seemed to swallow up his second shot. For Linus, it was thirteen. It didn't matter what kind of swing change he made, what he saw in his head as the perfect shot, or what club he used, he couldn't keep the ball out of the woods on the right side.

"Don't go right," Linus told himself.

"You should try the left side," Madison yelled, still picking at him. "I go left on this hole all the time, and I do it on purpose. I aim at the pavilion, put a little fade on it and then I'm all set up for my second shot. Easy."

"Okay," Linus said. "Give me room."

Sam and Madison retreated to the back of the tee box, giving Linus all the space he needed to swing his club. He stepped to his ball, but this time he turned his body to the right, allowing his feet and shoulder to aim at the tree line to the right of the fairway.

"What are you doing?" Sam asked.

"New plan of attack," Linus said. "I'm going to aim toward the woods and see if my body will autocorrect me as I'm swinging."

Libby moved out of her cart and joined Sam at the back of the tee box. "What the hell is taking so long up here?"

"He's trying something new."

"Oh, sweet Jesus. Hit the damn ball and stop thinking about it so much."

A couple of years older than Sam, Libby Price was a journalist for one of the smaller local newspapers. However, recently she had shifted over to putting most of her articles behind a paywall on the newspaper's website. She was short, only five feet tall, and broad-shouldered, her dark hair up in a bun.

Linus stood over his ball. He glanced down the fairway, looking for his target, then back at the ball. He remained frozen for a second, and Sam thought he might have said a short prayer; then he pulled the club into his usual slow, cautious backswing, accelerated down through the ball, and made contact.

The ball jumped off the tee and soared high into the air, flying down the right side. Then, as quickly as it had gone into the air, it curved to the right and entered the woods. The familiar sound of a golf ball hitting at least two trees echoed throughout the back nine loud enough for others on the course to hear.

"Nice shot, Hume!" one of the guys yelled from the sixteenth green.

Madison smiled. “Should I add another quarter to your tally now, or do we wait until you at least finish the hole?”

Linus dropped his shoulders and turned. “At least it went where I was aiming.”

“Next time, aim down the middle, genius,” Libby said.

Sam, Linus, Madison and Libby made up the foursome known in the Tuesday Night Mixed League as the Swing Squad. It was a terrible name. They all knew it, but Carey had thought it up back when he was on the team. Linus had replaced him when he left the league to tend to the course after Emmitt got sick.

While the foursome played as a team, doing their best to post a good score against other foursomes, Linus and Madison always had small side bets between themselves, with Madison usually coming out on top.

They jumped into their carts and pulled forward twenty-five yards, where the two women would hit from their tee box. As usual, Libby hit hers down the middle, about forty yards past Sam’s, while Madison did precisely what she’d said: She hit it up in the air, starting it down the middle, but the draw-biased swing she used gave the ball enough spin to curve it to the left.

“Whoa,” she said. “Not that far left.” The ball came down, bounced off the cement cart path, through the pavilion between the thirteenth and fourteenth hole and came to rest in the middle of the fourteenth fairway.

“That’s a nasty hook,” Sam said.

“What nasty hook?” she asked. “I did that on purpose. Didn’t you see how I gripped the club, then made sure my path was—“

“Stop talking,” Linus said. “You’re in the middle of the next fairway. You did nothing on purpose.”

“At least I’m not in the trees.”

Sam shook his head and laughed. He pressed the cart’s accelerator to the floor, taking himself and Linus near the woods where he thought Linus’s ball had landed. He stopped the cart as Madison pulled up next to him. The four of them exited their carts and wandered into the woods to look for Linus's ball.

"Fifteen years playing here, including ten in this league," Sam said. "I don't think I've ever seen this part of the course before."

"Glad I could open your world to new locations," Linus mumbled as he moved leaves around with his nine iron.

Sam moved a little farther into the trees. "Hey, there's a path over here. Where does it go?"

"I don't think my ball went that far. I'm going to head back a little."

Curious as to where it would lead, Sam continued walking toward the path. Behind him, a twig snapped as Madison approached.

"Follow me," she said. "I'll show you."

They walked another fifteen feet along the path before stopping at a bridge. She put one hand on the railing and pointed with the other. "There's a cemetery over there, then there's a main road, and across from it a housing development."

"Those giant houses on the lake?" Sam asked, also grabbing the railing and stepping onto the bridge next to her. "I've driven past there before. It's gated, isn't it?"

Madison nodded. "I grew up in one of those houses."

Sam stepped back and laughed. "Your family must have had some money."

"We did," she said. "Although I didn't even realize we had money until I was in high school. My dad invented something used in meat processing. To this day, I still don't understand what it does. He used to walk me over here on those evenings when he was home. He'd have a couple of golf clubs in his hand, and we'd practice our chipping and putting."

Leaves ruffled somewhere behind them. "I don't think my ball is this far into the woods," Linus yelled. "So, unless the two of you are going to make out, let's go back, and I'll take a drop."

Madison shook her head. "You realize if I do find his ball, I'm going to kick it deeper into the woods."

As they exited the woods, Libby was in the fairway, taking a practice swing. Up ahead, the green was surrounded by two sand traps, one on each side. The left-side trap was small and easily avoided with a good approach, and the one on the right was surrounded by orange cones and a rope as a construction crew had blocked it off a few weeks earlier. Late in the summer, Emmitt had put several holes under construction to give the course a facelift, hoping to increase its difficulty. He died before they could be finished, and the construction had halted until the new owners decided whether they wanted to continue.

Libby turned her body a few inches to the right, closing her stance, and took her swing. Her ball flew up into the air, heading left of the green, but at the top of its arc, it curved to the right. It landed fifteen yards short of the green, hit the ground, bounced up onto it and stopped ten feet from the hole. She dropped the club and put both hands into the air.

"I love this game!" she yelled. "If either of you hacks want a lesson, see me afterward."

Linus tossed a ball to the ground near the high grass around the spot where he thought his ball had entered the trees. He surveyed the area and pointed at the green while talking to himself. "What's the ruling if I hit into the under-construction sand trap?"

"Free drop but from behind it," Sam said.

A total of seven holes were under construction, and a new pond was being built on three. They were also ripping out most of the trees between sixteen and seventeen while lengthening four more holes.

"You'll definitely want to avoid the trap," Madison said with a smirk. "Could cost you another quarter."

Linus stepped back to the ball, took a slow backswing, accelerated on the way down and made perfect contact. The ball went up into the air, flew over the trap and landed on the green, a few feet from the hole. Thanks to the backspin he had put on the ball, it stopped almost immediately, giving him a chance to save par even though he had taken a penalty for the lost ball. He twirled the club as if wielding a sword and pushed it into the imaginary sheath on his hip.

"Nice shot," Madison said. "But you still have to make that putt."

Chapter Four

Each week, after their round, the group of four would get together at The Eagle's Nest, Savannah Palms' restaurant and bar. It had gone unnamed until Emmitt bought the place and decided he wanted it to operate as its own business, not depend on golfers as its customers. Before getting her dinner, Madison would usually go back to Emmitt's office and find Carey to talk about her round. Today, Sam would join her.

"How'd you hit 'em?" Carey asked as Sam and Madison walked into the small office.

"Not too bad," Madison said. "Linus has the card, but I'm sure I took at least a buck fifty from him."

"Why does he continue to bet you?"

"I've been asking her the same thing," Sam said, looking at Madison. As he turned back to Carey, his face softened. "How you doing?"

Carey said as he tightened his grip on the arms of his chair, "It's been tough, but I'm working through it."

"You sleeping yet, or are you doing that thing we did at camp where we pretended to sleep so the counselors wouldn't yell at us?"

"Don't mention camp," Madison said. "He'll start doing those voices again."

"Somewhere in between," Carey said with a smile. His eyes flicked toward the doorway, then snapped back to Sam. "I keep expecting him to come walking in here and bark his orders like he used to."

"Like I told you the other night, you never get over it, but you do get used to it, and it becomes easier."

"You should join us for dinner," Madison told Carey. "I'll make Linus go home, and you can take your old seat back, even if it's for one night."

"Can't," he said. "I need to get a jump on closing the books for November."

Madison leaned forward, rose on her toes and kissed him. "I hired people to do that accounting stuff so I wouldn't have to."

"If you need anything," Sam said. "You have my number."

The pair left the office and joined Linus at their regular spot. It was a small, rectangular table tucked against the wall in the back corner of the restaurant.

"How much do you owe me?" Madison asked, her hand already out and ready for the quarters they usually bet.

Next to Linus, Libby's chair was empty. She had made a stop in the locker room to change out of her golf clothes and into something more casual.

"Let's see," Sam said, snatching the scorecard from Linus.

He counted the plus and minus signs he had drawn on the scorecard to keep track of the side games. He had quit playing for money against Libby and Madison years ago because it was always a losing battle, but he continued to keep score for everyone else.

"Looks like she beat you six holes to one, so you owe her five quarters."

Madison took the scorecard from Sam. "Only five?"

"Maybe if you'd stop hitting left so much, you'd take more of his money."

She leaned into Sam, pushing her shoulder against him. "I already told you, I hit left on purpose."

"Sure," Sam said with a smile. "And I miss short putts on purpose."

Linus counted out five quarters. He set them on the table and pushed them toward Madison one at a time, counting as he went. "I played the best round of my life out there, and at the end of the night, I'm still handing her quarters."

"You played great. I was legit impressed, but I wanted to win, and I always get what I want." She flashed a smile his way. "You should know that by now."

Libby rounded the corner, nearly bumping into Kristie as they both neared the table. Libby took the empty seat next to Linus and reached for her water.

"Y'all eating anything tonight?" Kristie asked.

"You sticking around?" Linus asked Madison. "Or are you taking my money and leaving like usual?"

Her face fell, and she leaned toward Sam, her voice low, her shoulder touching his. "Any chance you can get my dinner tonight?"

"What's with you and money lately?" Sam asked. "Isn't your company like pulling in the cash?"

While she was still in college, Madison had begun running spring charity golf tournaments for small companies that didn't have the staff to do it on their own. As her company did well, she added corporate outings to her marketing plan. Within a year of graduating, she had built herself a business with a dozen employees, both repeat and new customers coming in faster than she could work them. At twenty-three, she had been mentioned in an article about young CEOs in Savannah, and her company exploded.

"It's seasonal," she said. "Thanksgiving slows down, then Christmas makes up for it."

Sam looked up at Kristie. "Yeah, we're all eating. Put her on my check."

Kristie dropped four menus on the table, and over the next few minutes, each of the foursome studied the menu as if about to order something different from what they ordered every other week.

As Kristie disappeared into the kitchen, Scott appeared in the doorway. Libby's face lit up. She tried to play it cool, but Sam had already noticed the sparkle in her eyes, the same sparkle he had seen the first time he had invited Scott to dinner after their league night. After that, he'd invited Scott more often. Sam wasn't the matchmaker type, but his curiosity around Scott's secret past had been piqued, and if he or Linus couldn't get it out of Scott, maybe Libby could.

Scott grabbed an empty chair and pushed it between Sam and Linus at the end of their table. "What the hell is this?" he asked as he held a pink piece of paper in the air.

Sam tilted his head to the side, reading the bold black letters across the top. "Seventeen years. Still missing."

He took the flyer from Scott. Below the headline were two pictures of the same girl; the first was from a school dance and the second was a grainy image taken at a convenience store. The name Juliet Summerfield was written below the picture. Under it was a short paragraph that included the date she'd vanished, information about her last known sighting and a line asking anyone with information to contact the police.

"I remember her." Sam set the flyer on the table. "It was back while we were still in high school. She went to Islewood on the north side, right?"

"She did," Libby said.

"Yeah, I do remember," Sam said while nodding. "They made it seem like she just disappeared off the face of the earth."

"We played volleyball against Islewood," Madison said. "I don't remember her that well, but I do remember when the story was in the news. There were rumors in my circle that she ran off with an older man."

"When I started at the paper as an intern, this was a hot story," Libby said. "I heard those rumors, too, but she was never found, and every couple of years, some amateur sleuth group puts these flyers out."

"What about her family?" Linus asked.

"As far as I know, they aren't in the area anymore. Her mom died, and her dad moved away. She also had a half-sister who no one has heard from in a long time."

"It's sad," Madison said. "Let's go back to talking about how I beat Linus for the umpteenth week in a row. That was a happier conversation."

"I wonder if I can write something for the paper's website about this. The world loves true crime nowadays."

"That seems a bit ghoulish," Madison said. "How about instead, we let her rest in peace."

"This many years later," Sam said. "I doubt she'll ever be found, or maybe she did run off with an older man."

"In that case, leave her be, and let her be happy."

"Where did you get this flyer?" Sam asked Scott.

"It was on your car. There's one on every car in the parking lot."

They stopped talking when Brock and Dexter entered the restaurant. The brothers weren't bickering, Sam noted, but they looked angry.

"Where's the kid?" Brock asked.

"In Emmitt's office," Kristie said. "What's wrong?"

His lips had formed into a thin line, and he folded his arms across his chest. "Peyton and Maryanne were married."

"Married?"

"We just came from Allen's," Dexter said. "He said they were married. Like three months ago, and they kept it a secret."

"Why keep something like that a secret?" Sam asked.

"Seems pretty obvious," Carey said as he emerged from the small hallway on the right side of the bar, coming from Emmitt's office. "She knew

Dad was dying, and she knew Peyton would get his money, so she convinced him to marry her."

"And now it's all hers," Dexter said.

Brock set his phone on the bar. "She's gonna blow through our money as if she had won a giant shopping spree."

"Not if I can help it," Carey said.

Chapter Five

Later that evening, Sam pulled his car into a parking spot near the front door of the Savannah Palms golf course. He killed the engine but kept both hands on the wheel, staring through the front windshield at the building. His knee bounced. He checked the clock on the dashboard, then looked back at the building, an empty pit forming in his stomach.

In the passenger seat next to him, Linus put his hand on his door handle, but paused and looked over at Sam. "What are we doing?"

"Something isn't right with Carey," Sam said. His grip on the steering wheel tightened, putting a crease in the leather that disappeared once he let go. "I didn't like the way he stormed out of here earlier tonight, and when I texted him, he didn't answer."

Linus pointed at the red Honda SUV parked at the far end of the lot. "That's his car, right?"

"It is," Sam said.

"Then he's here."

"If he's here, why is the building dark?"

"You always leave the lights off when you're the first one in the building at work. You talk about how nice it is to work in the dark."

"We're IT. It's expected from us. Carey's not like that."

"You're imagining things," Linus said. He grabbed the door handle again, but again he paused when Sam didn't move.

"I don't think so," Sam said. "Carey always stops by my house on Tuesday nights to chat about our golf. I think he misses being out there. But tonight he didn't."

"He came back to get some work done. What's the big deal?"

"I'm not sure. I'm just saying something isn't right."

Linus began to turn away from Sam but paused. "Hold on," he said, pointing to a small, narrow window high up on the left side of the building, in front of Carey's SUV. A pale blue glow had begun flickering in the window as if someone had switched something on inside.

"Simulator one. Maybe they're bonding over eighteen at Augusta."

"Maybe," Sam said.

Facing the parking lot, a large restaurant window gave anyone outside a clear look at the bar and the first few tables. Even on slow nights, there would be the glow from the television on the wall behind the bar, a bartender wiping down the counter or a shadow from the restaurant. But tonight, The Eagle's Nest looked dead, without lights or movement. It reminded Sam of the stories he had heard from friends up north about how golf courses went silent this time of year.

Sam glanced that way, then opened the door slowly. He hurried to the corner of the building opposite the light from the simulator with Linus trailing close behind him. Taking shorter, quieter steps, they moved along the building's side, but Sam stopped at the back edge, hesitant to move any farther. He pressed his back against the wall and eased his head around the corner an inch at a time.

"What are you—"

Sam put his hand up to silence Linus and moved his head a little more, gaining a better view of the back of the building. He expected to see something, maybe a figure in the pro shop, but there was nothing, not a single movement.

"Anything?" Linus whispered.

Shaking his head, Sam stepped around to the back of the building. Linus still followed. They moved through the outdoor seating area, which had a handful of high metal tables bolted to the concrete, each with four chairs and a yellow umbrella open above it. Sam turned the knob, expecting the door to be locked, but he heard the click as it opened.

"This door shouldn't be unlocked after dark," Linus whispered.

They crept inside and tiptoed through the dark pro shop. Sam's heart raced as they entered the restaurant and made their way past the bar toward the simulator room. Its door was closed, but through a small, narrow window in it, lights flickered as if the television had been turned on. Sam's hand trembled. He reached for the handle, his breath coming shallow and quick.

"I don't like this," Linus whispered.

Sam cracked the door wide enough for him and Linus to peek inside. His eyes widened, and he inhaled sharply. In the middle of the room, Carey stood over Maryanne's bloodied, motionless body, holding a blood-soaked golf club. Linus grunted and backed away, stumbling over a chair. Carey turned. Red spots dotted his shirt, and from his ankles down, his pants were soaked in blood.

"Jesus Christ, Carey," Sam said.

Carey's head shot up. The sound of approaching sirens grew louder by the second. Sam glanced at the club, then back at the floor beside Maryanne.

"Did you do this?" Sam asked.

Carey looked toward the window. "Get out of here."

Linus moved first, backing away from Sam. He tripped over the chair he had knocked to the ground earlier and fell to the floor beside it. Sam began to help Linus up, but from the pro shop, the flashlights swept in fast, the light quickly finding the pair. Radios hissed. Boots pounded the tile floor.

Sam stepped away from Linus, then stopped as the first officer rounded the corner, his gun already up, the light pinned on Sam's face.

"Don't move!"

Three more officers followed him, their weapons also raised, their lights finding Sam and Linus.

"Hands up, both of you!"

Chapter Six

Sam sat on a barstool, his wrists cuffed behind him, the metal biting into his skin whenever he shifted. Linus sat two stools down, hunched forward, his hands also cuffed behind his back. Neither of them spoke. Not because they didn't want to, but because they had been told not to.

Two uniformed officers stood between them and the simulator room, blocking Sam's view of the inside. As quickly as the police had put Sam and Linus in handcuffs and ordered them to stay put, they had taken Carey away. Sam had tried to speak to him as he walked by but was told to be quiet.

A paramedic stepped into the bar from the pro shop, moved across the restaurant and stopped at the door to the simulator room. He spoke with another officer outside the door, ducked under the yellow tape and vanished inside the room. The officer near the door spoke into the radio on his shoulder.

"Confirmed. Let them in."

More officers arrived, including a couple in plainclothes Sam had recognized from all the time he spent in the police station after his parents' car accident. Another officer with a cart rolled in, letting it bounce across the bar's tiled floor. The last man to walk in was one Sam knew better than anyone. His name was Randall Beaumont. He looked around the room, his eyes landing on Sam. He didn't smile. He never smiled.

He crossed the room and stopped behind the bar. Sam swiveled on his chair as best he could while wearing the handcuffs. Beaumont's eyes held Sam's for a beat.

"Mr. Norris," he said, his voice steady. "Didn't expect to find you here."

Captain Randall Beaumont was an older man, in his late fifties, early sixties, close to retirement, and had spent a lot of time with Sam after his parents' car accident. He was tall, thin, had a bit of gray in his hair, and loathed paperwork as much as he hated the new technology that would help reduce how much paperwork he had to do.

"Carey didn't do it," Sam said.

Beaumont's expression didn't change as another officer approached him. He turned slightly toward a uniform near the tape.

"Where's the victim?"

"In that room over there," the officer said. "Female. Blunt-force trauma. There's a large amount of blood. The male suspect was found holding the weapon, a golf club. He was standing over her. We've got him in a cruiser, and we're taking him downtown."

"Put him in an interrogation room and have him wait for me. Keep an eye on him while he's alone. See if he says anything."

Another uniformed officer appeared next to Beaumont. He wore white gloves and held a small plastic bag. He handed it to Beaumont.

"This was on the floor next to the victim."

Beaumont took the bag by its edge and tilted it, the officer shining his flashlight on it. Beaumont didn't react, only studied the item inside the bag. He turned to Sam.

"You're a member here, is that right?"

"For about ten years now," Sam said.

"You know the family that owns the place?"

"I do."

Beaumont angled the clear plastic bag toward Sam, holding it close enough for Sam to see it. He wanted to reach out, hold the item in his palm, but the metal from the cuffs only dug into his wrists more.

"You recognize this?"

"Can you take these handcuffs off me?"

"Not yet."

Sam exhaled and leaned forward as far as he could, his eyes narrowing on the piece of jewelry inside the bag. It was a small necklace with a pendant at the end of the silver chain. The upper half looked taller than it should have, as if someone had grabbed one end with a pair of pliers and pulled, stretching it into something resembling a heart but not quite right.

Sam hadn't known Maryanne that well, only seeing her here and there at the golf course. He remembered that she always wore jewelry, more than most people, but never really paid attention to what it looked like.

"I don't recognize it," he said to Beaumont as he shook his head.

Beaumont moved the bag toward Linus, but before Beaumont said anything, Linus also shook his head.

"Take them downtown," he said to another officer. "I'll be back to get their statements in a few minutes."

Chapter Seven

After a ride in the back of an uncomfortable police car, Sam found himself sitting in the small interrogation room in the city of Savannah's police station. The room's light was dim and harsh, worse than the lights over his desk at work. He settled into a hard-backed chair on one side of a small table.

Beaumont came into the room, his head down. He held a manila folder under one arm and a cup of coffee in his hand. "As I said earlier, Mr. Norris, I didn't expect to find you at the scene of a murder. What were you doing there?"

Sam forced a smile. He tried to make himself comfortable, but it was tough considering he was sitting in the same room where a decade earlier he had also sat, allowing tears to fall as this same man, then Detective Randall Beaumont, recounted what he knew about his parents' accident.

"Do I need a lawyer?"

Beaumont put the manila folder on the table and set his flip-phone and a small yellow notepad next to it. He opened the folder and scanned through the pages. Without looking up, he asked, "Did you do something wrong?"

"Other than showing up at the exact wrong time to see my friend standing over a dead body while holding what I'm assuming was the murder weapon, no, I didn't do anything wrong."

Beaumont pulled his notebook in front of him. "I need you to describe to me what you saw from the moment you entered the building until we showed up."

"Where's Linus?"

"Next door. He's talking with Officer Jackson."

"Jackson's a dick," Sam said. "He'll have Linus signing a confession in no time."

"We're running a bit thin tonight." Beaumont leaned forward, speaking lower. "We had a professor at the college get killed last night, the second murder over there in the last few months. I'm getting a bit worried we have a serial—"

"Carey didn't do it." Sam's voice trembled as he said the words. He knew what he had seen, but he refused to believe it. His fingers gripped the edge of the table, the cold metal edge biting into his hands.

"Sam—"

"Carey didn't do it." If he had to, he would repeat it over and over until it sank in.

The detective's eyes softened as he leaned back in his chair. "I know he's your friend, but you can't deny what you saw."

A smile appeared on Sam's face as a specific memory came back. "There was this one time while we were golfing. I saw him move a frog out of a sand trap before hitting his ball because he didn't want to cover it in sand." His eyes moved back to Beaumont, this time more focused. "I don't care what I saw. He didn't do it."

"He wasn't standing over a frog this time, Sam. He was standing over the dead body of his sister-in-law, a woman who, from what I've recently learned, inherited the golf course everyone else thought would be his."

Although Sam opened his mouth to speak, Beaumont kept going.

"He was also holding the murder weapon."

"I never saw him swing the club," Sam said. "Anyone could have done it, then tricked Carey into going in there while they called the police to make sure he would get caught."

"Did you see anyone else?"

"No, I didn't see anyone else," Sam said. "But who called you? How did you know to show up at that exact time?"

"Did you hear anyone else?" Beaumont asked, ignoring his question.

Wishing he had heard any other sound in the building, Sam again shook his head. Maybe the ice behind the bar could have broken in the cooler, perhaps a mouse could have sprung a trap, or maybe the building could have made one of those rattling sounds Sam's home made at night, which his dad always wrote off as the house "settling." But he had heard nothing. He closed his eyes and tried to bring the simulator room back into view, but all he saw was Carey's face.

"Okay, then tell me what you did see."

Sam sighed, and his shoulders dropped. "When Linus and I walked into the pro shop, the place was silent. The only thing we saw were the lights from the simulator room. We approached the door, I opened it, and Carey was there, standing over her, holding the golf club."

"Did he say anything?"

The chair scraped the floor as Sam pushed it back and stood, his legs pushing it back a few more feet. He turned to the bare wall and did his best to block out everything around him. Putting a hand against the wall, he closed his eyes.

"You're going to do that thing—uh, okay," Beaumont said.

The simulator room came to mind the way a television screen fades in as it's turned on. His synesthesia always came as a layout, a sequence arranged in space, the same way the sixth hole at Savannah Palms lived in his head even when he wasn't standing on the tee. Beaumont had been under the impression for a long time that Sam possessed a photographic memory, and Sam never corrected him. For years, he didn't even know himself what to call it. Not until Dani finally gave it a name while he was with her in Wyoming.

The room was plain, as if someone had built four walls and a ceiling, similar to the very plain interrogation room where he was currently standing. He saw Carey on a ladder, tightening brackets. Carey stepped down from the ladder and crossed the floor in measured lines, shelf up, shelf down, one inch left, then back to center. Two televisions had been stacked on the far wall, both black. A golf bag sat near the mat. Carey got a club from the bag and took a slow practice swing, checking the clearance overhead.

The sequence changed.

Maryanne lay on the floor where the fake green grass had been, blood soaking into it, turning the room into something else. The smell arrived next. The copper smell. Sam recoiled but held his eyes shut, tightening them. His throat narrowed, and his mouth went dry. His pulse pounded in his ears.

"I see him," Sam said through shallow breaths.

"What's the expression on his face?" Beaumont asked. "Is it anger? Rage?"

Sam concentrated on his friend, but he was drawn to Maryanne's bloodied and beaten body. His eyes snapped open.

"It's the blood," he said to Beaumont. "I can't look at anything else."

"Try again," Beaumont said, keeping his tone even. "Lock onto his face. Don't look at her."

Sam nodded. He closed his eyes again and pictured the room, this time from a different angle. The entire scene materialized in front of him. The only sound he could hear was Linus breathing over his shoulder.

"It's guilt," Sam said. "That's what I see on his face."

"He said he was guilty?"

His eyes fell to Carey's mouth, but no further. Sam wouldn't let them. "He's sad. He feels the whole thing is his fault. He expected the golf course. Everyone expected him to get it. But then Emmitt gave it to Peyton, and it threw everyone for a loop. It led to Peyton's death and now Maryanne's. He didn't do well enough for his dad to leave it to him. That's his guilt."

"You can see all that?"

"You asked me to tell you what I saw," Sam snapped at him.

Beaumont scribbled in his notebook. Without looking up, he asked, "Look at his mouth. Is he saying anything?"

Sam closed his eyes and rewatched the scene for a third time. He tried to slow his breath but couldn't. His breaths felt shallow, not giving him enough air. He pushed his palms against the interrogation room's wall, feeling the grit, proving he was still at the police station and not at the bloody scene of a murder. The copper smell hit him again, and he caught a glimpse of a few strands of Maryanne's bloody hair stuck against the fake grass. His eyes shot open. He turned to Beaumont.

"He said, 'You should leave.'"

Beaumont leaned back in his chair, setting his pen down on top of this notebook. "And with what you're seeing right now, seeing again and again, you're telling me you don't think he killed her?"

A knock on the door broke the silence, startling Sam for a moment. He turned his head, his gaze instinctively darting toward the sound. Beaumont remained still, his eyes never leaving Sam's face. The room seemed to hold its breath in anticipation of Sam's response.

"He's one of my closest friends. We go back twenty years. No, I don't think he killed anyone."

As Sam finished his sentence, another knock. Beaumont stood and walked to the door. "I don't like the tone of your voice, Sam. Regardless of what you're saying to me, I can tell that inside your own mind, you're questioning it."

"How can I not?" Sam said as he sat.

Beaumont opened the door wide enough to listen to the person on the other side. Sam couldn't see who it was or hear what they were saying, but it was a short conversation. Beaumont closed the door after no more than a minute and turned to Sam.

"The problem here is that he is one of your closest friends. Even if you think he would do it, would you admit it?"

Sam hesitated, his mind crawling with questions. "I don't know."

"In my experience, I've seen hundreds of people sit in that chair and lie to me. At least you're honest," Beaumont said. "That's more than I normally get in this room." He pointed at the door. "The story Linus told Officer Jackson matches yours, so the two of you can go."

"Can I talk to Carey?"

"Not at the moment. We're in the process of booking him."

"You're arresting him?"

"He'll be booked tonight. They'll fingerprint him, take photos, take his clothes, and put him in a holding cell."

"But what about—"

"In the morning, he'll appear in front of a judge. They'll read the charge and talk bond. After that, he can get an attorney involved if he hasn't already. Maybe you can talk to him tomorrow afternoon."

"What about Brock?" Sam asked, meeting Beaumont's eyes as if he were trying to force the seasoned officer into arresting someone else. "Didn't you hear how pissed he was at his inheritance? If anyone did it, it was him."

"We'll talk to Brock, verify where he was, and work the evidence where it takes us. But at the moment, Carey is the one we found standing over her, holding the murder weapon. Second death in three days in this family. We're not taking any chances."

"Second death? Are you talking about Peyton? You don't think his was a simple allergic reaction?"

Beaumont said nothing, but he gave a look Sam recognized. He had seen the same look on both Chase's and Emerson's faces while in South Plainfield. It was a look that said, "You're right, but we're not going to acknowledge it."

Sam straightened, the realization hitting him. "I'm right, aren't I? Peyton's death also wasn't an accident."

The detective's jaw tightened. He closed his notebook. "What happened to Peyton is still being reviewed."

"You're looking at it as if it were a murder?"

"I'm not ruling anything out with this family."

"But I can help," Sam said, almost pleading with Beaumont. "Call Detective Chase in South Plainfield. Ask her what happened out there. She gave me some leeway, and I solved the case for her."

Beaumont stepped closer. "I know what you did out there. She's called me a few times about you."

"There you go. You already know what I can do. Tell me more about Peyton. Why do you think—"

"We're not in South Plainfield. You're not a deputy or a consultant. You're a witness, and your friend is in jail for murder. You're biased, Sam, that's what you are."

"Give me a chance. If things point at him, I'll—"

Lifting a hand, Beaumont cut him off. "You want to help your friend? Make sure he has a good lawyer, and let me do my job. If you start screwing around with my case, you'll make it worse for him, and I'll make it worse for you."

"Carey didn't do this," Sam insisted.

"Go home," Beaumont said. "And if I hear you're interfering in any way, calling employees, or playing detective, I'll put you in a small room where the only thing you'll be able to do is watch this thing unfold on a jailhouse television."

Chapter Eight

Inside the interrogation room, Carey sat at a small white table bolted to the floor, his hands clasped so tightly his knuckles had turned white. The room smelled like bleach and stale air. Grey cinderblock walls surrounded them. One single fluorescent light, similar to the light over his desk at work, hung overhead.

As he sat, his eyes fell on the sign beneath the camera—AUDIO AND VIDEO RECORDING IN PROGRESS.

"You doing okay in here?" Sam asked. "Are you eating?"

"Yeah, bologna sandwich for lunch. Can't wait to see what dinner is."

"How about sleep?"

"Not much last night. You know I didn't do what they're accusing me of, right?"

"It doesn't look good."

"But you believe me?"

Sam wanted to believe him. Carey had never seemed capable of harming anyone, but considering how they'd found him and how angry he'd been over Maryanne's secret marriage, it was important to hear Carey's side of the story before deciding for sure. "Tell me what happened."

"After I left you at the course, Dexter and I went to see Allen. I was there for a couple of hours trying to work out what happened next with everything Peyton received in the will. None of us wanted Maryanne to end up with it."

Sam again glanced at the camera and the sign below it as Carey mentioned Maryanne's name. Everything Carey said was being recorded, and he wanted to warn Carey not to say anything negative. Still, he let Carey continue, wanting to hear his nonfiltered side of the story first.

"I don't care if they hear what I say," Carey said, following Sam's eyes. "I didn't do this, and everything I'm telling you right now is the truth."

"What did Allen say?"

"He said that since she was married to Peyton legally, everything was hers. Peyton had his own will drawn up a few days after they were married."

"Didn't that seem strange to you? That he would leave you and even Brock and Dexter out of it?"

"I wasn't the only one," Carey said. "Allen said he even tried to talk Peyton out of giving her everything. He told Peyton that Emmitt would want what he'd built to stay in the family, but Peyton demanded it."

Sam wondered if the police officers on the other side of the door were thinking the same thing he was. *They get married before Emmitt's death, and then Peyton creates a will leaving everything to Maryanne.* Pieces of the puzzle were missing, but those had to be two of the biggest ones.

"You show up at the course," Sam said. "What did you see?"

"Nothing out of the ordinary. Sometimes, after we close, I'll come back after dark and do some of the work to set up for the next day. Checking tee times, figuring out where we're going to mow, what greens need done, that kind of thing. I would either have to do it in the evening or get up really early to go in. I like to be there when Maddy wakes up, so I do it in the evening, and then I can be there to see her off to work in the morning."

"Any other cars in the driveway?"

Carey shook his head. "Just me."

"What door did you come through?"

"Front door," Carey said.

That made sense to Sam. The front door led into the restaurant, then it was a quick right into the kitchen, with Emmitt's office in the back corner, a small room he had built after he had taken over.

"And you didn't hear anything at all? You didn't hear Maryanne come in? You didn't hear the fight that left her dead?"

"No, nothing," Carey said. "And I would have. I didn't close the office door. The only noise I heard came from my phone. I played some music from my playlist, but the volume was low. I would have heard someone coming through the building."

"How about Security cameras?"

"We only have the one at the course. It points at the north side of the building and the first tee. We use it to make sure people aren't going off without paying."

"Nothing on the south side?"

Carey shook his head again. "We've talked about it but haven't put it up yet."

Sam stood. He turned and looked at the camera, then shifted his eyes to the door, wondering if Beaumont was listening. He tipped his head forward and kept his voice low, almost whispering, but loud enough that Carey could hear him.

"If I'm trying to come up with a timeline, based on what you're saying, Maryanne had to have already been dead when you showed up. You went inside, didn't check the simulator rooms—"

"Had no reason to."

"How long were you there before you found her?"

"Maybe, ten minutes?"

"If you didn't hear or see anything, what caused you to go up there in the first place?"

"From my angle at dad's desk, I can see out of the office to the exit sign above the front door. Out of nowhere, I saw these flashes of light. I left the office and realized they were coming from the small window above the simulator room door. I stood for a minute, watching the lights. It came from one of the televisions, which didn't make sense. It wasn't on when I arrived, and I didn't turn it on."

"I'll bet while you were standing there, you were only a few inches away from us seeing you."

"I was out there for thirty seconds, then I went to the simulator room, opened the door and saw her."

"Why did you go into the room? You should have called the police."

"I thought I saw her still breathing. I wanted to see if I could help."

"And in doing that, you touched the murder weapon."

"I thought I might have to do CPR, and it was lying across her."

"And as we're walking into the back door, you're realizing it's too late."

"Yeah," he said. "I messed up, didn't I?"

"I'm afraid so," Sam said. "Tell me about the night of the will reading."

Carey's shoulders tightened, and his clasped hands loosened, then locked. He leaned back a few inches, his eyes narrowing on Sam. "The police were asking me about it too, and I didn't understand why, but then I kinda got the idea that they thought whatever happened to Peyton wasn't an accident."

Sam glanced at the door, assuming Carey's comment had attracted Beaumont's attention. "Did they say that to you?"

"Not in so many words, but they kept asking me about the EpiPen in Maryanne's purse, the one she used on Peyton. They were asking who it belonged to and who had access to it."

"The EpiPen?"

"They asked me a few different questions about it."

"What did you tell them?"

"I don't know who it belonged to, but I'm sure everyone had access to it. It was a bit chaotic in there before Allen started reading, then again during dinner. Anyone could have gotten to her purse."

"Why would access to the EpiPen matter?" Sam asked.

"Not sure, but one of the officers mentioned..." Carey leaned forward, his voice so quiet he was almost mouthing the word to Sam. "Poison."

Sam didn't repeat the word but instead leaned back, his mind spinning. Had someone put something in Peyton's drink to make him react, causing Maryanne to stick him with a poisoned EpiPen?

"Did they say what kind?"

"No, the look Beaumont gave him after he let that word slip was enough to get him to keep quiet for the rest of the time they were questioning me."

"I don't understand. The EpiPen was in Maryanne's purse, but it was Peyton who had the allergies?"

"They both had the tree nut allergy. Peyton has told the story more than once about how they bumped into each other at a doctor's office somewhere in Florida."

"Who was there?" Sam asked. "Madison told me it was family and Kristie."

"Charlotte was there too, although she left before Allen began reading the will."

"Charlotte? Your neighbor? What was she doing there?"

"My dad has been treating her like family for the last ten years or so. Her husband died around the same time as my mom, and I think he liked the company."

"Madison told me there was a strange-looking man at the back of the room during dinner. She thought Kristie may have known him."

"Never seen him before in my life," Carey said. "He looked homeless, and Kristie shooed him away before he could come into the room."

"Do you think she knew him?"

"I'm not sure. She kicked him out so quickly."

"What's her relationship with your family?"

"Dad wrote how he felt about her in the will. She was the daughter he never had. I knew her pretty well since she worked for me at the course, but I'm not sure about the others. They didn't come by the course much, except Peyton. He and Maryanne would come in for dinner, and she would wait on them."

"And she would have gotten to know them a little."

"I guess," Carey said. "I did see Kristie arguing with Peyton as Maddy and I were walking in. I looked over, and Kristie stopped, then she stormed into the kitchen as if Peyton had told her she was fired."

"What were they arguing about?" Sam asked.

"I'm not sure. But she—" Carey's eyes narrowed. "Do the police think I killed Peyton?"

"I don't know, but I don't like that they're asking you these questions. Make sure you don't talk to them unless Allen is around."

"I need you to help me, Sam, like you did when you were in Wyoming."

"I've already been ordered to leave it alone," Sam said, his voice a little louder, making sure if the police were listening, they'd hear. "If I do, I'll end up in a holding cell next to you."

A knock on the other side of the door. "Wrap it up," an officer said.

"I gotta go," Sam said. "But I'll come see you again."

Chapter Nine

Sam sat at his dining room table with a bottle of water and his work laptop in front of him. Linus sat across from him, the fast food he had stopped to get on his way to Sam's almost gone. Sam had used the time while Linus ate to fill him in on his conversation with Beaumont and Carey.

"You've played in that simulator, right?" Sam asked Linus as he opened the TNT app on his computer.

"Why are you opening that?" Linus asked.

"I have everyone who was at the will reading written here," he pushed his notebook across the table to Linus. "But I need a way to organize my thoughts. Besides, Gil wants us to use this, so I'm going to."

Linus looked down at the list. "Charlotte? Who's she?"

"She lived next door to Emmitt. Carey said she was at the will reading but left before Allen began reading it. I'm curious why."

Linus slid the notebook back to Sam. Inside the TNT software, he clicked the tip of one of the triangles, which would have been for the project requirements. In this section, he was to give a title and a description for each requirement. Sam used the title field for the name and the description field to type what he knew about each person so far: very little.

"I need to know about the golf simulator, and I don't think the police are going to open the course for another couple of days. You've been in there. What does it look like?"

"It's small and narrow," Linus said. "That window we saw last night is at the back. There's a giant impact screen on the other wall, a couch for someone to sit and a high table with two chairs under that back window."

"Carey said a television was not only the light he saw from inside the bar, but also the light we saw while we were sitting outside. Where in the room are those televisions?"

"If you go inside the door and make a left, you'll run into the desk where the laptop sits. The two televisions are on the wall above it. One shows all the stats of your swing, you know, ball speed, launch angle, face angle, all those abbreviations we're not good enough to understand. You can also toggle it to show an instant replay of your swing from two angles. The other TV seems to perpetually be on the golf channel."

Sam's eyes drifted past Linus, not seeing his kitchen table, Linus or his own dining room anymore. He only saw the wall of the simulator room with the televisions on it. The detail Linus had said snapped into place, and an idea formed so fast in Sam's head, it made him sit up.

"It replays your swing? Like actual video?"

"Yeah, there's a camera pointing at you from the side and from the back. I'll show you." Linus wiped his mouth and hands, pushed his empty burger wrapper to the side and grabbed Sam's laptop, pulling it to him. "The company that put the simulators in is called ApexSim Golf. They have an online hub where you can access your data from anywhere."

Sam stood and walked around behind Linus, looking over his shoulder. Linus pulled up a web browser and typed the ApexSim golf URL. The page loaded, showing several products they sold along with a free promotion they were currently running. Linus scrolled to the bottom of the page and clicked a login link. He typed his email address and password, and it opened a new screen, a dashboard, showing the history of his simulator room usage.

"This is my profile. Here's my handicap when I play inside the simulator, and this," he said as he clicked a tab, "is my swing history."

A list appeared. It showed dates, which simulator room he was in and a series of thumbnails of Linus standing over a ball in the simulator. He clicked on one of the videos. A new window opened, showing a large video player with buttons below it to control the video. He clicked the play button, and it showed him swinging the club.

"It also does slow motion, and here is where you can toggle both angles or put them side by side. I'd like to get some lessons there from a pro while using this. It could really help me."

"Can we look at the video of the night Maryanne died?"

"We could see those if we were logged in as her."

Sam didn't have the faintest clue what kind of password Maryanne would use. He took a few steps around the table toward his chair but stopped. "I bet there's a master account for the course, someone who can manage the whole thing and possibly see everyone's history, right?"

"Probably." Linus clicked on the small picture in the upper right corner of the screen. "Under my account, it says 'User.' I would assume there is some kind of admin account."

Without answering immediately, Sam stared at the screen. It was well put together, very clean. "You remember when Carey worked with us?"

"I do."

Sam pulled a chair over next to Linus and took a seat, his pulse rate rising. He grabbed the laptop and clicked the Logout button for Linus's account.

"The thing about Carey is, he's a smart kid. Good at what he does, but he's shit when it comes to passwords. There was a time when we were sending out fake spam emails, trying to catch employees who would screw up and allow a hacker into our system."

"It obviously didn't work based on Scott telling us we just got hacked last month."

"And it didn't work on Carey either," Sam said. "We sent one out where we told people they had to change their password immediately. It had misspellings and a message saying it came from outside the company. It was so obviously fake, but he clicked it anyway and typed his password, then submitted it as if he were doing the right thing."

Linus laughed. "No, he didn't."

Sam held up his hand, showing two fingers. "Twice. The first time, I made him sit through a half-hour training video on how not to fall for those things. The second time, his manager got involved."

"You think he learned anything?"

"We're about to find out. Carey loves three things. His father, Madison and golf. He uses the same pattern for his passwords. He takes a word, adds a birthday, then, and only because he has to, he puts an exclamation mark at the end as if no one in the world had ever thought of that. He ought to use a dash or a semicolon. That would be a lot safer."

"And you're going to guess his admin password for this ApexSim website?" Linus asked. "You think you know him that well?"

"The first time he failed, he used Madison's name, her birthday and the exclamation point," Sam said as he typed exactly that.

Sam pressed the Submit button but was quickly denied.

"At least he's off that," Sam said as he began typing again. "On his second failure, he went with Emmitt's info."

He pressed the Enter key, and the page lit up, showing a dashboard similar to Linus's except with more controls, including simulator settings, a list of users, the amount of storage used and available and a camera configuration. The last tab was labeled Activity.

"You got it," Linus said with a smile.

But Sam didn't smile. He only shook his head. "Took me two guesses. That's not very secure."

The Users Tab, which he clicked first, showed a list of names, with Linus's about halfway down the screen. It showed Linus, Brock, Dexter and a handful of people Sam recognized from Tuesday's league, but no

Maryanne. At the top of the list was Carey's name with the word "Administrator" next to it. His was the only one marked that way.

Linus pointed at the screen. "History tab. If it's similar to what I see on my account, it should allow you to select a date."

Sam clicked it, and a timeline loaded. It showed rows of sessions, each expandable into shot-by-shot logs. He found the previous night and clicked. The shot log opened. It showed two players, Player 1 and Player 2, but no names. There was a file containing the information for each shot hit. Sam clicked it and saved it to his computer. Below it, where the same video thumbnails should have been, there were only gray boxes, each one with a small red x in the upper left corner.

"Do cameras come on automatically?" Sam asked Linus.

"They should. I didn't have to configure anything. When the simulator detects a club coming through the swing area, it takes a video."

Sam clicked the Activity Tab. Another list appeared. It showed settings changes, file actions, usage time and the user who made the change. Sam's eyes tracked downward, searching for the hour window around Maryanne's death.

Deleted: 14 video clips
Deleted: 9 video clips
Empty trash

"These were deleted by Carey's account," Sam said.

"Does that mean Carey deleted them?"

"Not necessarily," Sam said a little sharply. "It only shows his account as the user who did the deleting. It only took me two attempts to guess his password. Someone like Brock or Dexter could have done the same and deleted them to cover their tracks."

Linus held up his hands, his palms out. "Whoa, calm down, Sam. I'm not saying he did it. I'm saying the app is showing that his account did it. Someone is covering their tracks and making it look like it's him. The police have to already know this."

Sam's stomach tightened. He clicked into the User Security Settings Tab and changed Carey's password. It would no longer be a weak mess of someone he loved and a birthday. He typed a long passphrase, something golf-related Carey would remember once Sam told him, and no one else could guess.

Linus tapped the screen. "What now?"

"We need to know what the police know," Sam said.

"How do we find that?"

"You're going to have to make a phone call that I know you don't want to make and get some help for us."

Leaning back in his chair, Linus raised both hands in the air. "No. I haven't talked to him since I moved here, and I don't want to start now."

"Invite him down for Thanksgiving," Sam insisted.

"I would rather eat Thanksgiving alone than with my uncle."

"He's the only chance we have right now. If Beaumont sees me anywhere near this case, he'll lock me away." He grabbed Linus's phone and handed it to him. "Tell him to meet us at La Encina Taquería at noon."

Chapter Ten

"I can't believe you go to a Mexican Restaurant for Thanksgiving," Dani said to Sam as he drove toward La Encina Taquería, a Mexican restaurant near his office.

A few years earlier, Sam and Linus had begun going there on Thanksgiving Day, a small ritual they'd created after Linus moved to Savannah from South Plainfield. Scott had joined them last year. None of them had any immediate family in the area, so getting together for the November holiday was much better than spending the time alone.

"It's a tradition," Sam told her. He looked down at the clock display on his car's radio. "One that I'm apparently late for."

"I have so many questions," Dani said, barely able to hold her laughter. "Do you dip your turkey in salsa? Are there cranberry burritos? I bet a green bean casserole fajita would be amazing."

"Funny," he said. "You're funny. I'm pulling in now. I see their cars."

"Text me when you get home. Kenzie and I are hanging out at home all day."

"Tell her I said hello."

"You know I will," she said, then disconnected the call.

Sam pulled into a spot next to Scott's car. Being there on Thanksgiving was not much different than any other day. Other than the specials, which didn't include anything turkey-related, the menu was the same.

He pushed open the door and stepped into the warm air of the restaurant. The smell of grilled meat and lime hit him. A hostess stood near the door with a clipboard, but Sam pointed toward a small four-top in the back where Scott was sitting. Linus sat to his right, and across from Linus was a large man wearing a dark sweater, his shoulders wider than the chair.

Linus made eye contact with Sam, a strained look on his face. Sam took the empty seat across from Scott. Up close, the man was larger in all senses of the word. He was at least six feet five inches tall and pushing four hundred pounds. He had a thick neck, big, heavy forearms, and his hands rested on the table as if he could easily apply a little force and snap it in half.

Scott greeted him first. "There he is. Happy Thanksgiving, man."

Sam nodded at him and glanced at Linus.

Linus cleared his throat. "Sam, this is my Uncle Bruce."

"Bruce Hargreaves." The man offered his hand, although not to shake. Inside it was a business card. "Best Private Investigator in Atlanta and the surrounding counties," Bruce said, his eyes moving from one young man to another as the words he spoke echoed the exact words written across the bottom of the card.

"Sam Norris."

"Nice to meet you, Sam," Bruce said. "Your friend Scott here was telling me about your company getting hacked."

Sam flashed Scott a look that said, "You're supposed to keep your mouth shut," and Bruce must have caught it.

"Don't worry about it, Sam," Bruce said. "I'm on the clock right now, so everything we talk about here stays between us."

Sam blinked. "What do you mean you're on the clock? Who hired you?"

"No one yet. This part is free. It's like, when you're looking for a guy to blacktop your driveway. He comes out, he does some measuring, tells you what he sees, and then gives you a number if you want to move forward." He tapped the edge of the business card. "But the minute you start explaining your problem, you're a potential client, and I treat potential clients the same as paying ones. It's all confidential. No exceptions."

"Okay, great," Sam said.

Bruce leaned back in his chair. "Anyway, Scott said you paid these hackers, then tore the systems apart, rebuilt everything, and had it running before anyone realized what happened."

"Scott's good at that stuff," Linus said.

Bruce turned back to Scott. "The way you describe it sounds a lot like something that happened at my building a few months ago. I work at a big law office in downtown Savannah, Barrow, Denton and Shaw. I'm sure you've heard of them."

Probably the same blank look Linus had on his face was on his own, but Sam nodded at Bruce.

"I did some work for Denton's son a few years ago, got him out of some real trouble, and now his old man lets me use an office. A couple of months ago, they got hit by the same kind of virus. It spread its way through their system and forced them to pay. They didn't respond. A few days later, everything was gone. They had to hire a bunch of interns to come in and enter everything back into their system from years of paper files."

"Sounds awful," Sam said.

"It was, but they figured it out." Now Bruce addressed Linus. "It's about time you finally called me and took me up on an offer for dinner. I've left you multiple voicemails. I was starting to believe you didn't like your uncle."

"Sorry about that," Linus said. "I've been busy with work."

"Tell me about it," Bruce said. "I've been swimming in it. Lots of cases. Lots of people to find."

As Bruce spoke, recounting some of his latest cases, Sam didn't know what to think of the man. He had been there for a grand total of twelve minutes, and if someone had asked him to write an Amazon-style review of Uncle Bruce Hargreaves, Sam would have given him one star and written how the private investigator couldn't be trusted to find his hand in front of his face. But listening to Uncle Bruce recount the last couple of years to Linus, Sam found his opinion had changed. He had begun to wonder if there was anyone better at finding people in the entire world.

"You want to tell him why we're here?" Linus asked Sam. "Or should I do it?"

Bruce shifted his frame and leaned forward. "Linus said a friend of yours is in jail for murder, and you don't think he did it."

"Right," Sam said.

A waitress approached their table, balancing a tray of sizzling fajitas, one order for each of them. She placed the plates in front of them, each holding a combination of chicken, steak or shrimp, the shell and the vegetables. Steam from the fajitas filled the space between the four of them like a fog the morning after a heavy rain.

Bruce took a fajita and lifted it toward his mouth, but he paused and looked at Sam the same way Beaumont had a couple of nights earlier. "In my experience," he said, taking on a more serious tone. "The police get it right most of the time."

Sam's chest tightened as if Bruce had grabbed him with his large hand and began squeezing. In his mind, he saw Carey standing over Maryanne with the golf club in his hand. His mouth went flat, and his eyes stayed on Bruce a beat too long. Bruce's gaze narrowed on Sam, a smile forming at the corners of his mouth.

"You have that look in your face that says you're about to tell me how I'm wrong, and I'm usually not, but I'll listen. Go ahead, start from the beginning."

Bruce pulled a small tablet computer from his worn brown satchel. He set it on the table next to his plate, tapped the screen, and an app loaded. For the next few minutes, Sam recounted what he knew about both murders, with Linus jumping in now and then to let his friend take a bite of his food. Bruce scribbled notes into his app in what looked like some kind of shorthand that Sam couldn't read.

"What is that thing?" Sam asked, letting his curiosity get the best of him.

Bruce held the tablet in the air and turned it to face Sam. "I wrote an app a few years back to keep track of my cases. I could never find anything I liked, and I was tired of spreadsheets, so I learned some basic programming and used a little bit of AI to write my own."

"That's impressive," Sam said.

Despite Sam's "judge a book by its cover" first impression of Uncle Bruce, the man's dedication to his job and interest in Sam's story were becoming more evident as they spoke.

"After Linus texted me, I spent some time last night reading about this case." Bruce swiped the device's screen, moving his notes back a couple of pages. "From what I could find, Emmitt Layne took over a golf course and turned it into a place people vacation to so they can say they played Savannah Palms. He shows up in business features, charity photos, golf events, anywhere he can promote, he will promote." Bruce's thick finger scrolled. "Carey seems dependable. Brock's the loud one. Dexter's the boring one. Peyton's the successful one." His finger stopped on the last name on the list. "But then we have this Maryanne Preston character. I can't find a single thing on her."

Linus stopped chewing while Sam's eyes stayed on Bruce.

"She's a ghost," Bruce said.

"A ghost?" Sam asked. "What do you mean?"

"A ghost. Like she started existing ten minutes ago."

"I knew some ghosts back in Vegas," Scott said. Sam and Linus looked his way. "Ghosts love Vegas. It's an easy place to disappear and earn some money in some less-than-legal ways."

"You from there?" Bruce asked.

Scott nodded but went back to his lunch without saying anything more. There was a distance in his eyes, as if he were remembering things without sharing them with the rest of the table.

Sam turned to Bruce. "Can you get me everything the police have on Carey? Do they already know Maryanne is a ghost? I need to know what they know."

"Why?"

Swallowing the last bite of his meal, Sam pushed his plate away. "They've locked him up. I'm worried the only thing they're doing is looking for things to use to convict him and ignoring those things that could convict someone else. If something points away from him, I want to know what it is."

Bruce set his fork down and wiped his fingers on a napkin. "They're not going to hand me their file, and you're a civilian. You're best friends with the guy they arrested. They probably don't even believe you when it comes to what you saw. For all they know, you're lying. You saw him do it, and you're protecting him."

"The detective leading the case, Captain Randall Beaumont, is an—" Sam paused, looking for the right word. "He's an acquaintance of mine."

"From when your parents died," Bruce said.

Sam froze, his eyes flashing to Linus.

"I didn't tell him," Linus said.

"Homework is part of the job, Sam. I looked into your case, but I also looked into you. You can call him a friend, an acquaintance, your best pal, anything you want. But in the end, he's a cop and solving a murder is what he cares about most."

"He warned me to stay away,"

Bruce's eyebrows lifted. "Did he?"

"He told me not to interfere or there would be consequences."

Now Bruce's shoulders crowded the space as he again leaned forward. "Then you take that warning seriously."

"I can't sit on my hands," Sam said.

"Last night, while I was reading about this case, I read about you. I know what you did in Wyoming. The police here don't give a damn about that. Most of them would have arrested you for interfering with an officer. The only reason you got away with it is because one soft police officer bent rules she shouldn't have bent."

"What should I do, then?" Sam asked. "Maybe I can find out more about Maryanne—"

"No, Sam. You don't do anything. You let me handle it. I have some friends from when I was on the force. I'll talk to them and see what I can come up with."

"That's how it is on TV," Linus said with a laugh. "The ex-cops who become PIs always have friends still on the force."

"I appreciate that," Sam told Bruce. "I really do. It's what I was hoping you'd say. But I can't sit silently and wait. Maybe I could talk to Allen—"

"I'm not so sure about this Allen Bryce Foster character."

"Why?"

"I met him once. He came to Atlanta to represent someone I had found for the police. During the trial, it felt to me like he was throwing it, you know, like not trying hard enough. The guy I found ended up in jail."

"You think he lost on purpose?" Sam asked, surprised.

"It's hard to say for sure, but I was in the courtroom during the trial, and I didn't like what I was seeing. I'm not a lawyer, but I've been in enough courtrooms to know when someone is trying and when someone isn't."

He paused long enough to take a drink.

"Two years later, there was an appeal, and the judge awarded a new trial. Foster crushed it, presenting evidence he'd certainly had, but didn't bring out the first time. He asked completely different questions to the witnesses, and eventually, he won the case. The original verdict was thrown out, and my guy went free while loving his attorney for the job he did to get him out."

"Sounds like he messed up the first time but then figured it all out the second time."

"I think he threw that case the first time so he could have a second one."

"Why?"

"Lawyers get paid by the hour," Bruce said. "I assume the Layne family has money?"

"Lots," Linus said through a mouthful of food. "You should see Emmitt's house. It's huge."

"That's probably why. He takes on these big clients, people who will pay and not feel the amount of money he's taking from them. Then he'll string them along until he's made a little extra."

"What about Maryanne?" Sam asked. "It seems like her being a ghost is a big deal. Do you have a way to find out more about her?"

"There's always a way," Bruce said with a smile. "You want me to move forward with this thing? My rates are high, but I'll give you a nice family discount."

"I'm sure Carey would pay your bill once he's out of jail," Sam said.

"Sounds like you just hired me. I'll get a room down here for the next few days, and I'll take a look around."

Chapter Eleven

Sam stood in the foyer of a downtown Savannah apartment building. The warm Georgia sun filtered through the glass, a couple of rays hitting him in the face. He looked over his shoulder, realizing that he was standing only a few miles from where Maryanne's murder had taken place.

"I can't believe I'm doing this again," he whispered to himself.

The first time he had conducted an investigation, interviewing witnesses, looking for clues, trying to get someone he cared about off the police's radar, he hadn't thought of himself as a detective. He had fallen for Dani quickly, much more quickly than he had expected, and had acted mostly on instinct, a lot of which had been wrong. Until, eventually, it wasn't. This time it was for Carey.

"Is Linus going to be accused of killing someone next?" he muttered

He stared at the list of names on the wall, each with a small white-squared button next to it. They were arranged alphabetically by last name; starting from the top and slowly working his way down, he said each name out loud.

"Kristie Baker? No, that doesn't sound right. Kristie Bradford? Kristie Breckenridge?" He paused and moved his finger over the button. "Breckenridge. That sounds right."

He pressed the button, but as the buzzer sounded, more doubt crept in. Should he really be doing this again? Taking on a murder case was a huge responsibility, even without South Plainfield's most annoying police officer, Detective Alfred Emerson, pushing back on everything he did.

A female voice came through the speaker. "Yeah?"

"Kristie?" Sam asked.

"Yeah." Her voice was low, and she was breathing heavily.

"It's Sam Norris. Sorry to bother you." He paused for a second, waiting for her to respond, but she stayed quiet. Did she even know who he was? "I play in the Tuesday night league at the golf course. My friends and I have dinner afterward in the restaurant. Me and Linus and Madison and uh—"

"Yeah, okay. I know who you are. What do you want?"

"I wanted to ask you about what happened at the reading of Emmitt's will."

"I've already talked to the police."

"I know, but I have my own questions."

"Why?"

"They arrested Carey."

Silence filled the foyer. Sam stared at the speaker. What had happened? Why had she gone quiet?

"Second floor," she finally said. "First door on the left. It'll be open."

Her words had come out more quickly, and she'd sounded surprised. Had she not known about Carey? The door buzzed, and a click signaled it had unlocked. He went up the first flight of stairs, took a left, and stopped at her door. She had already left it against the deadbolt, keeping it open for Sam.

"Hello?" He said.

"I'm in the bedroom," Kristie yelled. "Give me a few minutes. I'm back from the gym. Get yourself a drink and take a seat."

Kristie's apartment was small and felt confined, almost suffocating. The curtains had been pulled back, but only a few inches, allowing a narrow band of morning sunlight inside. The carpeting in the short hallway leading from the door was worn. On the left, Sam passed by a small bathroom. Its tiles were slightly chipped, and the air inside carried a thick amount of steam along with the scent of soap and shampoo.

"There's water in the fridge," Kristie added.

To his right, the small, narrow kitchen seemed neglected. A few dishes had been piled in the sink, and on the tiny amount of counter space, a dirty plate with some silverware and an empty glass indicated Kristie hadn't bothered to clean up after this morning's breakfast.

Takeout menus were stuck to the refrigerator with different magnets, each representing something at Savannah Palms. Two receipts hung on the freezer, and on the side facing Sam, a doodle on a napkin of two people, one resembling Kristie, was held on by a Garfield magnet.

"I hate Mondays too," Sam said.

"What's that?" Kristie yelled from the bedroom, its door still closed.

"Nothing. I was talking to myself."

Sam's eyes were drawn to two couches, both facing the television. From what he could see, the fabric showed signs of wear, but piles of clothes had been stacked on it, forcing him to take a seat at the table. In front of him, a laptop sat half-closed within reach, its charging cord hanging off the edge, plugged into a wall outlet. On top of the laptop's case, she had stuck a large Savannah Palms Golf Course sticker. A spiral notebook sat next to it, a page dog-eared and covered in grease. Takeout napkins, a plastic fork, and a paper plate flecked with dried sauce crowded the edge. A grocery flyer, two crumpled receipts, a hair tie, and a tube of lip balm took up the remaining space.

"Sorry for the mess," Kristie said, peeking her head out.

"It's fine," Sam said. "I only need a couple minutes of your time."

"Good, because that's all I have." She disappeared back into the bedroom and shut the door.

Near the wall between the table and the bar, three empty suitcases sat next to three large, empty boxes. The suitcases were stacked inside each other, the largest on the bottom. Two drawers had been pulled out near the stove and set on the bar with two piles of kitchen utensils and other random items next to them, as if someone had pulled out each drawer and dumped its contents on the countertops.

The bedroom door creaked open, and she finally appeared. She wore black shorts and a matching T-shirt, her blond hair gathered into a messy ponytail. A bead of sweat fell from her forehead. She hurried toward Sam and cleared off the table in front of him. She smelled of perfume, something floral.

"Is this a bad time?" Sam asked.

"It's perfect timing," she said with a smile. "I have half an hour before I have to leave for work. I usually take Friday nights off, but Brock asked me to work the closing shift tonight."

"Brock asked you?"

"He texted me this morning." She paused and wiped the sweat from her forehead. "I'm glad it was him and not Maryanne. I can't stand either of them, but he's the lesser of two evils." She hurried into the kitchen. "Did you want something to drink?"

"What's your problem with Maryanne?"

"She's only interested in Emmitt's money."

Sam paused. He stared at her, trying to read her face. "Haven't you heard?"

"Heard what?" she asked. "How she's going to sell the course and put all of us out of a job? I heard her at the will reading saying that kind of stuff before Peyton, uh..." She trailed off and swallowed, not wanting to finish the sentence. "That was enough to know I didn't want her anywhere near that place."

"I don't think you'll have to worry about that anymore," Sam said.

"Why?"

"You really don't know?" he asked, tapping his phone with his thumb.

Her smile faded. She stopped what she was doing and turned to him. "Know what? What are you talking about?"

"Kristie, someone killed Maryanne two nights ago."

Kristie's eyes widened, and her face drained of color. She set her bottle of water on the table and sank into a chair across from him.

"You said you talked to the police. I assumed it was about that."

"I meant that I talked to them earlier in the week about Peyton." She grabbed her phone, lifting it to show Sam a missed call from the police on the evening of Thanksgiving.

"You didn't call them back?"

"I already said everything to them I needed to say. Yesterday was Thanksgiving. There are only a few days a year when I shut everything down and spend time with my family. Thanksgiving is one of them. I spent the day with my dad, drank a little too much, and instead of driving home, I stayed with him. When I woke up this morning, I had another missed call and a text, but I wanted to hit the gym first, so I came home, grabbed a change of clothes, did some shopping, then the gym, and now I'm here talking to you."

She pulled the phone back, tapped the screen again, and held it up for Sam to see. The most recent message was from Beaumont.

"Miss Breckenridge, you need to get a hold of us as soon as possible. We have additional questions."

He swept his eyes quickly through the list of the last ten people Kristie had texted with. At the bottom was Peyton's name, with "I'm so sorry about ly-" as the preview only showed the beginning of the text before the rest of it was cut off. The date and time were less than an hour before his death.

"They probably wanted to tell you about Maryanne," Sam said.

"What happened to her?"

"Someone beat her to death with a golf club."

For a moment, she was silent, and the only sound that filled the room was the low volume from her television in her bedroom. A soft gasp escaped her lips, and she reached for her phone.

"I should call them back."

"Wait," Sam said. He reached across the table and put his hand on hers. "Before you do, give me a few minutes of your time."

"Beaten to death? Are you sure?"

"Unfortunately, I am." Sam closed his eyes and tried not to see the body, but his brain forced him to, and his eyes snapped open.

"First, Peyton and now this," she whispered.

"What did you tell the police about Peyton's death?" Sam asked.

"Nothing too exciting. You know, what I saw, who was in the room. It's funny, though, the way they questioned me, it's like they think someone killed him."

Sam had already heard it from Carey, and now Kristie too. "What makes you think that?"

"They didn't exactly come out and say it specifically, but they kept hinting around, asking me if he had any enemies. They also asked me to provide a list of everyone who works in the kitchen and who was there that night."

"From your point of view, what happened?"

"He was arguing with everyone in the room, apologizing to Carey for his dad leaving him the course, then out of nowhere, he began to choke. Maryanne hit him with that EpiPen, and he died. I can't imagine why anyone would want to kill him. He was a good guy, and he treated all his dad's employees respectfully."

"Could that attitude from the employees have changed once Allen read the will?"

"No chance," she said. "The course was staying open, and the will specified they all got raises. They were overpaid as it is, and he was giving them more. It was sweet of Emmitt to take care of his people one last time. Besides, no one knew Peyton was getting the course until that night."

"What did Peyton eat for dinner?"

Kristie stiffened, and a small amount of defensiveness crept into her voice. "Why?"

"Simple curiosity."

"No, Sam. You're asking specific questions. The same questions the police asked me multiple times. Why is everyone asking about his dinner?"

Sam hesitated, "Is there any chance someone could have tampered with his food, maybe dropped peanuts or something into it to cause the reaction?"

"He was allergic to tree nuts, not peanuts."

"Is there a difference?"

She smiled. "If I had a nickel for every time I heard Peyton tell a waiter the difference, I'd have a whole bunch of nickels."

Sam's brow furrowed. "You seem to know a fair bit about him."

"He ate at the golf course all the time, and his father was my boss," she snapped. "I don't like this line of questioning."

He held his hands in the air. "I'm not accusing you of anything. I wasn't there, so I'm trying to work out who was there and what they saw. If the police asked about his dinner more than once, it must be important. What was the dinner?"

She hesitated and stood. "It was chicken or steak with a potato and a couple of options for vegetables. Some bread and a dessert. It's the same menu we put out for every golf outing."

"Did he have steak or chicken?"

"Neither. A couple of nights before the will reading, Peyton called and asked if I could make him something vegan." She smiled. "I've known him for years. I didn't know he even knew what that word meant. Then suddenly, he calls and asks for it."

"Why?"

"Isn't it obvious?"

"Not to me," Sam said.

"It had to be Maryanne. She had this hold on him that I, uh, well, let's just say she had a hold on him. I never did like—" Kristie waved a hand. "I mean, I shouldn't speak ill of her now that she's gone." She paused briefly, but then looked up at Sam. "And before you ask, yeah, I'm the one who prepared his meal and took it to him. There's no way anyone else could have touched it without me knowing. Whatever caused him to have the allergic reaction, it wasn't in his dinner."

"What did he drink?"

"He had carbonated water."

"Did you prepare anyone else's food?"

"Only his," she said. "Once he veered away from the regular menu, I told the cook I'd handle it."

Sam frowned. If Kristie prepared the dinner, and nothing suspicious was in the food, how could Peyton have had an allergic reaction unless she was involved? He glanced past her at the suitcases on the floor.

"Did you see Carey leave the room or come into the kitchen?"

"I wasn't paying attention to him the whole time, but he definitely didn't come into the kitchen."

"Who did?"

"The only one I remember was Allen," Kristie said. "The cook threw a piece of chicken on a bun for him. He wanted something to eat for the road."

"No one else?"

"Brock got all pissy when he found out I got more money than him, and he stormed out that way, but he came back for dinner."

"What was everyone else doing while Peyton went through his reaction?"

"Nothing, really," she said. "Maryanne was the only one who really did anything. Emily tried to help, but Maryanne had one of those EpiPens." Kristie's eyes narrowed, and she glanced up as if she were replaying it in her head.

"What's wrong?" Sam asked.

"I remember her looking at the pen like she didn't know which end was the needle, which was strange because she had the same allergy as him. But the way she stared at it, she looked confused."

"But she did use it, right?"

"Stuck him in the thigh. Then he died."

Neither spoke. They let those words hang in the air as if they had decided to have a moment of silence for Peyton.

"Are you going somewhere?" Sam pointed to the suitcases.

"Doing some spring cleaning."

"It's November," Sam said.

"You can spring clean anytime."

"What else did the police ask you?"

"They rattled off a list of nuts and asked which ones we had in the kitchen. We didn't carry any of them."

"I assume they'll talk to the cook too?"

"They already did. But since I made his dinner, she didn't have much to say."

"Could she have any reason to hurt Peyton?"

"She's a sweet old lady who's been at the course for a few months now. We hired her away from the Legends Golf Course at the beginning of the summer. Emmitt discovered how much the customers there liked her, so he made her an offer she couldn't refuse. She also brought along her regulars as customers."

"You really loved Emmitt, didn't you?"

"He was like the father I didn't have growing up. Even now, with my father back in the picture, Emmitt was still the one I went to if I needed a dad. When I was a little girl, my mom worked two jobs, and I wasn't an easy kid to raise. If I had a nickel for the number of times she had to come down to the police station to get me—"

"You'd have a lot of nickels."

"So many nickels," she said with a smile. "Shoplifting, vandalism and pretty much any rebellious thing I could think of."

"What changed?"

"I was working as a bartender at Playmakers when I was nineteen, to uh, well, let's just say, to support some habits. I'm sure you know the place. It's downtown."

Sam knew the place. Linus had gotten him there once after work. Wall-to-wall TVs, free appetizers on the tables and waitresses in crop tops and short shorts. The wings were terrible and way too expensive.

"Emmitt came in one Friday afternoon for lunch. We were talking, and he seemed like a nice man. He told me how he was buying Savannah Palms and wanted me to come run the kitchen."

"That sounds like Emmitt," Sam said.

"I was shocked. My dad went into a tailspin after he lost his business, and I had to look out for myself. I ended up working at a skin restaurant. Emmitt knew my dad. He came in one day to tell me to ditch the place and work for him. I agreed almost immediately, ditched my short shorts, and the rest is history. He changed my life."

"What about the brothers, Brock and Dexter?" Sam asked.

"They're shit."

"Blunt. I assume you didn't get along with them?"

"I didn't see them much," she said. "Peyton stopped by once in a while because he was the good son. Brock only showed up when they needed money, and Dexter never showed up."

"What about Carey?"

"Of the four, I knew him the best. A few years back, in my only attempt at windsurfing, I fell and broke my leg." She reached down and touched a spot below her knee. "Emmitt invited me to stay at the house. I agreed, and when I showed up on that first day, he had hired a live-in nurse to help me get through it. Carey was living there at the time, and we got along like brother and sister."

She stood and went back into the kitchen, rinsing her plastic water bottle, then filling it with water from the tap. Sam followed her, stopping at the entrance to the kitchen. The doodle on the napkin caught his eye. Below it was a dinner receipt. The total was $51.77, with the tip of $9.61 and total of $61.38, an odd amount. Underneath the total, the word "Kings" was written.

"You had an argument with Peyton before the will was read," Sam said. It wasn't a question. He wanted her to know that he already knew about it. She shut the fridge, her fingers fidgeting with the cap of the water bottle she had grabbed.

His eyes moved back to the doodle. It showed two figures, one with a ponytail and the other wearing a tie. Sam glanced at Kristie, her ponytail swinging slightly from side to side as she spoke.

"We talked," she said, avoiding eye contact. "But I wouldn't call it an argument."

"What did you talk about?" he insisted.

"Nothing too important."

"Seems like if you argued, it would be important."

"It wasn't." She grabbed a dish towel and began wiping down a sink that didn't need wiping.

Sam leaned back and looked at the doodle on the side of the fridge. The figure on the left was clearly Kristie, and on the right, the other figure wore a tie. He had broad shoulders, and he held his hand in the air as if he were throwing a football. There was a little heart drawn between them.

Without looking her way, he said, “When did the two of you stop sleeping together?”

Chapter Twelve

Kristie set the dish towel flat on the counter and folded it in half. She smoothed it, pressing it down so there were no wrinkles. "What are you talking about?"

"I'm talking about you and Peyton, sleeping together. When did it stop?"

"We weren't doing that," she said through gritted teeth.

"I think you were."

She grabbed the salt-and-pepper shakers, saying nothing as she re-arranged them near the sink. Sam stood in the narrow entrance way to the kitchen, blocking her exit, hoping she would feel trapped. After a few seconds, she turned to face him, her shoulders slumped. "How did you know?"

"You have a drawing hanging on your fridge of you and him together with a little heart on it. That's generally something two people don't get unless they're more than friends. I also noticed he had sent you a text on the day he died, apologizing for something, and there are only a handful of things he would have apologized for. I didn't think it was money. That led me to sex. When did it end?"

"A few weeks ago," Kristie finally said. "When I found out he and Maryanne were married."

"But you were as surprised as we were earlier this week when Brock told us."

"Peyton asked me to keep it a secret."

"Did you tell the police about it?"

"I didn't kill him, and I certainly wasn't going to give them the motive they were fishing for."

Sam leaned in, his eyes locked on hers. "When they find out, they'll know you lied, and they'll see that motive even stronger than it already is."

Her voice wavered, but she held her ground. "I would never harm a hair on his body."

"How long had it been going on?"

"It started a few weeks before he and Maryanne had begun going out. He stopped by the bar alone one night after we had closed. Emmitt was gone, and I was the only one here. We started talking, drinking and things happened."

"And you kept going once they began dating?"

"I didn't think it would last," she said, shrugging. "No one did. I figured they would do what they were doing for a little while longer, he would realize how terrible she was, and get rid of her."

"But that didn't happen," Sam said.

"Eventually, they moved in together, but Peyton and I kept things going. He came up with this way of communicating with me when he and Maryanne would come into the golf course for dinner. It's how I knew where to find him when she wasn't around."

"Did she know about the two of you?"

"Not as far as I knew."

"Why did you stop?"

"Once he and Maryanne looked like they were serious, I told him, the minute they were married, I was done with him. I may not be an angel, but I'm not messing around with a married man."

"But then he did get married, and I assume he didn't tell you?"

"That's what we argued about. I told him I was pissed that he didn't tell me, but he said he didn't want to lose me. Numerous times over the past few weeks, he apologized to me for lying whenever he could, including that text message you saw, but I told him I was through with him. I was pissed."

"Pissed enough to kill?"

"No way," she said.

"You sure?"

"I know I make a pretty good suspect, Sam, but I didn't do it."

"Revenge is a nice motive, and according to your own words, you were the only one who had access to his dinner. The police will call that opportunity. In terms of the means, you run the kitchen. I'm sure you know what things could lead to an allergic reaction strong enough to kill someone with a peanut allergy."

"Tree nut, Sam, and I don't like how you're talking to me." Kristie squeezed past him and hurried to the dining room table, where she grabbed her phone. "I need to talk to the police right now. They can't think I did this."

Sam followed. He put his hand on hers, keeping her from picking it up. "At the will reading, there was a man. You made him leave. Do you know who he was?"

"For someone who wasn't there, you sure know a lot about what happened."

"Do you know him?"

"No, Sam, I don't know him."

"You know where I can find him?"

"It was some homeless guy who wandered in off the street."

Sam's phone buzzed, and he looked at a picture of Linus on the screen. It was probably the bell he needed to get him out of there, as he was starting to wear out his welcome.

"Let me grab this call," he said.

"That's fine. I need to call the police anyway. You can let yourself out."

She took her phone and disappeared into her bedroom. Sam let himself out of Kristie's apartment and tapped his phone to answer Linus's call.

"What's up?"

"Simulator Two is open again, and the police are gone if you're interested in hitting some balls."

"Is Brock there?"

"Oh, yeah," Linus said. "He's sitting at the bar, half in the bag, giving orders as if he runs the place."

"He thinks he does. You said the cops are gone? All of them?"

"It's back to being a regular old golf course again," Linus said. "Unless they find another body around here."

"I'll be there in a few," Sam said. "But not to hit balls."

Chapter Thirteen

Sam hurried along the south side of the building, checking for cameras. Carey had told him they weren't there, and even though he believed in his friend, he had to see for himself. At the back door, he paused, not exactly excited to have a conversation with Brock but also knowing he had to.

Behind him, on the back nine, the construction company had restarted its work on a few of the holes. He watched as a backhoe cleared dirt near the seventeenth tee, curious if anyone had consulted Carey about restarting the course's makeover.

He moved into the pro shop and continued to the bar. The door for Simulator Two was open, and Linus was inside hitting balls.

A few foursomes in from their rounds of golf, one of them including Dexter Layne, sat at tables eating a late lunch. At the end of the bar, Brock sat alone nursing a drink while a cigarette burned in an ashtray. He looked up at Sam briefly with a flash of recognition in his eyes, then went back to the newspaper in front of him.

"Your annoying friend is in there," Brock said. He pointed toward the simulator room.

"I was hoping to get a drink first," Sam said as he took a seat at the bar, leaving an empty stool between himself and Brock.

Without asking, Brock reached over the bar, grabbed a glass and filled it with diet soda. He set the drink down in front of Sam hard enough for some of it to spill.

"Diet, right?"

"Yeah, that's fine," Sam said. He grabbed a cocktail napkin, wiped the wet spots, and put the drink on it.

Sam took a sip, the ice clinking against the glass. He took another, glancing at Brock, trying to find the right opening line. Brock's paper rustled, then went still; the silence in the room was only broken by the mumbling of the patrons behind him or the thump of Linus smacking the ball. Sam cleared his throat. Brock folded his newspaper in half and set it down. He looked at Sam.

"What do you want, kid?" he finally asked. "You're sitting there staring at me as if you want to ask me for a date."

"It's a shame what happened," Sam said. "With Peyton and Maryanne. And now Carey in jail. This place doesn't feel like it used to."

"It's more than a shame, kid, it's shitty. That's what it is."

"Any idea who did it?" Sam asked, purposely keeping the question vague. Brock could easily interpret it as a question about Maryanne's murder, but if he wanted to bring up Peyton, Sam wouldn't stop him.

Brock leaned in slightly, his words coming slowly. "No way, man, I don't know nothing about that. Murder's not my thing."

"What is your thing?" was the question Sam wanted to ask, but instead, he stared at Brock. He had dark circles around his brown eyes, his hair was messy, and a five o'clock shadow had attached itself to his face.

Brock showed a crooked smile. "I'm talking about enjoying the finer things in life, if you catch my drift."

He lifted his half-empty glass in a mock toast and took a slow sip, his eyes never leaving Sam's face. Sam hadn't caught his drift, but he lifted his glass anyway. He peered down at the paperwork in front of Brock. Alongside the newspapers displaying horse- and dog-racing outcomes, a collection of Savannah Palms-related paperwork, invoices, and course layouts was spread out. A small black notebook also sat next to the newspapers. It was closed but looked well-used.

"Are you running the course now?" Sam asked.

"Why shouldn't I be? Maryanne is gone, and there ain't no kids. Common sense says it comes to me."

"Common sense isn't necessarily law, though, right? Everyone expected it to go to Carey."

Brock sat up and laughed. "Not a damn thing he can do from inside, is there?"

Anger flashed inside Sam, and he felt the heat rising in his chest. "He's your brother. Isn't that a little harsh?"

"Allen told me to take control while he checked into it. He said it could take some time, and someone had to make the decisions around here, so being the businessman of the family, I took it over."

"Shouldn't the relatives of Maryanne end up with it?"

"There's not a snowball's chance in hell I would ever let that happen." Brock's voice was steady at first, but it grew more heated. "They probably weren't even married. She's the one who said it, and she didn't tell any of us until after Peyton was gone. She's probably lying to get all his sh—"

Brock's chest hitched, and he coughed hard enough to lean forward, his forehead almost resting on the bar. The cough was wet and raw and ripped through his lungs. He slapped a palm against the bar. Sam took a glass and filled it with water, pushing it toward him. Brock grabbed it and drank it down.

"Thanks," he said as he held his cigarette in the air. "I gotta stop smoking these things."

"I don't think you're supposed to be smoking those inside."

"I'm running the place, junior, I can do what I want around here."

Sam turned his head and took in a breath of fresher air than what was in front of him. “Did you ask Allen if they were really married?”

“He’s looking into that too.”

“For a price, I bet,” Sam said.

“He don’t do that shit for free.” Brock took a drag from the cigarette, held it in, and blew the smoke from his nose and mouth. “He said once he has some answers, he’ll get us all straightened out.”

Brock’s phone rang. He looked down at it and grimaced, an expression that wasn’t too far off from his normal expression. “Running a business is hard fuckin’ work.”

Sam leaned forward, trying to see the phone’s screen. “Who is it?”

“Construction company. I started them back up. Once this place is mine, I’m gonna sell it and get the hell out of here.” He reached for his glass and, realizing it was empty, hit the bar with his fist a few times. “April, get out here!”

From the kitchen, a young woman emerged. She couldn’t have been more than twenty-one, her blond hair tied back in a ponytail. She greeted the two men with a warm, friendly smile.

“Come on, April, you let my glass go empty without bringing me another. We talked about this.”

April’s smile faded slightly as she took the glass. “Sorry, Mr. Layne.” She filled it to the top and set it in front of Brock before turning her attention to Sam. “Can I get you anything, sir?”

Sam, taken aback by the formal address, politely declined.

“A new bartender?” he asked.

“Remember that girl Dad hired a few months ago to help Kristie? She didn’t come in today. I don’t put up with that kind of shit, so I let her go.”

“And you hired this one that quickly?”

“April’s my buddy’s daughter.” He turned and looked at her. “Cute, isn’t she?”

April blushed. She moved a few strands of hair away from her eyes, tucking them behind her ear while offering a half-smile.

"What is it with you guys nowadays? Drinking soda as if you were still fifteen years old?" Brock asked him. "Peyton usually drank water, Dexter will have a beer every now and then, but only rarely, and Carey just drank soda. If I wanted someone to drink with, my only option was Maryanne, but all she drank were those fruity colorful drinks. I hate those things. The last time I saw her drinking, it was an Aperol Spritz. That seemed to be her drink of choice lately. I hadn't even heard of that until I saw her drinking one at the will reading."

Sam glanced over his shoulder toward Dexter, who was in a conversation with the people at his table.

Lowering his voice, Sam leaned toward Brock. "Speaking of the will reading, I heard you and Dexter were in a pretty heated argument before Allen read the will. What was that about?"

His fingers tracing circles on the surface of the bar, Brock offered a shrug. "Dex gave me twenty-five thousand dollars a few years back to invest in a business deal that wasn't going to fail."

"What happened to it?"

Brock laughed. "It failed miserably, and I haven't paid him back yet. It wasn't my fault, though. The guy I gave my money to was a goddamn thief." He paused to take a drink from his glass, let it sit in his mouth for a split second, then swallowed it. "I was hoping I would get enough from Dad's will to pay Dex back, but for some reason, Peyton got everything, and the rest of us got the shaft."

"Were you surprised by that?" Sam asked.

"Of course I was," Brock responded more loudly. His lips curled into a half-hearted smile.

Sam looked back again, but Dexter still hadn't turned toward them.

"Even the kid got more than me. I was one of four sons. I should have gotten at least one-fourth of his money." The upper half of Brock's body filled the empty spot between them. "Look, kid. I may have my vices." He looked around. "Some even a tiny bit illegal, but Dad showed me exactly what he thought of me that night." He took another drink. Alcohol dribbled from the corners of his mouth as he spoke. "I'll tell you what, though." This time, it was Brock who looked back. "I wouldn't be surprised if we find out at some point that Dex did that shit. He was here Wednesday night in that very simulator room. He probably did it to get a bigger piece of the pie."

Sam matched Brock's low, conspiratorial tone. "With Peyton and Maryanne both dead and Carey in jail, don't you already have a bigger piece of the pie? You've taken over running this place even though Emmitt left it to someone else."

"I'll end up in charge, anyway." Brock leaned back, sparing Sam of the scent of alcohol being spat his way. "And as I said, I'm gonna sell it."

"Why sell? It made your dad a ton of money."

"Golf isn't my thing."

"What is your thing?"

"Horses," Brock said as a spark appeared in him that Sam hadn't yet seen during their conversation. Brock grabbed the remote and turned on the TV above the bar. He flipped through the channels, stopping on a horse race. "See that horse right there." On the TV, the third race at Penn National had already started. "That horse in the lead is owned by a buddy of mine. He owns five horses in tonight's races."

"Another business deal with a buddy?"

Brock's laugh quickly evolved into another coughing fit. "I met him in a bar in Jacksonville," he said, choking the words out. "He bought me a beer, and we ended up chatting for a few hours. He's looking for investors. He wants to expand his stables, and I'm gonna help him."

"And you're going to do that to the family?"

"What the fuck has the family done for me?" He scooted his stool closer to Sam. "I'm not as stupid as you think. I know a good business deal when I see one. This morning, I met with a high school kid who's gonna build me a new website for the stables. I'm going to rebrand it as Brock and Kroll Stables. How cool is that? I'm Brock. He's Bobby Kroll. Like Rock and Roll!"

Sam let the name hang out there. Brock and Kroll. Brock had met a buddy in Jacksonville, and all it had taken was one beer: He was going to sell the course and lose the money. It wasn't a matter of when but rather of how quickly it would happen.

"Clever," Sam said while Brock stared at the TV, not picking up on his sarcasm.

"You should see the logo I designed."

"You put this together pretty quickly. As if you knew you were coming into money."

Brock laughed again. "Don't throw your accusations my way. I didn't kill my brother or my brother's supposed wife. When I found out about the ten thousand, I called Bobby and told him I had part of the money. I assured him I would get the rest. I wasn't sure how, but things always seem to find a way of workin' themselves out, don't they?"

Maryanne's battered body popped into Sam's head, followed by the look of guilt on his best friend's face as he knelt over her, holding the murder weapon. Sam had never thought of himself as violent, but the urge to punch that stupid grin off Brock's face was as strong as it had ever been. Before he could say anything, Brock jumped off the stool and ran behind the bar.

"What the fuck. Did you see that?"

He pointed behind the bar near a corner of the room. A small gray mouse sat up on its hind legs, chewing on something. Brock threw his pencil at it, the mouse disappearing through a small hole.

"I told Kristie to deal with those fuckin' things. It'll kill the value of this place if the kitchen's shut down."

Sam shifted his eyes from the hole the mouse had used back to Brock. "You told Kristie to deal with a mouse problem?"

"Apparently, she doesn't listen either. I never understood what my dad saw in her." He elbowed Sam and smiled. "That's a lie. I know exactly what he saw in her."

"How was she supposed to be dealing with the mouse?"

"I didn't give a shit how she did it. I just wanted it done."

"But do you know?"

"Some kind of poison, I think."

"Where do you keep your poison?"

Brock walked toward a small closet behind the far end of the bar, unlocked the door and opened it. He pointed to an empty spot on the floor. "We had some rat poison."

"Where is it now?"

"She probably moved it somewhere else."

Sam grabbed his phone and did a quick search, finding the image of a common type of rat poison sold at most stores. He zoomed in on the label and began reading out loud to himself. At the second item on the list, he inhaled sharply. He turned his phone around and showed the picture to Brock.

"This one?"

Brock leaned in, swaying as he stood a few inches from Sam's phone. "Looks about right."

"The main ingredient is strychnine alkaloid," Sam mumbled.

"What the hell does that mean?"

"It means I need to go."

Chapter Fourteen

Sam steered his car to the right, pulling into the apartment complex's large parking lot. He paused, his foot touching the brake pedal. Parked next to the steps were three police cars. None of the officers were outside, but the security door had been propped open. Had they found out about the rat poison? Had they come to arrest Kristie?

He hurried up the concrete stairs, pulled open the first door and rushed through the open security door. At the top of the staircase, he paused to catch his breath. The hallway was empty. He went to Kristie's door. Voices came from inside, of at least one female and two males, including one he recognized as it grew louder. Sam took a deep breath and pushed open the door.

Officer Beaumont's eyebrows shot up as he turned to face Sam. "What are you doing here?"

Behind him, a female officer Sam hadn't met stood in Kristie's bedroom, her hand against her holster as Beaumont spoke. Jacobs stood in the living room, his eyes also on Sam.

"Is Kristie okay?" Sam asked.

"Why shouldn't she be?" Beaumont asked.

Sam's eyes narrowed as he studied the three officers. One in her bedroom, the other in the living room, with Beaumont standing near her dining room table. No sign of Kristie anywhere.

"Okay, but why are y'all here if she's not here? You don't even know if she's missing or headed out to the grocery store. It looks like you entered her apartment without her knowing, and you're searching it as if she were your top suspect."

"I've got two dead bodies in under a week. The door was open, and I saw the mess. I'm not taking any chances. Why are you here? I told you to leave it alone."

"And I told you Carey is innocent."

Beaumont grinned and looked over his shoulder at Jacobs. He closed his notebook and held it at his side. "Sam," he said, keeping his voice flat. "You keep walking into my scenes, and I'm going to arrest you."

Sam stood in the apartment's doorway, not taking a single step back or forward. In South Plainfield, Detective Emerson had threatened him with an arrest more times than he could count, but he'd never found a reason that would stick, something he suspected Beaumont also lacked.

"For what?" he asked. "Visiting my friend in prison? Having a conversation with Brock Layne at the golf course I'm a member of, and he is currently running? Or standing in the hallway of an apartment building asking the police about a woman who I consider a friend?" He didn't add that he hadn't been able to remember her last name a few hours earlier.

Beaumont took a step closer; Sam could smell the coffee on his breath and see remnants of the man's lunch on his chin. "How about interfering with my investigation?" He looked at Jacobs and back at Sam. "Or maybe obstruction. I'm in a good mood today. You can pick."

Holding out his hands, Sam kept his wrists together so Beaumont could put the handcuffs on him. "Then do it. But first, tell me what I've obstructed or what evidence I've touched or how I'm interfering. Unlike y'all, I'm still out here in the hallway. I'm not the one who entered her apartment illegally."

Sam's heart was beating in his ears. He wasn't sure if his hands were shaking as he held them out to Beaumont, but he didn't back down. He held the veteran detective's eyes a beat longer than was comfortable.

"You want to be helpful," Beaumont said, "go home. Because if you keep doing this, eventually I will have a reason."

All at once, it hit Sam. "You figured out they were sleeping together. That's why you're here."

"Do you know where she is?"

"I told you, I don't know." Sam rubbed the back of his neck, then took one step inside the apartment.

"What did the two of you talk about?"

"We mostly reminisced about Emmitt and what a great guy he was. She told me how she met him, and I told her my story."

"And that's all you talked about?"

"She also said she didn't know about Maryanne's death. In fact, I'm the person who broke it to her."

Beaumont's head flinched back slightly. "You're telling me she worked at the golf course that the dead woman now owned. She was technically an employee of Maryanne's, and thirty-six hours later, she still didn't know her new boss was dead? No one told her? No one texted her?"

"It surprised me too. She told me she was with her dad yesterday, and she drank too much, so she spent the night at his place. She showed me your calls and your text messages, but they were vague, and she said she never checked her voicemail."

"You believe her?"

"I did until I learned about the rat poison."

Inside the bedroom, the female officer stopped and looked toward Sam. She had released her grip on the holster, but her expression hadn't changed. In the living room, Officer Jacobs had been rooting around the piles of clothes on the couch. He also looked toward Sam.

"What rat poison?" Beaumont asked.

"Brock told me she had access to rat poison."

Beaumont flipped through his notebook. "He didn't tell me anything about rat poison."

"Rat poison's main ingredient is strychnine, and that's how Peyton died, wasn't it?"

Beaumont's pen clicked at his side as Sam said the word "strychnine." Sam smiled. Beaumont didn't need to verbally confirm anything. His actions had done it for him.

Sam continued, "Someone put strychnine in the EpiPen. Peyton and Kristie argued during the will reading, and you think she may have spiked Peyton's dinner or his drink, which would cause the allergic reaction. Then Maryanne would jab him with the EpiPen, killing him."

"What else did you two talk about?"

"Nothing much," Sam said as Beaumont took a seat across from him. "I was confused by the mess, and I think she sensed my confusion, as if I were suspecting her of something, maybe wanting to leave. She apologized before I even said anything about it and told me she was doing a spring-cleaning thing."

"In November?" Jacobs asked.

"You can clean anytime you want and call it spring-cleaning."

Sam took another step forward into the apartment. Beaumont didn't move, and although he wasn't near Sam, it was clear he was keeping Sam from going any farther.

"When I was here earlier, there were three suitcases on the floor next to the dining room table. How many are there now?"

Beaumont looked back at Jacobs, who walked over to the table. He knelt, out of Sam's view, but quickly jumped to his feet. "There's two, sir."

"That means she left," Sam said.

Beaumont's eyes moved to the suitcases, then to the open bedroom door where the female officer stood. Silence filled the room as the wheels in the police veteran's mind seemed to be working. His mouth moved slightly as if he were talking to himself, the same way Sam talks to himself when he's fixing a bug in a program at work. Beaumont wasn't stalling. He was deciding what to do next.

"Jacobs," he finally said, lifting his chin, "I want a BOLO put out on Kristie Breckenridge. Adult female, blond. Approximately five feet, six inches tall. One hundred and twenty-five pounds. Her last confirmed sighting was earlier today at her residence at..." He looked at Sam. "What time?"

"Uh, around noon, I guess."

"Noon," Beaumont said, continuing to give orders to Jacobs. "We're treating this as a possible flight."

"Who would she be running from?" Sam asked, talking more to himself than anyone else. "We talked about both Peyton's and Maryanne's deaths, and she seemed shaken up by them. At the time, I didn't get the impression she had anything to do with them."

"She had access to his dinner," Beaumont said.

"So did a lot of people," Sam said. "The number of people who came and went during that will reading was almost everyone in the room." He looked Beaumont in the eyes. "Except Carey. He never left the room."

"She knew about the rat poison."

"So did Brock," Sam said.

Beaumont did a quick scan of the apartment. "Jacobs, head back to Savannah Palms and look into this rat poison."

"It was in the small closet behind the bar," Sam said.

"Was?" Beaumont asked.

"When Brock opened the door to show me, it was gone."

Beaumont waited until Jacobs moved past Sam and was gone from the apartment.

"You have anything else?"

"Who called you guys Wednesday night to come out to the course to find Maryanne's body? What did they say?"

"You're done here," he told Sam. "Go home."

Sam folded his arms across his chest. "Why won't you answer my question after everything I just gave you? I'm trying to help." He watched Jacobs as he disappeared down the flight of stairs toward the building's front doors. "In fact, I think I did help you. How much of that did you actually know? It didn't seem like much at all."

"No. You're trying to help your friend. Those are two different things." Beaumont nodded toward the doorway.

Sam shook his head and turned. He still had the deleted simulator videos along with the scoring records. He had been the one to talk to Kristie, seeing her face when he told her Maryanne was dead. It didn't matter what he told Beaumont; he would get nothing in return, and Carey would continue to sit in jail for something he hadn't done.

Chapter Fifteen

Another Tuesday league night was coming to an end in The Eagle's Nest. Sam, Madison, Linus and Libby sat at their usual table. The police had finished their investigation of the murder scene and allowed the bar to open to the public, although they kept the kitchen closed until a thorough search of it could be completed. With the rat poison now missing, the kitchen was becoming ground zero for Peyton's death, something the police still called accidental in public. At the same time, simulator room one was also sealed off, with only the police allowed to come and go.

Sam had talked with Dani for most of the weekend, including Monday, when he had spent the first half of his workday with a bud in one ear while she did the same during her hotel shift. He took out the earbud only when her shift ended, and she was ready to go home and sleep while Kenzie was at school.

He had also spent part of his weekend watching his phone, waiting for Uncle Bruce to call him back with anything new. After leaving Kristie's the previous Friday, he had stopped by the hotel where Bruce was staying and given him what he had learned. But Bruce hadn't gotten back to him yet.

"One of these days I'm going to beat you," Linus told Madison as he counted out six quarters, setting each in front of her.

"Why do you keep betting?" Sam asked.

"Because the day I do beat her is going to be the sweetest day of my life."

"I do take checks if that would make this easier, but since it's you, I'll need to see some identification with it," Madison said.

"Funny. You're funny." Linus turned to Sam, dropped his head, and mumbled, "I should never have gone double or nothing on that putt on seventeen."

"What made it worse was that you missed the next one," Sam said with a laugh. "You really do stink at golf."

Their regular league round had ended about an hour earlier with the foursome doing what they did every week, eating dinner together, adding up their scores and watching Linus pay Madison.

Sam pointed at the scorecard. "Seventeen was the only hole you even had a chance on." He looked at Madison. "And you went left again on thirteen. You could hit ten straight drives on that hole if you wanted to, but you step up to that tee and hit it left toward the pavilion."

"And then I par the hole. Every time." She pulled the card away from Sam and pointed to her score. "Golf really is a simple game if your course management is on point."

Brock's new waitress, April, brought out a tall glass of dark beer and set it in front of Linus. "Does anyone want anything else?"

"Any idea when the kitchen will reopen?" Sam asked.

"I'm not sure. You'll have to ask Brock."

After a few seconds of silence, she shrugged and returned to the bar. Sam's stomach growled, reminding him that he hadn't taken a single bite of the burger he usually ate on a Tuesday night. He looked at Madison and Libby, remembering how his mother always carried food in her purse for times when he was hungry, but they weren't at home.

"Either of you have anything to munch on?"

"I may have string cheese," Libby said as she dug into her purse.

"No, thanks," Sam said.

Madison was next, pulling out a half-eaten fruit bar in a torn wrapper, a crushed package of crackers and some cough drops.

"I'll take this," he said as he grabbed the fruit bar.

She shoved the other items back into her purse. "I can't believe Brock has taken over this place as if it's his own. I told Carey he should press Allen to work harder to determine what happens next."

"What did he say?" Sam took the last few bites of the bar and shoved the empty wrapper into his pocket.

"He said he'll talk to Allen, but you know how he can be, passive, not wanting to cause any problems."

"I wouldn't worry about it too much. Once Carey is shown to be innocent, he'll get out, and it will be his to run."

Another league foursome consisting of two older men and their wives came through the door. They were usually the last group to finish, and they always put the highest scores on the board, but they had about as much fun as anyone in the league. They sat at a table near Sam and his group.

"Hey, Brock," one of the men called out. "Something's going on out there on thirteen."

Brock looked up from his newspaper and spun around. "What are you going on about, Tony?"

"A bunch of police cars are parked on the street next to it. Their lights are on, and they're walking around the green."

Brock went to the far window, grunting something unintelligible. He squinted and craned his neck. A few others from the course, including Libby, jumped up and joined him.

"I think I see lights," Libby said.

Sam, Linus and Madison joined the group. In the distance, the blue and red lights were dim but still visible, though the oncoming dusk and the distance to the hole made it hard to tell if anyone was walking around the green.

Linus nudged Sam. "Check it out." He looked past Sam toward the door to the pro shop. "Things are about to get interesting."

Dexter rushed into the restaurant, making a beeline for Brock and waving a piece of paper in the air. "What the hell is this? You already listed this place for sale?"

Brock stood his ground, allowing his brother to get within a few feet of him.

"Whatever you get for it, I'm taking half."

Madison shot to her feet. "It's not yours to sell!"

Brock's eyes flared. "You, shut your mouth," he said to her. He turned to Dexter, his jaw now tense. "The only thing you're getting from me is the money I owe you. Not a penny more."

Dexter lunged at his brother. Brock, caught off guard by the sudden attack, tried to defend himself by raising his hands, but he was too late. Dexter's punch landed in Brock's stomach, below his ribs. Brock exhaled sharply and doubled over, using his hands to keep himself from crumpling to the ground.

"What are they doing?" Madison asked as she fell back into her chair, talking to Sam, Linus and Libby. Her knee bounced, and she cleared her throat. "Why are they like this? First, they restart construction, and now they're doing this, all while Carey sits in a jail cell for something he didn't do, unable to do anything to stop these two idiots from burning it all down."

"Over there," Libby said.

In the pro shop's doorway, two police officers stood watching the two brothers make asses of themselves. One of them was shaking his head.

"Jacobs and Jackson," Sam said. "They're working on Maryanne's murder with Beaumont."

"Jesus Christ," Madison said. "What now?"

Brock threw another punch, but Dexter moved aside, his laughter more mocking than triumphant this time.

"Enough," Jacobs said.

Officer Jackson placed himself between the two brothers. He pulled a pair of handcuffs from his belt and slapped them on the bar. "You both will stop at this instant."

The brothers backed away, with Brock taking a seat on his stool and Dexter standing near the pro shop's entrance.

"Who the fuck called you guys to my course, anyway?" Brock turned to the golfers at their tables. "Which one of you snitches called the police on two brothers having a discussion?"

"Your construction crew called us," Jacobs said. "They found something under a sand trap that resembles human remains."

Chapter Sixteen

Sam and Linus glanced at each other while Libby moved closer to the two officers. She had taken her phone out and began tapping the screen.

Brock stepped forward. "You guys are out there digging without telling me? I own this place. You, uh, you need a warrant."

"Special circumstance," Jacobs said. "We contacted your lawyer. Legally, it belongs to the state until a decision is made on what to do with it."

"Allen told me it was mine," Brock said.

"He lied to you," Jackson said.

"That son of a bitch," he mumbled while shaking his head.

Jacobs pointed at Brock and Dexter. "The two of you, come with us."

The officers, along with the two brothers, left the restaurant, and the room fell into an eerie silence. Outside the window, the brothers jumped on separate golf carts and followed the police officer across the driveway to the cart path leading to the thirteenth hole.

Sam stood in silence as the carts carrying the police, Brock, and Dexter disappeared into the darkness, heading down the cart path running alongside the eighteenth hole. Madison hurried to the window, standing on her tiptoes as they disappeared.

"Did he say human remains?" Linus asked.

"I'm following them," Libby said.

She hurried outside. Madison grimaced and shoved her hands into her pockets, then followed behind Libby. Sam and Linus were close behind them. The foursome jumped onto their carts, still parked with their golf clubs strapped to the back, and followed Brock and Dexter.

"I can tell by your face that you're confused," Linus told Sam as they rode together.

"I don't think it's Kristie. It can't be. It doesn't make sense," Sam said.

He drove the cart along the path toward the bottom of the eighteenth fairway. Once there, he made a hard left and found the path for the fifteenth green, a short par three where Sam tends to hit his ball on the side of the hill on the left side of the hole.

"Why doesn't it make sense?" Linus asked. "She works here. She disappeared. It makes perfect sense to me."

"When I was talking to Kristie at her apartment, she had suitcases out. I thought she left voluntarily as if she was running from the police."

"And now they find human remains at this specific golf course, where she has worked since Emmitt bought the place," Linus said.

Sam guided the golf cart along the path toward the fourteenth green, one of the lowest points of the course. What Linus said made sense. Sam knew that, but he was sure it wasn't Kristie.

He crossed the fairway, moving his faster cart ahead of Libby's. Other than the sound of crickets and the hum of the cart, the course was as peaceful as he'd ever seen. When he drove up the long hill of the fourteenth fairway, the entire backside of the course opened up, giving him full view of the chaos playing out on the thirteenth green. He continued forward, moving to the pavilion between thirteen and fourteen, slowing as he reached it, stopping the cart as the grass turned into cement under the cover of the pavilion.

A hundred and fifty yards down the thirteenth fairway, red and blue police lights flashed. Floodlights had been set up around the hole, illuminating the entire green and the two sand traps flanking it. A couple of officers were talking to Brock and Dexter while other officers moved back and forth, crossing over the green from the sand trap on the right side of the hole to the street behind it, where at least five police cars sat.

"That is a lot of police," Libby said as she pulled her cart next to Sam's and stopped.

The foursome sat in silence, their eyes trained on what was going on ahead. Sam couldn't look away from the police officers digging into the dirt of the empty sand trap, pulling out human remains. Possibly Kristie's. Libby was the first to press down on the accelerator, taking her and Madison toward the chaos.

"It can't be her," Sam said under his breath as he accelerated.

Libby jumped off the cart and hurried closer to the green, eventually being stopped by a police officer. Madison had followed her. Between them and the officer, a line of police tape had been stretched across the entire fairway, twenty yards in front of the green.

On the green, giving orders as usual, stood Randall Beaumont. As if he had sensed Sam's presence, he turned, looked past the two women and made eye contact with Sam. He began walking, ducked under the police tape, and strode toward the golf cart. Libby and Madison followed him.

"What did you find?" Libby asked as she stepped up next to Beaumont, almost cutting him off.

He kept walking, stepping around her and ignoring her question.

"Do you think it's Kristie Breckinridge?" Libby asked, her voice louder this time.

Beaumont paused. He looked down at her. "I don't talk to newspapers, Miss Price, especially yours."

"What's that supposed to mean?" she asked.

Beaumont stopped next to Sam's cart. "Funny how you keep ending up where the bodies are located."

"Tuesday is our golf league. I'm here every week at this time. It's purely a coincidence."

"I'm sure it is." Beaumont considered the sand trap. "How long has this hole been under construction?"

"Maybe a month."

"It's Kristie, isn't it?" Linus asked.

Before Beaumont could answer, Sam jumped in. "It's not Kristie. It's Juliet Summerfield."

Madison jerked her head toward Sam while Libby peered up at Beaumont, her pen ready to write down every word he said.

"Juliet Summerfield?" Linus asked. "The girl in the flyers from seventeen years ago? You think that's who it is?"

"There are a lot of missing women out there, Sam," Beaumont said. "Keep your hunches to yourself, and let's deal with facts. Our crime scene people are on the way. All we can do for now is not disturb the scene, which means you."

Sam looked past him toward the edge of the sand trap. Next to him, Madison held her hand to her mouth. She took a step away as her face had gone gray. Sam stepped back with her and put his hand on her back, trying to comfort her.

Beaumont addressed Libby. "And I mean all of you, including you, Miss Price. You all stay back here."

Libby leaned to one side, trying to see around the uniforms, her eyes fixed on the trap as if she were already writing her first paragraph in her head. Without another word, Beaumont turned and walked back to the green, chatting with officers along the way. Libby pulled her phone from her pocket and began zooming in and snapping pictures.

"It's gotta be Kristie," Linus said.

"It's not," Sam said.

"But she went missing a few days ago. She's linked to Peyton and Marianne, and she works here."

"How is someone getting her down here? There's a camera on the North side of the building, and putting a body on a cart and driving it down here would attract attention. I don't care what time of day it is."

"They probably came from the street," Libby said as she pointed toward the police cars behind the hole.

Sam shook his head. "Look at those houses. At least one, and probably all of them, have security systems installed. No one is risking that either."

Sam took a few steps away from the cart toward the tree line on the right. "You know what's not risky, though?" he asked as he walked toward the path he and Madison had followed the previous week while looking for Linus's ball.

"No way," Madison said. "There's no way someone could carry a body along that path. It's too bumpy, and the bridge is too narrow."

Sam stopped at the entrance and stared into the dark woods. "You said it yourself," he told Madison. "There's nothing here until you get to the road. No cars, no cameras, no nothing."

"Hey!" Beaumont screamed behind them.

Beaumont and another officer approached. They had flashlights pointed along the ground as they walked, occasionally shining them on the faces of the group. Sam and Madison took a few steps into the woods as Linus walked forward, stopping the police.

"I, uh, lost a ball over here earlier this evening," Linus said. "Since you won't let us hang with you on the green, we decided we would take another look before we headed back to the restaurant."

"This whole area is a crime scene until we get a chance to look around," Beaumont said.

Sam and Madison took a few more steps, keeping their heads down.

"Can't you give me a couple of minutes?" Linus asked. "Pro Vs are like four bucks a ball. It's like finding gold."

"Let's go, Sam," Beaumont yelled, ignoring Linus. "I need you all out here."

"You see anything?" Sam asked Madison.

"Nothing that looks important. How about you?"

"Nothing here either."

Beaumont moved past Linus and into the woods. He caught up with Sam and Madison, standing between them.

"What are you two doing in here?"

Sam pointed into the darkness toward the bridge. "Whoever buried those remains may have brought them in from here."

The detective shined his flashlight around the ground at his feet, eventually shining it down the path.

"No way anyone carried a body from the clubhouse," Sam continued. "They would have risked being seen or caught on camera. They're not parking their car on the street over there where you guys parked and walking them to the green. Again, houses and cameras. This is the only place it could have come from."

The flashlight stopped. Beaumont didn't look at Sam right away, but his posture changed. His shoulders squared, and his chin lifted. "Where does the other side of this path lead to?"

"Near the graveyard on Maple," Madison said.

Silence from Beaumont as he walked across the bridge, then back toward Sam and Madison. Jacobs arrived, frowning at Sam and Madison.

"Body's been there for a long time," Jacobs said.

"How long?" Beaumont asked.

"It's too soon to tell, but it's definitely not recent. Soft tissue is gone, and there's no odor. Nothing about it looks fresh."

"Clothing?"

"Bits and pieces. Enough to tell us they were there."

"It's Juliet Summerfield," Sam said.

"Go back to your carts," Beaumont said, "Or else I'll—"

"I know, I know," Sam said. "You'll arrest me and throw away the key." He turned to Madison. "Come on, let's give them their space."

Chapter Seventeen

Sam sat at his desk at the Morello Manufacturing corporate office, staring at his dual monitor setup. He leaned back in his chair, straightening his body as if he were lying flat, and stretched his arms high in the air while resting his feet on the box of printer paper he had put under his desk many years ago to act as a makeshift footrest.

On the left-side monitor, he opened the source code for the system he had installed in South Plainfield to a specific screen where an error had been reported. It was the screen that users at South Plainfield regularly used to report bugs.

Sam scrolled to it from top to bottom, his eyes barely focused as he searched for something causing the bug he had recently been alerted to. On his right-side monitor, he had opened his database management program but wasn't paying much attention to it.

His phone buzzed. He wasn't surprised. Dani usually texted him a good morning on nights she didn't work the overnight shift at the plant but still had to get up for her morning shift at the hotel. He glanced over and inhaled sharply, sitting up in his seat. The name on the phone's screen, Randall Beaumont, was not one he expected to see.

He stared at the phone for another half second as it vibrated against the desk, then cleared his throat and picked it up.

"Morning, Beaumont," he said, doing his best to sound relaxed.

"You were right," he said.

For a second, Sam didn't breathe. He wasn't sure what Beaumont was talking about. Something to do with Kristie? Had he let Carey go free after learning something? If so, why would he call Sam to tell him? What was the catch?

"About what?" Sam asked.

"The remains we found. They belong to Juliet Summerfield."

Sam's eyes moved to his monitors, his source code on the two screens blurring into a big blob of symbols. His chair creaked as he leaned back.

"You can test it that quickly?"

"We had her dental records on file. I passed them on to the coroner last night. We'll still do the routine DNA testing, but her dental records confirmed it."

Sam's shoulders fell, and he relaxed, not because he had been right, but because Beaumont had listened to him.

"Has this been made public yet?"

"No, and I'm not sure when it will be, so keep it to yourself for now."

"Yeah, absolutely," Sam said.

"I'm trusting you with this, Sam," Beaumont spoke slowly, almost as if there was a warning somewhere between each word. After a few seconds of silence, he spoke again. "How did you know?"

The question took Sam by surprise. Not because it was a bad question, but because he didn't have a good answer. He answered the only way he could while staying honest.

"It was a hunch."

"A hunch, huh?"

"Yeah, just a hunch."

Beaumont disconnected the call without saying goodbye, surprising Sam. He pulled the phone away from his ear and checked the display, making sure Beaumont was gone.

As he set down his phone, Linus rolled the chair from his desk across the aisle into Sam's cubicle.

"Why are you so happy?" Linus asked.

"You read this support ticket from South Plainfield? Any idea what the hell they're talking about?"

Linus didn't bite. His expression stayed the same. "What did you do last night after I dropped you off? I logged in to the network to check the help desk tickets and saw you were online. Since when are you working after hours?"

"I wasn't working."

"What were you doing?"

"I don't know. I guess I spent most of the night talking with Dani."

"You don't need to be on the network for that, Sam."

Sam squeezed his eyes closed for a second or two, then opened them. He took a breath and minimized his database management application. Underneath, he had TNT open, showing his murder project as if it were any other software project that needed planning before it could be written. On the screen was a large triangle. Sam had made a considerable number of changes, adding to it everything he had learned about everyone involved.

"You're still using that?" Linus asked.

"It's not as terrible as it sounds," Sam said as he moved the mouse around the screen. "I had originally been overwhelmed when I opened it. It does a lot of stuff, so I went into the app's forums and found a quick-start guide one of their developers made." He recited the first paragraph to Linus as he read it. "'The TNT principal uses a triangle to represent a three-point system while working on a project for a customer. The corner labeled T is for Teamwork and Transparency. The second corner is labeled N for Nimbleness and Adaptation, and the third is for the Three Core Principals.'"

"That is the most corporate-speak bullshit sentence I've ever heard anyone mumble ever," Linus whispered, making sure Gil wasn't around to hear him speak poorly of it.

"I know, but after I spent the first hour staring at it, I began to understand how I could use it. After that, it wasn't so bad. I took the first T for Teamwork and Transparency and set it up to represent me, you and Uncle Bruce. It's cloud-based, so any update we make, the others can see, and we're able to chat inside the app. I'll send you an invite link."

"What about this?" Linus asked as he pointed to the second point of the triangle. "What was it? Nimbleness and Adaptation? Is Nimbleness even a word?"

"Let's say we're working on an application together. In this section, we would enter what we worked on based on customer requests and production issues. I'm using it to hold questions or things I need to follow up on."

"You don't have much in there."

"That's my biggest problem. I'm grasping at straws here, putting things in there that don't matter, trying to make it look like I have something to do. I'm not quite at a dead end yet, but I can see it off in the distance."

Linus moved the mouse to the third corner. "How did you incorporate this part?"

"I'm using it to keep track of things I learn."

"Gil's gonna make you employee of the month once he sees how much you've learned about TNT."

"Yeah, about that. Let's keep this between us. I made it private, so internally only you and I can see it. This TNT app isn't something I want to incorporate into our day-to-day programming lives, regardless of what Gil says. It's overkill and way too complicated for the apps we create."

"How much time did you spend working on this?"

"I didn't go to bed last night," Sam said. "Apparently, I'm back to not sleeping again."

"Looking over it, what's it telling you?"

"Nothing. I stared at it all night. I rearranged things, added and deleted things. I even joined a message board that other companies in the area use to discuss TNT exclusively."

"That must be the most boring message board on the internet."

"You'd be surprised," Sam said. "Five percent of it is related to TNT. The other ninety-five is a mishmash of random topics, everything from people talking sports to pictures of food to a section where TNT members can date."

"Sounds like so many horrible social media sites that I stay away from."

"Yeah. Although I did find a tater tot casserole recipe I'm going to try this week."

Linus rolled his chair back and reached into his pocket. He pulled out his phone and stared at the screen. "Uncle Bruce."

"Great," Sam said. "We could use some good news."

Linus pressed the green button on his phone's screen and stuck the phone to the side of his face.

"Hey, Bruce," Linus said.

Sam could only hear the murmur of his voice. Bruce spoke fast; his words did not come through, but his excitement did. Linus sat up straight, his hand clapping down on Sam's desk.

"What is it?" Sam asked.

"Hang on, let me get Sam," Linus said to Bruce. "We'll go to an empty conference room." He pressed the mute button on his phone and motioned for Sam to follow him.

Conference Room B was the smallest of the company's four conference rooms. It was tucked away in the back of the building, along a hallway that very few people ever used. The only reason to even wander into that hallway was to go to that conference room, nothing else, but it was usually the last one anyone chose. Sam quickly reserved it, marking it in use so no one would have a reason to get anywhere near them. He grabbed his laptop and followed Linus.

Once inside, Linus pushed the door shut and sat at the small table. It held a maximum of eight and was a favorite hiding space for Sam when he wanted to get away from people and feel like he could speak more freely. Linus set his phone on the table and tapped the button to unmute it.

"Hello?" Uncle Bruce said. "Linus? You still there?"

"Yeah, Bruce," Linus said. "Sam and I are sitting in a conference room, and you're on speaker. What news do you have?"

"I found something that I'm pretty sure you're going to want to hear."

A few seconds of silence. Sam and Linus looked at each other.

"Go ahead," Linus said.

"Maryanne Preston-Layne isn't who she says she is. According to her fingerprints, her real name is Evelyn Delaney."

"Okay," Sam said, nodding along with Bruce's words. "That makes sense. That's why Maryanne Preston was a ghost."

"There's more, and this is where it gets good. She used her mother's maiden last name; her real last name was Summerfield."

"Summerfield?"

"Yep. The girl they found last night in the sand trap at your golf course, Juliet Summerfield? She's the half-sister of Maryanne Preston-Layne, aka Evelyn Delaney."

Chapter Eighteen

Sam ran his palm down his face and pinched the bridge of his nose. "Did you say, sister?"

"You're goddamn right I did," Bruce said. "There's no way that's a coincidence."

Linus shifted in his chair. "It's been seventeen years since that girl disappeared. It could very easily be a coincidence. Two unrelated things can certainly happen to the same family over that period of time."

"You could be right, but I'm not so sure," Sam said as he pulled his phone from his pocket and set it on the conference table. "Bruce, did you find out anything more about Maryanne?"

"She shared a father with Juliet, but they had different mothers. I can tell you everything you want to know about Evelyn Delaney up to a certain point. You want middle school, even her high school and college years, that stuff was easy to find. I can tell you what clubs she belonged to, who her friends were and even where she worked out. But not long after college, she disappeared, fell off the face of the earth. Then, eight months ago, Maryanne Preston popped up in Las Vegas."

"Did you say Vegas?" Linus asked.

Sam lifted a finger to say something to Linus, but Linus had already begun tapping out a text message on his phone. He pressed send and put the phone back in the center of the table.

"Yeah, Vegas, but I have no idea how she got there."

"We may have a way to figure that out," Sam said.

"It's moments like this that make me love this job."

Sam's knee began to bounce, and with his middle finger, he traced a triangle on the top of the desk. "Thanks for all of this, but can you do me a favor?" Sam asked, talking more to Linus than Bruce. "Let's keep all of this between the three of us for now."

"You never have to say that to me, kid. It's part of the job."

"Thanks, Bruce," Sam said.

"I'll be in touch," Bruce said. He disconnected the call, and Linus pulled his phone back in front of him.

Sam stood and took a few steps, stretching his legs, listening to his knees crack as he walked. "Okay, Maryanne Preston wasn't Maryanne Preston? She was Evelyn Delaney, and she was also Juliet Summerfield's half-sister?"

"And apparently she was off the grid for like fifteen years," Linus said. "Then she popped up in Vegas eight months ago."

"That's about how long Peyton and Maryanne have been together."

Linus asked the question that had been forming in Sam's mind. "You think she knew Emmitt was going to die and leave a whole bunch of money to Peyton, so she found him, began dating him, eventually convincing him to marry her so she could kill him and take all the money for herself?"

"I guess it's possible, but we're still stuck with the fact that someone went and killed her."

"But who? Could have been any of them. Brothers watching all their dad's money going to some stranger? A bartender who was also a jilted lover?"

The door swung open, and Scott came in holding a twenty-ounce soft drink and a cup of coffee from the cafeteria's coffee machine. He set the coffee on the table in front of Linus. "If you called me in here because you wanted coffee and for no other reason, I'm going to be pissed."

Linus took a sip of the coffee and pointed at Sam.

"Tell me more about the ghosts you talked about in Vegas," Sam said.

Scott set his drink down. "Why?"

"We need your help."

Chapter Nineteen

An officer pushed open the door and let Sam into the visitation room at the County Detention Center. Carey sat at a table near the back of the room. Sam took a few steps, then stopped. The room had twelve tables, each with four chairs. There was a counter with a microwave on it and multiple vending machines in the back. The lights overhead were bright, much brighter than the ones in the room the first time Sam had visited Carey at the police station.

"This looks like the cafeteria at our Benton Falls Plant in Ohio," Sam said to Carey as he sat across from his friend. "And I think it's nicer than the one in South Plainfield."

"Yeah, it's not bad in here," Carey said. "It does get kinda boring sometimes, but at least Madison shows up. Other than you, she's the only other person who's come to see me."

"Neither brother?"

"Nah, but we've never been like brothers. We're really only family by name. Dad held all of us together, and with him gone, I feel like an only child."

Sam looked around the room. "How do you pass the time?"

"There's a small library, so I get some books, and I've been working on this jigsaw puzzle. It's one of those puzzles with a thousand pieces, a picture of some European castle. It almost makes me feel like I'm planning an escape to someplace grand."

"Are you?"

"Not a chance," Carey said with a laugh. "They're treating me pretty well so far. I think they know I didn't do it."

"If they knew that for sure, you wouldn't be sitting here."

"I do have access to a small yard for a bit of fresh air, and I've also been trying to get into chess. They have a few boards here. Keeps the mind sharp."

"Good," Sam said. "'Cause I'm gonna get you out of here."

Carey sat up. "Do you have something?"

"Did you know Juliet Summerfield?"

"Sounds familiar," Carey said. "She disappeared from the area when we were in high school, right?"

Sam nodded. "She was at Islewood, a couple of towns over."

"Right, I was a senior. I think she was a junior. It was right around the time my dad bought Savannah Palms."

"Funny thing about that," Sam said. "Last night, they found human remains that have been positively identified as hers."

"That's good, right? I bet the family will be happy to have some kind of a resolution, even if it's that one."

"Yeah, except it's a little more important to you than you think."

"What do you mean?" Carey asked.

Sam sat up in his chair and leaned forward, his voice low and flat. "They found those human remains under the sand trap on the thirteenth hole of your golf course." Sam pulled out a newspaper article written by Libby that had appeared in the afternoon paper.

The color slipped from Carey's face. He took the article from Sam and quickly read the first few paragraphs. "All these years, she was right there? How terrible."

"The rumor is that whoever killed her must have buried her under that trap at the same time your dad was doing construction on that hole. Do you remember the exact dates of that construction?" Sam asked.

"I don't, but you could ask Dexter," Carey said.

"Dexter? What does he have to do with the course? Hasn't that been you and your dad this whole time?"

"He designed the original construction changes on the course when Dad bought it. He used some computer program to do all the design."

"Hold on. Dexter used a computer program? I always had the impression he was—" Sam paused for a beat, then continued. "No offense. I know he's your brother, but isn't he kind of a dope?"

Carey laughed. "A lot of people think that, but he's pretty good with computers. With this program, you could plug in your current course layout and move things around until you find the design you like. Once you like what you have, you could save it and print out the blueprints for the construction people."

"That's surprising," Sam said.

"I felt the same way when I found out. He's my brother, and I had no idea he was working with computers until Emily let it slip to me a few years ago. We were talking about vacations, and she said they hadn't taken one in a while because he's always in their basement working on something big as if he's designing the next great game."

"Let it slip?"

"Her reaction was kinda strange when she told me. She looked like she was sorry she had started the sentence. I asked him about it not too long after, but he wouldn't tell me anything. He said he was afraid I would tell you, and you would steal his idea."

"Me?"

"You're a computer programmer, and he can be a little paranoid."

Not knowing how much time they had left, Sam changed the subject. "When did Peyton and Maryanne start going out? Do you remember how they met?"

"Back in March, I think," Carey said. "It was on St. Patrick's Day. My dad hosted a party for the family and some of his friends, and that's when Peyton introduced her to everyone. It was the first time we had all gotten together after he told us he was sick."

"A couple of weeks, huh?" Sam asked, the dots beginning to connect. "You know anything about her history? Where's she from? Her family?"

Carey shook his head, his lips pursed together. "Come to think of it, no, nothing. Why?"

Sam was about to answer, but he stopped. He wasn't supposed to know anything about the relationship between Maryanne and Juliet. Letting someone else know wouldn't be smart.

"You think she found out he was sick," Carey asked, filling the silence, "then went after the firstborn male to get the money? Is the marriage even legal?"

"I don't know."

"What about Peyton? You think she killed Peyton?"

"I think it's a possibility."

"But then someone killed her?" Carey said. "Someone who could have found out and been upset that she was taking our money?"

"Right," Sam said as Carey's speculation moved to his brothers the same way his had earlier that afternoon. "Unfortunately, that group includes you."

"What about Kristie?"

Kristie had nothing to gain from Peyton's death, but if she was still in love with him and suspected Maryanne of poisoning him, revenge was as good a motive as money.

"Her and Peyton were close, and she's disappeared, right?" Carey asked.

"Closer than you think," Sam said.

"Seriously?" Carey shook his head. "For how long? Did dad know?"

"A long time, and I doubt it."

"What is this family that I'm a part of?" Carey said. "I'm the only normal one, and I'm the one sitting in this cell."

The door opened, and a guard stepped inside. "Times up, Mr. Norris. Time to go."

"Sam, next time we talk, any chance you can bring me good news for a change?"

"I'll do my best," Sam said.

Chapter Twenty

Sam and Linus sat in the booth across from Libby and Madison at Calloway's Corner, a small restaurant on the boardwalk down the beach near Sam's house. Linus had insisted on the place ever since Sam had taken him there, not too long after Linus moved from South Plainfield and began working at the corporate office. Jenna Calloway, the restaurant's owner, had made him a plate of shrimp and grits, a dish he could never find in South Plainfield. He always said it would be the one thing he would eat every day for the rest of his life if he had to pick something.

"Here you go," Jenna said as she set Linus's plate in front of him.

"You're seriously going to ruin eating anything else for me," he said to Jenna as he loaded up a fork and shoved it into his mouth. He groaned as he chewed. "It's so good."

She continued serving the others, setting down Sam's burger and fries, Libby's chicken sandwich and Madison's cobb salad.

"Y'all need anything else?"

"We're good, Jenna. Thanks," Sam said.

Libby looked up from her mail. "Okay, the reason I asked for this lunch is because with this Juliet Summerfield murder now back to being an open case and no longer cold, I've been doing some digging."

"Why?" Madison asked. "A young girl getting murdered like that. We were all the same age back then. I don't even want to think about it."

“You don’t find it interesting?” Libby asked as she took a bite of her sandwich, then pushed her plate back a little, making room to set a manila folder she had taken from her bag in front of her. Sam leaned forward, trying to get a look inside the folder.

“Not at all,” Madison said as she looked at Sam. “It’s morbid. Don’t you think?”

“I’m actually kinda curious,” Sam said, although he wasn’t ready to say the exact reason as to why he was interested.

“So am I,” Linus said.

Madison shook her head and said to Sam, “I know you’ve been doing everything you can to help Carey, and I appreciate it, I really do, but is every dead body going to be interesting to you going forward? I’m not sure how I feel about that.”

“No,” Sam said. He looked toward Libby. “But I am going to support my friend in her work. If she can write something that will get eyes on it, I think we should try to help her.”

“Thank you,” Libby said.

She set a few pictures in the middle of the table. The first was the same double image that had been on the flyer Scott had found on Sam’s car before Thanksgiving. It showed Juliet at a school dance on one side, and the grainy image of her getting into her car, taken outside a convenience store. Another was from a school newspaper. It showed Juliet and another boy, Joseph Weller, starring together in a school play. They were in costumes, and their faces were covered in makeup.

“What play is this?” Sam asked.

“It’s West Side Story. According to the school’s principal, whom I talked to last night, the school did that play the year she disappeared.”

The next photo was from a party: a bunch of teens crowded together, having a good time. The last photo was from a security camera behind a store counter.

"What's this one?" Sam asked as he popped a couple of French fries into his mouth, then lifted the last picture. "Is this the same store as the one on the flyer?"

"It is. They were taken the same night," Libby said. "That one outside is the last known picture of her, and the one taken from behind the counter was taken a few minutes before that as she waited in line to check out."

"What store is this?" Linus asked.

"There used to be a convenience store around the corner from the golf course. I think it's a shoe store now. The night she disappeared, she stopped there for a couple of things, got into her car and was never seen again."

In the black-and-white photo, Juliet stood in line, facing the security camera, though not looking directly at it. Her dark hair had been pulled back into a loose ponytail with a few strands falling across her face. She wore a dark hoodie that looked at least one size too big, the sleeves covering part of her hands.

"She doesn't look rushed or scared," Sam said. "If anything, she looks bored."

He showed the photo to Linus, whose hands were full of food, then handed it to Madison. She looked at it quickly, set it back in the middle of the table and returned to her lunch.

Sam grabbed it again and squinted, holding it closer to his face, looking for some kind of resemblance between her and Maryanne. "Do you have any pictures of her that are clearer?"

"I do," Libby said. She pulled an Islewood Yearbook from her bag and opened it, showing Juliet's picture. In this one, she wore a red blouse with a small pendant hanging across her neck with two letter Js inside it.

Sam grabbed the picture of Juliet and Joseph Weller in the school play and held the two photos side by side.

"Let me guess. The other J is for Joseph Weller?"

"Good guess. They were dating at the time she disappeared, but the police cleared him quickly."

Libby took the photo of her in the convenience store from him and tapped her finger on the security image of Juliet's face. "Imagine being her and not knowing that at that exact moment in time, within a few hours, it would be the last time anyone would ever see you."

"Any family?" Sam asked.

"It was just her and her dad," Libby said. "Her Mom had passed away a few years earlier. There was a much older half-sister on her dad's side. Her name was Eve, but she was long gone by the time Juliet disappeared."

Sam kept his face still and took a slow sip from his drink. Next to him, Linus kept quiet.

"Long gone, huh?" Sam asked. "You know anything else about her? Where she went or anything like that?"

Libby shook her head. "Not much, and she hasn't reappeared since. The police are hoping that finding Juliet's remains will bring her out of hiding."

"What was this Joseph Weller's alibi?"

"He was out of the country at the time. There are plenty of records and witnesses that back up his story."

"A boyfriend would make the most sense," Linus said. "But if he was cleared, who does that leave?"

"At the moment, no one," Libby said. "I've read every witness statement the police pulled together, and not a single person knew where Juliet was going after she left that convenience store."

Jenna appeared at the booth, coffee pot in hand. "Everything okay over here?" she asked, her eyes moving across the pictures and papers Libby had spread out.

"I think we're fine," Sam said.

Jenna poured coffee into Sam's mug without asking, then topped off Libby's water. She looked down at the center of the table at the items Libby had spread out. "You folks look like you're planning a bank robbery," she said.

"Something like that," Sam said with a smile.

"Well, if you do, you can count on me to keep it a secret." She returned his smile and put her hand on his back before turning to walk away. "Yell if you need anything."

Madison's phone buzzed, making the table vibrate. She picked it up, her eyes moving across the screen, and pursed her lips together, letting out a small breath from her nose.

"Something wrong?" Sam asked.

"It's Charlotte," she said. "There's a family dinner Friday night at the house. She says it's important. She wants the family to come together to remember Peyton."

"What's wrong with that?"

"I don't want to go."

"You should go," Sam said. "Since Carey can't be there, you should be there to represent him, speak on his behalf."

"They don't like me, and I don't like them."

"I heard the same thing about Maryanne, but she always showed up at family functions to support Peyton. Carey can't be there, so you should go. Someone needs to keep an eye on that family."

"Don't ever compare me to her," Madison said with some unexpected anger in her voice. "She was an awful person." She held for a beat, then gave an exaggerated smile. "I'm a joy to be around."

"You should go," Sam said, a little more sternly.

Madison picked up her phone again, thumb hovering. "Fine. I'll go, Dad, but I'm telling them that you're coming with me."

Sam blinked. "Why me? I'm not part of the family."

"You've always said Emmitt was like a second father to you."

"That's true," Linus said through a mouthful. "You have said that."

"No one asked you," Sam said.

"You said you wanted to talk to Dexter and Emily," Madison said. "They'll be there. This is your chance. Maybe you can figure something out to help Carey."

Sam nodded. "Okay, yeah. You're right. Count me in."

Madison's face softened, and she smiled. "One thing I should tell you, though. Dinners at their house are formal. Like, really formal."

Sam's eyes narrowed. "Define formal."

"Jacket. Maybe a tie."

Linus laughed into his napkin. "Do you even own a tie?"

"I have one," Sam said. "But I may need some help tying it."

Chapter Twenty-One

The Morello manufacturing breakroom always smelled the same around ten in the morning, a combination of coffee and caramel. For the first couple of hours of each workday, coworkers would come in looking like zombies, as if they were programmed. They'd stand at the small coffee maker, pour themselves a cup and move along.

Sam was one of the few employees who didn't drink coffee, but he still needed the same caffeine that kept everyone else awake. In the cafeteria, there was a small, unmanned store. He grabbed his normal breakfast, a twenty-ounce bottle of Pepsi and a package of Zingers, then swiped his card across the sensor, paying the same three dollars he had spent every other day.

On the other side of the snack machines, the employee door swung open, and Scott walked in. Sam glanced at the clock on the wall; Scott looked like he'd just gotten out of bed. His hair stuck up on one side, and his dark polo was wrinkled. He had slung his backpack over one shoulder and was rubbing his eyes.

"You look terrible," Sam said. "You just wake up?"

Scott paused and eyed Sam. "You look like you've been awake longer than me," he said with a smile.

"You're not completely wrong," Sam said as he poured a cup of coffee from the machine and handed it to Scott. He swiped his card again, paying for his friend's drink. "This whole Carey thing is keeping me up at night."

"I guess it's a good thing I showed up at all today," Scott said. He took a sip of his coffee, swallowed it, and exhaled as if it had already begun to work its magic. "I may have something that could unstick you."

***

Ten minutes later, Sam and Linus sat across from Scott in Conference Room B, again, taking the conference room in the back where no one would overhear their conversation. Sam had his laptop open, the TNT app loaded, ready to scribble down anything important.

"I went back to some of my friends in Vegas and found out more about Maryanne, or Evelyn Delaney, as they knew her." Scott tapped the table's edge, occasionally referring to his phone, where he had taken notes. "In Vegas, she wasn't anyone special, not a socialite, not anything. In fact, she was kind of a mess."

"A mess?" Sam asked.

"What kind of mess?" Linus asked.

"A gambling mess. Some of my friends bumped into her on the underground poker circuit a few times. Their exchanges with her weren't usually friendly. She drank too much and smoked like a chimney."

"What is the underground poker circuit?" Sam asked.

"They weren't the kind of games you'd play in a casino. You'd end up in an abandoned building, usually in the basement, to not attract unwanted people from the outside. Other games took place in people's houses, and they took a generous cut to keep things private. These places didn't have cameras, and there was no gambling license to keep things civil. There was always a greater than zero chance a fight would break out over how someone played a hand, and you'd be 'politely' asked to leave."

Sam leaned forward on the table, his elbows bumping his laptop. He had stopped typing as he listened to Scott tell tales of something he had only seen on TV. Linus also stared at Scott, engrossed in his story.

Scott looked past them, staring at the wall above their heads, as if memories were coming back. "Those were the kinds of games you only played in if you were invited, and you couldn't get through the door unless you had a roll of cash on you."

"How often did you play?" Sam asked.

"A few times."

"Is that where you got that?" Linus asked, pointing at the scar near Scott's right eye.

Scott paused for a beat as if he were deciding how much detail he wanted to give about his old life. When he did speak, he ignored Linus's question. "It wasn't too long before they stopped inviting her to games."

"Why?" Sam asked.

"She'd run up tabs, borrow from people and then vanish. They had heard stories of her going back to her old man for cash, but he didn't have anything. Eventually, she was blackballed from any of those games the same way a casino asks a card counter to stay away. Only difference, if she had shown up, they would have hurt her."

Sam kept his face still, but a knot formed in his stomach. "What happened next?"

"She showed up one day with an apology and a lot of money, more than they'd ever seen."

"Did she say where she got it?"

"People out there don't care how she acquired it, only that she paid them back what she owed. And she did. All of it. No one really knew for sure, but it seemed small-time at first. Running cons on tourists, then some fraud. Some claim she was involved in a theft ring. Then she ended up in jail."

"For how long?"

"A few years," Scott said. "After she got out, she tried to go straight, you know, earn her money the right way. She ended up as a waitress at a restaurant. Not one of those casino restaurants, but an actual restaurant off the strip somewhere in downtown Henderson. That's where we lose her."

"Lose her?" Linus asked.

"None of my guys can find her after that. She stopped playing poker. She stopped scamming. She was another person living in the desert."

Sam moved the mouse across the triangle on the TNT app where her name was typed. "How does Evelyn Delaney start as the half-sister to Juliet Summerfield, then end up in Vegas, only to eventually find herself marrying Peyton Layne as Maryanne Preston?"

"Did she ever talk about her past?" Scott asked. "I can give my guys whatever information you have. They'll be thorough, probably more than the police can be."

Sam double-clicked her name. A small window opened showing where he had typed everything he learned about Maryanne. He copied it, opened an email and sent it to Scott's personal email address. "You have everything I know about her in your email. It's not much, but it's a start. Carey told me she never talked about her past."

"I can see why," Linus said. "Who are these friends of yours that can be more thorough than the police?"

Linus put a question out there that Sam had also been curious about but wasn't sure if he should ask.

"It's a long story."

"We have time."

Scott shook his head. "Not today. Besides, it's not as glamorous as you think."

Linus looked deflated.

"I'm going back to my desk," Scott said. "Let me know if you need anything else."

Chapter Twenty-Two

The Savannah police department's interrogation room was as plain and boring this morning as it had been the last time Sam was here, sitting across from Beaumont, fresh from seeing Maryanne's dead body, while at the same time telling the veteran officer that his friend hadn't done it.

Sam tried to stay loose. Beaumont had called and asked him to come down, but he hadn't said why. He was pretty sure he hadn't done anything wrong. He had thought the old man was softening, but now this. The woman at the front desk had escorted him back here without so much as a "Hello" or a "Good morning."

"Any idea why I'm here?" he had asked her as they walked through a sea of blue, with the officers staring at him as if he were a criminal.

"He'll explain when he gets here." She opened the door and motioned Sam inside. "You want a water while you wait?"

"While I wait? He's not here yet?" Sam asked.

"He's running late. Have a seat." She pulled the door closed.

Sam sat alone. His pulse beat a little quicker than the clock on the wall. He stared at the door. He wasn't under arrest. She hadn't told him to stay. If he wanted to leave, he could leave.

***

It had been ten minutes, the same amount of time he would wait for a late professor. He stood, feeling more relaxed. Whatever it was would have to wait, but as he took his first step toward the door, it opened, and a haggard-looking Captain Randall Beaumont walked inside. His suit jacket hung open and his tie was loosened. The man was tired, as evidenced by the lines around his mouth and the dark circles under his eyes.

"You look like you were run over by a bus," Sam said as he retook his seat.

"I hate working midnights," Beaumont said. "Criminals apparently don't need to sleep like the rest of us."

He closed the door and took a seat across from Sam the same way he'd probably done a thousand times before, ready to question a criminal. He didn't hurry, but he also didn't go slow. Instead, he pulled a manila folder from his briefcase, set it on the table and tapped it once.

"Why did you call me down here? I don't think I did anything wrong," Sam said.

"Are you sure?" Beaumont asked.

Sam's stomach tightened. He held Beaumont's gaze, but in his mind, he was replaying the events of the last few days as if he were rewinding through a movie.

"I'm positive," Sam finally said. "Unless it's illegal to show up at the golf course where I'm a member and talk to people that I've always talked to."

"You're talking with them about my case."

"So is everyone else," Sam said. "I assume you're going to drag them down here and question them next?" Sam wanted to stand. He wanted to leave, but something was holding him there. He glanced at the folder under Beaumont's finger. "I assume there's something in there for me. Otherwise, why would you bring it here with you?"

"Is that another hunch?"

Beaumont watched him for an extra few seconds as if he were trying to look into Sam's brain, trying to read what he knew. Certainly, by now, they both knew Maryanne was Evelyn Delaney, though Sam suspected he knew more about her history than Beaumont did. He glanced at the folder again. Saying nothing, Beaumont slid it across the table to Sam.

"We've gone through and catalogued Maryanne's belongings, and we found something I'd like to show you."

Sam opened the folder. Inside was a single sheet of paper. On the paper was a series of letters someone had cut from newspapers and magazines. It was the kind of threatening note Sam had seen on TV and movies, never believing that anyone would send such letters in real life.

"We found it in a safety deposit box," Beaumont said. "It wasn't under the name Maryanne Preston, but under a different name."

"Let me guess," Sam said. "Evelyn Delaney."

Beaumont didn't react the way Sam expected him to. He expected surprise, maybe anger, but instead Beaumont sat still, almost like a statue. His eyes stayed level, and Sam had no idea what was in the veteran officer's head.

"You've been busy," Beaumont said.

"I've heard things."

"You know she was related to Juliet Summerfield, don't you?"

"Half-sister," Sam said.

"What does that gut of yours tell you about that?"

Sam shook his head. "Could be a coincidence."

"I don't like coincidences."

"Me either, but two members of the same family killed seventeen years apart. It's not unheard of."

Beaumont nodded at the paper. "What do you make of that?"

Sam reached for the paper and lifted it carefully. Each block was a letter or a combination of letters.

If you don't leave him alone, I will kill you.

There was no name, no signature, no nothing to give away who had put it together.

"Fingerprints?" Sam asked.

"There were a few, but they didn't match anyone we have in the system. We'd like to know who gave it to her."

"The obvious answer is Kristie, right?" Sam said. "Is that where you're leaning? She was sleeping with Peyton before Maryanne entered the picture. Kristie ended the affair after she found out they were married. She wanted revenge. She killed them both and ran."

"That's what some of us think," Beaumont said. "But until we find Kristie, we can't answer that."

"Only some of you? What about the rest of you?"

"A few of our guys think it was a mob hit. She owed money that she couldn't pay back."

Sam exhaled. Beaumont knew about Vegas, or at least a part of it, and now Sam had to decide if he would let Beaumont in on how much he knew. If Sam acted surprised, Beaumont would surely pick up on his lie. How many men did he say sat across from him in this room and lied to him? Hundreds?

"Could be," Sam said. "Maybe somewhere along the way, Eve disappears into the Vegas nightlife, does someone wrong, maybe borrows money she can't pay back."

Beaumont's eyes narrowed, and he tilted his head.

Sam continued, "She ends up in jail, maybe she's safer there, although it seems like if someone wants you dead, knowing exactly where you're at would be bad for you."

Sam reread the letter, not sure if the words on the page matched a threat to someone owing money to the mob. Unless 'leave him alone' referred to the person she's blackmailing. A mob boss, maybe? Someone high up?

"She gets out of jail and reappears as Maryanne Preston, goes after Peyton because of his eventual inheritance, but then gets killed anyway?"

Beaumont blinked once. He tilted his head and studied Sam. "You've been really busy."

"What about you?" Sam asked him, "What do you think?"

"I'll tell you this," Beaumont said. "I don't like to make guesses without all the facts, but if you were forcing me, I wouldn't say blackmail. I'd say she was being threatened. I've seen notes like this in the past, although not so much recently. They're usually a ransom note."

"You check her bank accounts?"

"We couldn't find anything in either of her names."

Sam put the letter back into the folder and slid it across the table. Beaumont slapped his hand on it before it hit the floor.

"Why are you showing me this?" Sam asked.

Beaumont stood. "You should get back to work."

"Come on," Sam said. "Enough of this game you're playing with me. You're threatening to arrest me, but then giving me information, information you're keeping from the public. How about you answer something for me? Just one question, and then I'll leave."

Beaumont was silent, staring at Sam, but he didn't demand for a second time that Sam leave. That had to be progress.

"Who called you and told you to go to the golf course to find Maryanne dead?"

"We don't know," he said. "Whoever it was disguised their voice, and we can't track the number it came from."

"Any leads?"

"Nothing right now, so go back to work, and I'll be in touch."

Chapter Twenty-Three

Later that afternoon, Sam sat at his desk. Both monitors showed the source code he should have been working on. He pulled up a browser window, keeping it tucked in a small corner of one screen so no one could see it unless they walked up behind him. He typed "Evelyn Delaney," hit Enter, and skimmed the short list of results, most of which had nothing to do with the Evelyn Delaney he was searching for. The few that did looked like high school track results and a blurry newspaper photo showing the nine students who'd made the honor roll in sixth grade.

Footsteps approached. He quickly minimized the window and sat up in his chair.

"Minimizing the window doesn't make it so Gil can't see your search history."

Sam spun his chair around. Scott stood there holding a plastic cup from the water dispenser in one hand and his phone in the other.

"I don't think Gil checks our search history," Sam said.

"I have news you'll want to hear."

"What kind of news?"

"I know how she became Maryanne Preston."

Sam's pulse jumped. "Tell me."

Scott grabbed the second chair in the back corner of Sam's cubicle and pulled it closer. He sat, took a sip of the water, and set the cup on Sam's desk.

"She bought a new identity."

"Bought it? Is that something you can do?"

"It's a lot easier than you think, trust me. I know a few guys in Vegas who, for a few thousand dollars, will set you up with a driver's license that will get you past most things. But if you get into the five digits with your payment, you can get a social security number, a fake history and even a passport."

"How much did she spend?"

"Just under twenty thousand," Scott said.

"That's not money you earn being a waitress." Sam glanced past Scott into the empty hallway next to his cubicle. With no one around, he leaned forward and lowered his voice. "The police called me downtown and showed me something this morning. It's why I was late."

He explained the letter to Scott, its words, and how it was put together, with newspaper and magazine clippings.

"Beaumont told me a few of the officers think it was a mob hit."

Scott let out a few quick breaths through his nose and laughed. "No."

"You don't think?"

"Dude, I'm not gonna sit here and pretend there's not a mob in Vegas. It's not like you see on TV, and it's not like it was in the fifties. I also won't deny that they threaten people. They do. Trust me on that. But they're not doing their threats with arts and crafts."

"No?"

"If the mob wants to scare you, they do things that make you scared. They don't leave a ransom note made by a third grader, and they don't say, 'I'll kill you' like they're nose to nose with you on the playground. They do things to prove they're serious."

"Then who writes something like that?" Sam asked.

"Don't focus on the who," Scott said. "Focus on the money. You always look at the money, and it will lead you to the who."

"Where do I start?"

"My guys talked to the person who set her up with the new identity. As he was setting her up, she did some talking to him about where she was going."

"She came here."

"Not at first," Scott said. "She moved in with another woman in Vegas who had been looking for a roommate."

"Who was she? You're have her—"

Scott handed him a piece of paper with a name, address, phone number, email and her place of employment. There was also a photo on the other side.

"My friends are thorough, and I knew you'd ask."

"Cassandra Whitaker," Sam said. He flipped the folder over, looked at the picture, then turned it back to the side with her information. "She's in Florida, now, and only an hour away."

"Go talk to her." Scott stood. "And with that, I'm out. The rest is up to you."

Chapter Twenty-Four

Linus drove his car along the two-lane highway. With the exception of the dim streetlights spread out in large intervals and the occasional car coming the other way, the trip was mostly dark. Sam had told Linus about the note Beaumont showed him, asking him not to tell anyone, since it was not yet released to the public.

"You think someone was threatening her?" Linus asked.

"Beaumont told me some of the police officers thought it was a Vegas mob hit, but Scott says no way. Scott said the mob doesn't do things that way."

"What do you think?"

"I don't know," Sam said, remembering Beaumont's words about not making guesses with all the evidence. "I think she was blackmailing someone, or at least threatening them with notes like that."

"It would make sense if she changed her identity and left town."

A Christina Aguilera song played on the radio, bringing Dani back into Sam's thoughts. During one of his first meetings with her, his first real interrogation of a suspect, the same singer had been playing on her station's boombox, and she had been dancing along with it while she worked. Linus reached over and turned down the radio.

"Hey," Sam said. "I like that song."

"Since when?"

Sam grabbed the knob and adjusted the volume. He smiled as he stared through the passenger side window. His mom had always told him how pretty the coast was at night. As a child, she had talked him into going to bed with his window cracked to let the sound of the waves hitting the beach creep in. Over time, it became the one sound he could always fall asleep to.

***

After another fifteen minutes of mostly listening to the radio and staring out the window, Linus pulled off the highway, heading east toward the ocean, and entered the small neighborhood of Cedar Shoals, a city in Florida of less than a thousand people. Most of the houses were dark, except for the glow of porch lights or a flickering television screen in the houses where the curtains hadn't yet been closed.

Again, Sam cracked his window. The scent of saltwater hung in the air. It reminded him of home. Linus pulled down another road, a narrow one-way that dead-ended into the library's crowded parking lot.

"Look at this," Linus said as he stepped out of the car. "The book club at the Cedar Shoals Public Library on a Thursday night is apparently the place to be."

They entered the library and found a few spots to sit at a table in the middle. Against the far wall, a young woman who looked like the photo Scott had given Sam was reading to a group of fifteen kids, aged from five to ten. Parents filled the rest of the library, most likely happy to get some time to themselves. A few sat at the hard tables while others occupied the chairs at the end of the aisles. Some read books of their own. A few others browsed the shelves while a young couple sat together at one of the computers, looking at a travel website.

"Do we wait?" Linus asked.

Cassandra Whitaker, the woman they had come to see, looked up, her eyes briefly meeting Sam's. They narrowed, and she tilted her head, confusion on her face. She probably knew everyone in that building at almost all times. Small-town libraries were like that. But she didn't know them.

"She's confused at our arrival." Sam looked over at Linus, who was staring at her. "Okay, well, I'm confusing her. You're creeping her out."

"She's beautiful," Linus said.

Cassandra had shoulder-length brown hair and bright green eyes that seemed to see the room and the words in the book she was reading at the same time. She wore a simple cardigan over a t-shirt and jeans with white sneakers. If someone ever said to Sam, "Imagine a librarian," she was what would pop into his head.

"You stay here," he whispered to Linus. "Make sure she doesn't leave."

His eyes briefly met Cassandra's again before he turned and walked to the back of the library. "It should be here," he mumbled to himself as he scanned the authors' names on the shelves.

"What are you looking for?"

Sam turned to find Linus behind him. "I told you to keep an eye on her."

They squeezed past a woman, probably another of the young mothers. She sat on the floor, her back against one of the shelves as she thumbed through a magazine.

"It was uncomfortable out there," Linus said, his voice a little louder than Sam's. "She was watching me as if she thought I was going to walk off with one of these kids."

The shelves, though not towering, were densely packed with books whose spines displayed an array of colors, some bright, others dulled by time. Sam reached the section he was looking for and stopped about halfway into the empty aisle. He dropped to his knees and grabbed a copy of short stories by Edgar Allen Poe.

"What are you doing?" Linus asked.

"Checking something."

He flipped it to *The Tell-Tale Heart* and read the first few lines. Next, he felt the back of the book, but it seemed normal. Nothing had been added to it. Finally, he reached to the back of the shelf, pushing books out of the way, ensuring the shelf itself wasn't concealing any secrets.

"Dude, seriously. What the hell are you doing?" Linus's voice cracked slightly, and the corners of his mouth twitched. He scanned the room as if worried about what one of the other patrons in the crowded library would think. "Another hunch?"

"Something like that," Sam said, his attention still partly on the shelf.

Linus shifted his weight from one foot to the other, the crease in his forehead deepening. He walked to the end of the row, glancing back at Sam one last time.

"Can I help you?"

Linus spun, and Sam looked up. At the other end of the aisle stood Cassandra Whitaker. She smiled at Sam, but not in the same welcoming way as when they had walked in. She noticed the book in his hand.

"Let me guess," she said. "Savannah College of Design?"

Sam paused. A quick smile flashed across his face, and he nodded.

"Guilty," he said.

"There's nothing there. I check every few months. I've had to keep my eyes on people like you over the years. No one in this town reads Poe, so when I see someone heading back here, I follow them and make sure they're not ripping apart my shelves."

"Sorry about that," he said. "It's not why we're here, and I do promise I don't rip shelves apart anymore."

"What are you two talking about?" Linus asked.

Cassandra approached Sam, took the book from him, and put it back on the shelf. She straightened the rest of the books Sam had disturbed.

"Now," she said. "How can I help you?"

"I understand you lived in Las Vegas for a little while around eight months ago, is that correct?"

She tilted her head a little and narrowed her eyes. "I did," she said. "I did my Grad school out there at UNLV, then came back to Cedar Shoals once I graduated."

"And you had a roommate named Maryanne Preston, is that right?"

She frowned. "Who are you guys? You don't look like cops. You look like—" She paused again, her eyes moving from one to the other. "An insurance salesman or something."

"We work IT for a manufacturing company," Linus said, the words coming a little too fast.

"Then I wasn't too far off," she said with a laugh as she turned to walk away.

Sam stepped in front of her before she could disappear down the aisle. "I'm Sam Norris." He offered his hand. "This is my friend Linus Hume. We're asking about her because of some things going on in Savannah that have to do with her."

She took Sam's hand and released it, her attention moving back to the corner of the building where she had been reading. Most of the kids had gone, although a few lingered, standing with their parents.

"What's going on with Maryanne in Savannah?" she asked as she headed down the aisle. She grabbed a stack of books from a cart and began shelving them.

"She's dead," Linus blurted out.

Sam turned his head slightly toward his friend, his mouth contorting into a thin line, but he quickly turned back to Cassandra. Her expression had barely changed. She didn't put her hand to her mouth or step back or anything. She only blinked once, slowly.

"How?"

"Someone beat her to death with a golf club."

This time, Cassandra raised her eyebrows. "Sounds like a terrible way to go."

"You don't seem as disappointed as I thought you would be," Sam said.

"I didn't really know her that well, and it only took a few weeks of living together before I realized what kind of person she was."

"What kind of person was she?"

"It's hard to explain. She was just odd. She was only with me for a couple of months. I was going to ask her to move out, but I came home one day, and there was a note with a wad of cash for her half of the rent for the rest of the month."

"What did the note say?" Sam asked.

She pulled a book from the shelf, wiped her arm across the spine, and put it back a few spots from its original location. "She had found an opportunity in Savannah and had to go."

"An opportunity? Like a job?"

"She never said job, but I know she had traveled back and forth there a few times after she moved in with me."

"To see Peyton?" Linus whispered.

"Is Peyton her boyfriend? I was under the impression she had met someone here in town who was from there. She would spend her weekends at the casino, then about every other week, she would fly back and forth to Savannah, where I think he lived."

"And that's why you didn't see her much?"

"She was hardly ever home."

Sam took a breath, letting the thoughts settle in his brain. "What made you think she was odd?"

Cassandra pushed the cart to the next aisle. Sam and Linus followed her.

"One night, a few days after she moved in, she drank way too much and began ranting and raving about her childhood. Her dad was an alcoholic, awful to her mom, and when she died, he ran out and married someone else so quickly that she suspected he'd been having an affair as her mom lay dying in the hospital."

Sam moved beside her, putting his hand on the cart, stopping it along with Cassandra. "Did she mention a sister?"

"Oh yeah, that story," Cassandra said with a laugh. "She claimed her sister was murdered. The next morning after she left the house, I did some searching on her name but couldn't find anything. I suspected she was making up the whole thing."

Sam's pulse kicked so hard that he felt it in his throat. He kept his face as calm as he could, but he tightened his grip on the cart. He wasn't going to let Cassandra move away from him until he asked his next question.

"Any chance she told you who she thought did it?"

Cassandra's eyes shifted away from Sam for a second as if she was re-playing that evening, deciding how much of it she thought was true versus fiction. As she looked back at Sam, any annoyance or disinterest she had been showing disappeared from her face. "Hold on," she said. "You're asking these questions as if she were telling the truth."

"She was," Linus said.

Cassandra fell still. Her mouth opened a fraction, then closed again. "I thought she was drunk and making things up."

"There's been a case in Savannah, a girl who'd been missing for seventeen years. They found her bones in the sand trap of a golf course."

"I read about that," Cassandra said. "Juliet something, right?"

"Summerfield."

"That was her sister?"

"Yes."

"That's so sad. She never said anything about who did it, but I didn't like how happy she seemed to be while talking about it."

"Happy?"

Cassandra nodded once, firmly. "Almost as if she thought this younger sister deserved it." She looked away and muttered under her breath. "Oh, this is so terrible. I feel so bad for this poor girl. Maryanne hated that family."

"Hated, why?"

She pushed the cart, and Sam loosened his grip, allowing it to move. At the next set of shelves, she began sliding books into place.

"She once told me this story." Cassandra was almost whispering. Linus moved next to Sam so he could hear. "Her dad used to sit in this chair, drinking beer and watching TV. The TV would be turned up so loud that her mom couldn't talk over it. If she tried to turn it down, he'd snap at her. Everything in that house was his, including the sounds."

"Sounds like a real piece of work," Linus said.

"One night, her mom made dinner and put the plate in front of him. He took one bite and shoved it away. He complained it was cold, then he went on a rant on how useless she was. Her mom didn't even argue. She picked up the plate, took it back to the kitchen, and started over."

Sam watched Cassandra's face as she spoke, seeing the emotion she felt for Maryanne's mom, a woman she didn't know.

"Maryanne told me how she stood in the doorway as an eight-year-old watching her mom reheat food for a man who didn't even like her. She vowed at that point she would never be like that."

"When Maryanne first showed up at your place," Sam said, "what was she like? Her attitude. How'd she act when she moved in?"

"For the first week or two, not great, but then she was happy, like she had finally caught a break."

"More like caught a fish," Linus mumbled.

"How did she pay for rent?"

"Cash," Cassandra said. "Always on time, and always cash. I don't think she had a bank account."

Sam nodded. Evelyn, or Maryanne, had been able to afford twenty-seven thousand dollars for a new identity. She paid rent with cash. She was taking trips back to Savannah, sometimes coming home with money."

He turned to Linus. "That note," he said. "I don't think she was being blackmailed or threatened. I bet she was the one doing the blackmailing, but I'm thinking it wasn't someone in Vegas."

"Are you sure?"

Sam asked Cassandra, "Did she ever talk about Savannah?"

"She didn't."

Sam glanced toward the front of the library. Most of the parents had cleared out, taking their kids after Cassandra had finished reading to them, but a few stood near the desk, staring at her as if they were waiting for her to come and help them.

"How long were you in Vegas?"

"Two years," she said.

"I'm sure the people around here are glad you're back. We appreciate your help, Cassandra. I think we've taken up too much of your time."

She walked over to the reference desk and returned, handing Sam and Linus each a business card. "It's Cassie," she said. "Once you find out what happened to her, let me know. I do think there was something off about Maryanne, and I'd be curious to know what it was."

Chapter Twenty-Five

Sam eased his car off the main road, passing a set of pine trees that eventually cleared away and showed the perfectly manicured lawn before the Layne family home. It was bigger than your average home, but Carey always shut Sam down whenever he called it a mansion. It had stone columns, high windows and a roofline that seemed to go on forever. White strings of lights laced the gutters and wound down the porch posts, each light blinking in a rhythm that lit up the early December evening.

Madison pressed her palms against the dashboard and leaned forward, getting a better view of the house. "They've decorated since I was here last."

"How long ago was that?"

"A few days before Emmitt died." She faced Sam. "I still don't understand why they invited me."

Sam slowly pulled the car up the driveway, through the gravel and onto the paved portion, stopping behind a black SUV next to a silver coupe. "Why shouldn't you be here?"

"I already told you how much they hate me," she said.

Sam laughed as he opened his car door, hurried around the front of the car and opened the door for her.

"Look at you," Madison said. "All gentlemanly."

"I need to practice. Between you and me, I think Dani is going to be moving here sooner rather than later."

"That's exciting," she said as she stepped outside. "I'll finally get to meet the girl who stole your heart. Libby and I assumed you'd stay alone forever."

Madison's heels sank into the grass near the edge of the driveway. A pair of lanterns on each side of the garage gave enough light for Sam to see her fully. She wore a small gold necklace and earrings framed her face, sparkling as they caught the porch light.

Sam took a breath. "People normally stare at me when I enter a room," he teased, a wry smile on his face. "But tonight, a few of them may look your way."

"You're the one who decided not to dress up." She looked at Sam from head to toe. "Seriously, khakis and a boring black shirt? I'm surprised you wore something with buttons. Did you even change after work, or is this what you wore on casual Friday?"

"I've always hated buttons," Sam mumbled as he adjusted his shirt.

She leaned forward and looked down to his feet. "You're wearing sneakers, for crying out loud. I told you this was formal."

"They're black," he said, sticking his arm out for her to take. "I like to call them my dress sneakers."

She interlocked her arm into his. "The sooner Wyoming moves out here, the better. You're in desperate need of a makeover if you're going to come to shindigs like this."

They stepped onto the front porch, and before Sam could ring the doorbell, the door opened. Charlotte Windsor, Emmitt's next-door neighbor, quickly pulled Madison close for a hug. "Oh, sweetie, it's so nice to see you again." She released Madison and glanced at both. "Sam and Madison. The two people Carey talks about the most. I'm saddened at what has happened, but I'm so glad you could come."

She stepped back inside the house and held her arm out, guiding the pair through the large oak doors and into the foyer. Charlotte's green gown caught the light of the large chandelier hanging overhead. As Sam moved past her, a waft of her perfume hit him. It was something floral, a scent he remembered smelling more than once while golfing with Emmitt.

Madison stuck her arm through Sam's and pulled him closer. "At least one person here likes me," she said.

Charlotte led them through a foyer that itself had more square footage than Sam's entire house. To its right, the door to Emmitt's office was closed, and next to it, a small guest bedroom had been built, its door also closed. They turned left, into a spacious living room with plush green furniture and large windows offering views of the front yard.

"You two should head into the dining room," Charlotte said. "Everyone else is already here."

Passing through the living room to the other side, they crossed another set of large, wooden doors. All eyes focused on them as they entered the dining room. The guests paused mid-conversation, their attention moving to Sam and Madison as if they were on display at the circus. Brock stood by the fireplace, a small glass of something in his hand. He raised it toward the pair and took a long sip and finished it off.

Dexter and Allen Bryce Foster stood at another corner in what appeared to be an intense discussion. From what Sam could hear—words like "confidentiality" and "data security"—it seemed to be about a business Dexter was running.

Emily Layne, Dexter's wife, sat at the dining room table. Her eyes met Sam's briefly before she returned her attention to her restless son, who was clearly not where he wanted to be. He stared at his phone, ignoring whatever it was Emily was saying to him.

"About fucking time," Ethan mumbled as he looked up from his phone at Sam and Madison.

Sam had heard stories of Ethan, the fifteen-year-old who caused trouble for most of the adults in his life, including teachers and his own parents, but had never met him. As if she were swatting a fly, Emily's hand shot out and caught the back of his head. His cell phone jumped from his hand. It hit the floor at his feet and bounced twice, ending up under his chair.

"Sorry, we're late," Sam said. "It's a bit of a hike from the island. Plus, it took me an extra few minutes to get across town to pick her up."

"Way to shift the blame," Madison whispered.

"They like me more than you," Sam said, keeping his voice low and trying not to move his mouth. "No need to change that now."

With her arm still locked in his, Madison jabbed her elbow into Sam's side. Charlotte indicated two chairs on the side of the table with their backs to the large front window. "You two have seats over here." She looked toward the kitchen, then at Emily. "And before anyone says it, yes, we know appetizers are meant to be passed around before dinner, not served at the table. Tonight we're pretending it's fashionable."

"Or maybe we could finally hire some staff for this house," Dexter said. "So Emily doesn't get roped into helping again."

Charlotte shot him a look. "Your father didn't like strangers in the house when we could manage it just fine. I was always happy to help him. Emily, let's get dinner started."

Charlotte left the room with Emily following her into the kitchen. Sam walked behind Madison around the table. He held the chair for her, pushed it in as she sat, and took the seat next to her. Across from Madison, Ethan glared at Sam, probably looking for any reason to get out of there.

"This is fancy," Madison said to Brock. He sat to her right at the head of the table. "It's nice to see you away from the barstool."

Brock grunted a response and looked away from her.

Emily emerged from the kitchen, carrying a tray with appetizers. She took her seat next to Ethan, across from Sam. Among the items, one in particular caught Sam's eye. It was something he couldn't quite identify: small, oblong morsels wrapped in bacon gave off an amazing smell, something he couldn't quite recognize.

He leaned closer to Madison, whispering, "What are those?"

"No idea."

"Those are dates wrapped in bacon," Charlotte said.

Emily set the tray in the middle of the table, and Sam reached for them, using a fork to put two on the small plate in front of him. "I'll eat my own shoes if you wrap them in bacon."

He was the only person who seemed to appreciate his own joke. Along with the dates, there were mini quiches, something his mom had unsuccessfully tried to get him to eat, and a classic shrimp cocktail. The chilled, cooked shrimp had been lined neatly around the edge of a glass bowl filled with cocktail sauce.

"We thought it would be good to get everyone together," Emily said as each of the guests carefully placed a few appetizers on their plates.

She continued, her voice carrying as much warmth as she could put into it, "It's been tense around here lately, and a good dinner party always helps to smooth things over." Turning to Dexter, who had taken his seat across from Brock at the other end of the table, she added with a gentle smile, "Right, sweetie?"

Dexter shoved a whole piece of shrimp into his mouth. "Yeah, sure," he said, and paused to add, "It's a great idea. I've been excited about this night ever since you told me we were doing it."

Emily continued, recognizing her husband's sarcasm at the same time as everyone else. "It's important that we remember Emmitt and Peyton for the years we had with them."

Charlotte came back into the dining room, setting another tray of appetizers on the other side of the table. She took her seat between Emily and Dexter, with Allen sitting between Sam and Dexter.

Emily looked at the group, her voice shaking. "We haven't taken the chance to do that yet as a group, so let's talk about the good times. Who wants to go first?" The ensuing silence quickly became unbearable, so she picked someone.

"Charlotte. You knew Emmitt as well as anyone. What do you remember?"

Charlotte's fingers tightened on a locket hanging around her neck. A quiet smile formed, and she took a breath. "I remember lots of good times. Emmitt was so sweet to me, inviting me into his house and allowing me to help him out when he needed it."

"You were certainly good for him," Emily said. "Here when he needed you most."

"If she was so good for him, why didn't he leave her anything in the will?" Brock asked.

Everyone looked his way as the grip Emily had on her fork tightened. All at once, the warmth she had tried to create in the room disappeared.

"You didn't get anything?" Sam asked. As uncomfortable as it made him, he leaned into the comment. Everyone talking nicely about Peyton and Emmitt wouldn't get Carey out of jail any quicker, but the yelling and screaming, with people saying something they shouldn't, had a better chance of working.

"I told him I didn't want any of his money," Charlotte said, looking at Sam. "The time I was able to spend with him was much more valuable."

"I'm surprised he listened," Emily said. "He was always so generous."

"He could have been more generous in the will," Brock mumbled.

As if they were at a tennis match, all eyes on the long sides of the table moved from Charlotte to Brock.

"You have something intelligent you want to add, Brock?" Dexter asked.

Eyes to Dexter, then back to Brock.

"He didn't say anything," Emily said as if desperately trying to stop the impending fire with a thimble of water. She looked toward Sam, her voice shaking. "How about you, Sam? I've heard him say he was like your second father."

Sam held her gaze, wondering what Beaumont would do. Emily's mouth formed a thin line, then opened a tiny bit as if she were begging Sam to answer, team up with her, help her extinguish the flame—but on this night, she and Sam weren't going to be on the same team.

"How come you didn't mention Maryanne?" Sam asked, hoping the added gas would push the fire higher. "You said celebrate Emmitt and Peyton, but not Maryanne. Why not say nice things about her?"

Emily's smile thinned. She reached for her water, missed the glass by an inch, then found it and took a sip. "I, uh, certainly didn't—"

"I was saying..." Brock's voice rose a little. Emily's head snapped to him. The rest of the table turned as well. "He could have been nicer to Charlotte in his will, regardless of her wishes. She took care of him every day until he died, and he left her nothing." He looked toward Allen. "Did he ever tell you why?"

Allen held one hand in the air as he jabbed a small piece of shrimp deep into some cocktail sauce. He seemed thrown off by the question, making Sam wonder why he was there at all, other than maybe to get a free meal. Allen stuck the shrimp into his mouth, chewed for a few seconds, swallowed, and finally spoke. "She said she didn't want anything. He listened."

"How could you not want anything?" Brock asked Charlotte.

"My husband did very well for us before his untimely passing."

"I understand that, but it's the gesture, you know, the thought. Everything you did for him. He could have been a little more fair to you."

"I wasn't his maid expecting payment, Brock. He was my friend."

"Come on, Brock, we know this isn't about her," Dexter said. "This is about you."

Brock nodded. "You have to admit I got the shaft. We both did."

Next to Sam, Madison stiffened. "Carey too," she whispered.

"I didn't need his money like you did," Dexter said. "I was smart in my decisions."

"In the first version of the will," Allen said as he dabbed at the corners of his mouth with a napkin. "He left everything equally to the four boys, with something left over for both Charlotte and Kristie."

Forks paused in midair as each member of the table looked up at Allen.

"First version," Brock said. "What are you talking about?"

Instead of looking toward Allen, Sam let his eyes move to each of the people at the table, checking their faces. They all had a similar look of surprise, although Brock's carried a bit of anger in it, while Dexter seemed more confused than anything.

Allen raised his hands in the air as if to calm everyone. "Charlotte convinced him to take her out of the will, so he changed it. When he changed it, he moved almost everything to Peyton."

Brock glared at Charlotte. "That means it's all your fault."

"I didn't tell him to take everything from you." She set her palms flat on the table like a teacher looking down on a rowdy class. "I asked him to leave me out of the will. That's the only thing I ever asked, so lower your voice and stop blaming me."

As if he'd had an epiphany, Brock smiled and leaned back in his chair. He took a sip from his drink as the anger changed into something else, something that looked more like satisfaction, or like victory. "Okay, I'm willing to accept that he rewrote it and put almost everything on Peyton. Peyton's gone, and as the oldest living brother, it all comes to me."

Sam frowned, surprised by how Brock went from "Peyton died" to "it all comes to me" as if it should be an easy transition. He remembered when he lost his parents; it took him years to spend any of the money they had left him. If he spent it, it felt like they were truly gone.

"You're not even going to pretend to be sad to have lost a brother?" he asked Brock.

"I am sad, but life goes on for us. The course still needs someone to run it, and since Carey's not going to walk through that door anytime soon, I'm going to make the decisions."

Next to Sam, Madison stiffened.

"Sorry, big brother," Dexter said. "But it's not that easy. Maryanne was his wife. Everything went to her, and with her gone, what happens next?"

Allen looked at his plate. He fidgeted with his fork, jabbing at the last piece of shrimp, dipping it into the sauce. Feeling everyone's eyes on him, he said, "I'm still checking on it."

Sam glanced at Allen, then around the table. The police had to have told them, at least Allen, that she was not Maryanne Preston, but instead Evelyn Delaney, but he said nothing about it.

"There are two of us now," Dexter said. "I say we split everything down the middle."

"Three," Madison said, tapping her fork against the table.

"I'm fine splitting it with you," Dexter said. "Splitting it two ways still gives us both a good amount."

"I'm getting pissed," Madison whispered to Sam. Her heel began a steady drumming under the table.

"Keep your cool," Sam said.

Dexter continued making his plea. "We can split it fifty-fifty with no arguments or legal junk or anything, and then we go our separate ways."

"Three brothers," Madison said, her voice loud enough to be heard above everyone else.

The room seemed to pause. The two brothers, whose expressions had hardened as they spoke to each other, turned to face Madison.

"Do either of you even give a shit that your brother is sitting in a prison cell?"

"He made his bed when he killed Maryanne," Brock said coldly, as if he were the judge banging the gavel at the murder trial moments after the jury had declared Carey guilty.

"You say that as if he's already been sentenced."

Sam felt the urge to speak, to stand and defend his friend, to add his voice to Madison's. Everything she said was correct, he knew it, they all knew it, but he restrained himself. His role there was not to argue. He had decided before walking through the door that he would observe only.

"Why are you even here?" Brock asked. "Just because you happen to be the girl Carey is banging doesn't give you access to my house."

"I care about him more than you do."

"You only care about his father's money. You're worse than all of us. I can't believe you have the nerve to get all pissed off because he didn't get the golf course you think he deserved. Why do you even care what he ended up with?" He looked toward Emily. "Why is she even here? Why are either of them here?"

Madison kicked her chair back. It collided with the wall behind her, the top of it smacking against the glass of the window. Color rose in her cheeks, and she glared at Brock with an anger Sam had never seen in her.

"You're a real piece of shit, Brock," Madison said. "You probably killed Maryanne so you could take control of all this and call it yours. I'm surprised you haven't already gambled it away in one of your drunken stupors."

Before Brock could speak, Ethan erupted. He had been quiet all night, hardly looking away from his phone. But now he was standing.

"Shut up, all of you!"

In one swift motion, he grabbed his plate, spun, and hurled it at the fireplace. Shrimp and cocktail sauce flew from it, covering the floor. The plate shattered against the stonework with a crash. Fragments scattered across the hearth.

“I hate this family, he yelled. “You’re all fucking awful.”

Chapter Twenty-Six

"Ethan!" Emily yelled.

She stood to face him, but he pushed her away. Tears streamed down his face. He bolted from the table, throwing his chair to the floor, and stormed out of the dining room.

Emily shot a look at Madison before leaving the room to chase after her son, who had gone up the stairs and slammed a door somewhere on the second floor. Madison had also begun to cry, her mascara running down her face. She stormed out of the dining room, finding a bathroom near Emmitt's office.

Sam watched Madison leave, torn between the urge to comfort her and the need to stay for the outbursts; they were why he'd agreed to come. People said stupid things during a fight. Another door slammed on the second floor as Ethan could be heard stomping down the hall and going into another room.

"Ethan," Emily yelled while pounding on the door.

Near Emmitt's office, the door to the spare bedroom also shut as Madison had found her spot to cry. Sam stood, but something one of the brothers said had stuck with him. It was a question he hadn't yet asked himself.

Charlotte said, "Dexter, go get your wife. Bring her back here. I'm sick of all this fighting. We're going to sit down as a family and have a nice dinner."

Dexter stood. "Sorry, Charlotte, but the last time I checked, you weren't my mom, and you certainly aren't part of this family. Dinner is over for me. Tell Emily I'll be in the car."

"Sit down," Charlotte said. It was not a question. It was an order.

But Dexter didn't listen. "I told Emily over and over this was a stupid idea," he mumbled to himself as he left the room.

Allen was next to stand. He shoved another piece of shrimp in his mouth. "I'm going to take off too."

Brock walked to the fireplace, picked up the larger pieces of the broken plate, and took them into the kitchen. Sam followed Dexter to the front door, leaving Charlotte by herself at the table.

***

"Hey, Dex, you have a minute?" Sam asked outside.

Dexter paused before stepping off the porch. He turned to face Sam. His jaw clicked, and his heel tapped against the floor. Sam cleared his throat and tried to come off casual.

"Crazy thing, finding those bones on the golf course?"

"I don't know anything about them, if that's what you're suggesting."

Sam raised his palms. "I'm not suggesting anything. But it was crazy how they ended up there. Carey told me you were in charge of the construction when your dad first took over the course. He said you were writing a computer program of some sort to map the whole thing out?"

"I tried, played around for about a week, but I gave up. I didn't have the patience for computer programming. I'm not sure how you do it."

Sam had worked on this lie for a day or so, making sure he said everything correctly. "Listen, I need to be honest. I didn't want to come to dinner tonight, but I did because I wanted to talk specifically with you, and you're a hard man to get a hold of."

Dexter squinted at Sam, his chin tucked almost to his chest. "Why?"

"My girlfriend's in-laws are working on the same thing back at their home course in Wyoming, helping the owner redo a few holes. She asked me to find some software for them to use, so I told her I would ask you."

Dexter seemed to relax. "The software package we used was called the Golf Designer. It's a terrible name, I know, but it did a great job for what we needed."

"How did it work?"

"It was pretty basic." Dexter put his keys into his pocket. "You sketch the property line, then drop the tees and greens where you want. After that, you create fairways, moving from tee to green. There are settings that allow you to control the slope, the rough width and the depth of the bunkers. You can also tilt the greens and watch the runoff lines."

He made a small arc in the air, tracing an invisible contour.

"It also has a library of trees that match what we have down here in Savannah, pines, live oaks and maples. You stamp them in, put yourself at any point on the course, and you can see what the user sees if they were really standing on the course."

"Sounds complicated."

"It was, but it was also thorough," Dexter said. "You could design a hole right down to the blades of grass, and it was realistic. It would also determine the handicap and slope of the course as you were designing it. Expensive, but well worth it."

"Any idea how it worked behind the scenes?"

"Not really, but I did contact the manufacturers. I had the same questions. They said it used something for terrain generation based on a Perlin noise algorithm."

"A what?" Sam asked, although he already knew the answer.

It was a basic computer science term he had learned in his sophomore year of college. But hearing lately from several people that Dexter had been working with computers, something he didn't expect to be true, made him curious as to how Dexter would answer.

"Beats me," Dexter said, shrugging. "Something to do with a seeded function, fake random gradients, octaves."

"Sounds like you know some of the fancy terms," Sam said, impressed that Dexter knew enough to throw those words out there. He thought about the golf simulator and Maryanne's records being deleted by someone with access.

"I'm sure there's more to it than that, but I got tired and bailed. Too many big words."

"Did you also pick the software for the golf simulator?"

"I helped Dad a little when he was building it, why?"

"Did you have a chance to use it? Someone told me you were in the simulator the day Maryanne was killed. What time did you get out of there?"

Dexter pulled his hands from his pockets and leaned against one of the porch posts. He smiled. "Nice try, Sam, but getting me talking about one thing then trying to flip it so you can interrogate me about Maryanne's murder? Not so smooth for someone Carey once described as the smartest person he knew."

The front door opened, and Emily came rushing out, Ethan a step behind her. They moved past Sam as though he wasn't standing there.

"If you want to know what I've been doing the last few weeks, ask the real police," Dexter said. "I already talked to them."

He hurried the family to the silver Coupe, leaving Sam alone on the front porch. His mind drifted to Madison, who should also be ready to leave.

Chapter Twenty-Seven

At the door of the spare room, Sam smoothed his shirt with the palm of his hands, trying to simulate what an iron would do, then he tapped lightly. "Hey. You okay in there? I'm ready to go if you are." His voice was soft, but he spoke loudly enough for Madison to hear him on the other side.

Silence was the only response he received, so he turned the knob slowly, listening for the click so he could push it open. One last look over his shoulder; Brock was still upstairs, and Charlotte in the kitchen, but at that moment there was only silence. The house felt big and empty.

Once inside, he closed the door. It was a smaller room, used by guests when they stayed over. A few family photos hung on the wall, mostly Emmitt with the boys, one with their mom and one of only Emmitt and his wife at the wedding. She had died a few years before Sam had met Carey.

Madison's green purse sat on a simple twin bed in the middle of the room. She had said the purse's color was sea-glass because, according to her, it matched her eyes. Against one wall, a roll-top desk sat half-open, and a dresser had been pushed against the opposite wall. Madison had left the overhead light off when she came in, and the room was lit by two small lamps on nightstands, one on each side of the bed.

She stood at the window, her back to Sam. She had pushed a curtain aside and was looking into the darkness.

"We can go now," Sam said quietly.

She sighed and turned, shaking her head. "I'm so tired of being polite to what's left of this family."

Somewhere upstairs, Brock's laughter rang out while the clinking of dishes was most likely Charlotte clearing the table. Sam stepped closer to Madison. She didn't move.

"Sorry for forcing you into being here tonight," he said.

"No, don't apologize. You were right. I needed to be here to help represent Carey, make sure they weren't slandering him."

"I know—"

"And of course they did," she said, tears beginning to well up again. Her hands hung to her waist, pinching her dress, rolling it between her fingers and thumb. "They couldn't even get through the appetizers before pretending he didn't exist."

Sam took another step forward, and she looked up at him, her eyes red from crying. She moved to press her forehead to his chest and put her arms around him, pulling him close.

"Carey's going to be okay," he said as he embraced her.

"I can tell by the tone of your voice that you don't believe that."

He set his chin on her head, feeling her hair. "No," he said. "Not yet, but we'll get there. I have some ideas on who it—"

Then she kissed him.

He went still for a beat; his arms falling and locking in place at his sides. For a second, he didn't pull away. Her lip gloss tasted sweet, and his mind took him back to when he had first met her. He remembered how her eyes looked, her smile and how he had immediately fallen for her. He remembered being silently jealous of Carey for a while before those feelings finally faded. As quickly as those memories popped into his head, his brain switched it up, showing him the two most important people in his life. Carey, currently sitting in a jail cell, and Dani, standing in her workspace in South Plainfield, her hips swaying to the music from her boombox.

He pulled back. "Madison."

As if she hadn't realized what she had done, her eyes widened. She stared at him like she couldn't believe it, then glanced at the door. "I'm so sorry," she said. Her hand rose to her mouth and dropped again. "I don't know why I—That was wrong."

Sam nodded once. Silence filled the room.

"Please don't tell Carey," she breathed out.

"I'm not telling anyone."

"We don't talk about this."

"We don't," Sam said.

Chapter Twenty-Eight

It was late on Sunday night, and Sam sat at his dining room table, hunched over his laptop. An empty bag of potato chips sat behind the laptop next to a large water bottle he had begun drinking from after running out of Pepsi. He'd spent most of his weekend at the house, talking with Dani on long calls and messaging her on longer text threads. Even when they hung up, her voice seemed to linger throughout the house.

Several times, he had fought the temptation to call Rick, one of the supply chain managers, and ask again if they had made a decision about her transfer. Dani had told him not to. She didn't want him to be a pest, but he liked her voice around his house and desperately wanted it to be there more often, live.

He had turned off all the lights and left only the soft glow from the laptop in the room. Anyone peeking through his window right now would surely be afraid of what must have looked like a horror show: his face lit up with nothing else visible at the dining room table. He had rubbed his eyes raw and red, and though he had slept this weekend more than in a while, he still felt the fatigue of a college weekend spent cramming for a Monday test.

The TNT application filled the screen. He went through everything he had, moving it around, trying to put the puzzle together with very little luck. Despite the late hour and another Monday morning that would come way too soon, the urgency of updating TNT with everything he had learned kept him in the chair.

More than anything, Charlotte was in his head. Why was she there? What was her real relationship with Emmitt? Although he was confident she hadn't killed anyone, he added her name to the larger of the two triangles.

The room around him was silent, save for the occasional creak of the house settling and the soft tapping of his keyboard. He stopped typing and leaned back. Behind his laptop, under a stack of unopened mail, his phone buzzed. He glanced down, noticing Emmitt's number.

He shook his head, wondering if Charlotte knew he was thinking of her. The phone buzzed again. He tapped the screen twice, first answering the call and then activating the speaker phone.

"Hi Charlotte," he said.

"You need to get over here tomorrow night."

There was a tremor in her voice, and her breaths were shallow and quick. She wasn't the same calm, cool woman who'd sat near him at the dinner party.

"Why?"

"Did you know that Brock is using Emmitt's money to acquire a horse with some shady business partner?"

"Yeah, he told me about it a few days ago. Brock and Kroll or something silly like that."

"I bet he didn't tell you everything."

Sam sat up. The exhaustion that had filled him for hours slipped away. He closed his eyes tightly, then opened them. "What didn't he tell me?"

"I overheard him with this new partner on the phone earlier. They were talking about plans, something to do with a virus and how they would score a ton of money once they released it. I think he's planning to poison the other horses in the race."

"Poison?" Sam asked. "Did he say how?"

"That's all I heard. He hung up and left in a hurry."

"What do you want me to do over there?"

"I want to search his office, but I'm afraid I'll miss something. I'd rather you did it instead."

Sam stared at his TNT screen. He wasn't the type of person to go sneaking around someone's house to steal something or, even worse, to get caught—especially by Brock. The man was unhinged. At best, he only had a temper, but at worst, he might have killed his own brother and sister-in-law. When given a chance to show some emotion about the deaths, Brock hadn't. All he cared about was how things worked themselves out for him.

"You're sure he won't be there?" Sam asked, his mind showing him Carey sitting in that jail cell.

"He has dinner plans with whatever girl he's tricking into sleeping with him this week. Be here at seven. I know the combination to the safe. Whatever he's hiding has to be in there."

Chapter Twenty-Nine

The next evening, Linus cut the headlights on his car as he drove past Emmitt's house.

"Next street," Sam said from the passenger seat. "First house on the right."

Linus made a quick right, then another, and pulled into Charlotte's driveway. It was long, and as Linus drove toward the garage, he also moved closer to the back of Emmitt's house, which was butted up against Charlotte's side yard. Her house was smaller than Emmitt's, although not by much. Christmas lights flashed around the doors, windows and the two pine trees flanking the house.

"No wonder she didn't want any of his money," Sam mumbled.

Linus inched toward the garage, stopping next to a large SUV that shielded his car from the windows at the back of Emmitt's home.

"How do I get myself one of these houses?" Linus asked.

"Marry a rich guy."

"Is there another option?"

"Work hard and save your money," Sam said. "Advance up the corporate ladder until you're CEO."

"I don't like that, either. Is there a plan C?"

Emmitt's house was dark, offering Sam very little visibility as he hurried across Charlotte's side yard and into Emmitt's garden. He stepped onto a walkway made of red bricks. It was lined with small black solar lights, currently lit and showing the way along the path. Thick green shrubs were set against the house, set off by flowers of many colors. Their scent hit Sam, and he stopped for a split second to inhale. Charlotte stood inside the back door, and the darkness inside only let him see her silhouette in the threshold.

"As many times as I've been to this house," Sam said quietly, "I've never been back here. It smells amazing."

"I did most of it," Charlotte said, her lips curling into a smile that held a touch of pride. But almost as quickly as it had appeared, her smile dimmed. "Emmitt liked to sit back here."

Sam raised his eyebrows. "There was something between you two more than friendship, wasn't there?"

"There was something, but not what everyone wants to assume." She pushed open the door, and Sam slipped inside. He stopped at the large table in the middle of the kitchen.

"Anything in particular we should be looking for?"

"Brock has a notebook," she said. "It's small, almost like something a teenage girl would use as a journal, but even smaller."

Sam thought back to the conversation with Brock at the course when a notebook had sat among all the other things he had spread out on the bar. Brock had made sure to keep it close to him.

He nodded to Charlotte. "I've seen him with it at the golf course."

"He's almost never apart from it. Except for tonight; he has a date, and he never lets his ladies know his business. I was here earlier cleaning up the place, gathering up some of Emmitt's belongings to give them away, and I wandered into his office. Brock was sitting at Emmitt's desk, writing in that notebook. I could hear him mumbling. I don't know what he said, but he was angry about something. I asked him what was wrong, but he slammed the notebook shut and shoved it into Emmitt's safe."

"You didn't see any of what he was writing?"

"It looked like shorthand, but I'm sure it's important. Why else would he slam it shut like that?"

Sam paused, stopping Charlotte before they left the kitchen. "How come you were at the will reading if you knew you weren't getting anything in the will?"

Charlotte stopped, her hands resting on the back of a chair. She didn't answer right away, instead turning to look at Sam, a smile on her face. He wished he could tell what was going on inside her head. He had little doubt she had anything to do with either murder, but that question had been bothering him since the dinner party.

"I went because I wanted to make sure from Allen that Emmitt kept his word and didn't leave me anything. I left early because I didn't want to be around that family as Emmitt handed more money to them. That's all he ever did, write checks. Handouts. Anytime they asked. All except Carey, who was working harder than any of them."

"Even Peyton?" Sam asked. "I thought he was the golden child."

"He was not as golden as everyone thought."

"What do you mean?"

"Well, I don't know the details, but more than once, he came to Emmitt for money, calling it a business investment. He always had the proper paperwork, a business plan, and everything looked legit, Allen's signature on everything, but I wasn't so sure."

"Did Emmitt never question or ask for more details? Did he ever follow up?"

"No, and neither did I," Charlotte said. "I wish I had. There was something off there, and I was never able to find out what.

He followed her out of the kitchen and into the dining room. "I'm curious, do you know how Brock was able to move into this house and take over the golf course as if Emmitt had left it directly to him?"

"Carey's in jail, and Dexter doesn't want to deal with him. Dexter believes in the legal system, always the family's goody-two-shoes. But the problem with Allen is that he'll take his sweet time and milk them for everything he can. I told Carey that once he took over the course, he should get rid of Allen and find someone a little less expensive."

She moved him into the foyer. The house was mostly dark, with small lamps by the windows turned on to give them enough light to get where they were going.

"You should get moving. I'm not sure how long Brock is going to be gone."

"You're sure the notebook is in the safe?"

She nodded and shoved a folded piece of paper into Sam's hand. "This is the combination."

"I'll be out here," she said, pointing to a chair next to the front window. "If I see headlights, I'll let you know."

Sam hadn't been in Emmitt's office since he was a child, but it was obvious the room had fallen into a state of disarray since Brock had assumed control. The room, filled with mahogany paneling and two large grand windows overlooking it, felt more neglected than ever. Dust had settled on the polished surfaces, and stacks of papers and files cluttered the once perfectly organized desk.

Sam moved further into the room, the smell of tobacco still there from when Emmitt would spend his evenings going over paperwork. Sam could almost see the old man, still dressed from his work at the golf course, sitting at his desk. He almost expected to hear Emmitt speaking to him, telling him to leave because danger was lurking.

He hit the switch on a small lamp at the back edge of the desk. It added a little more light to the room, although not much. The walls, once covered with artwork Sam knew had value, stood bare. He wondered which brother had gotten to them first, and how much he had gotten paid for them.

In the corner of the office, a ladder leaned against the wall. It led to the second-story balcony overlooking the room. Sam's eyes fell upon a familiar sight behind the ladder. It was the secret closet Carey had shown him so many years ago.

"This is the perfect place when playing hide and seek with my dad," Carey had told him. It reminded Sam of the cubbyhole in his father's office. It had been his own perfect spot. He remembered Carey telling him, "Dad always pretended not to know where I was, but he always found me. Turns out, it's a pretty obvious hiding spot."

Sam wiped his brow and moved around behind the desk. He dropped to one knee and crawled underneath. Attached to the underside of the desk was a small safe. He unfolded the piece of paper Charlotte had given him and held it in the light. As he turned the combination lock, the clicks could be heard. The last number fell into place, and he pulled.

The door was heavier than expected, especially for such a small safe, but once it opened fully, a light on the inside clicked on. Sitting on a stack of paperwork was a small black notebook. Sam pulled it out, stood, and set it on the desk. Quickly rifling through it, he found a mess of letters and numbers on each page, nothing making sense at first glance.

"Shorthand," Sam muttered.

He dropped to his knees and began digging through the stack of paperwork. He pulled folders apart while skimming the headings of the pages inside. Most of it looked like the boring paperwork Sam shoved into a filing cabinet at home, things having to do with owning a home. There were also items relating to a second home in Florida and items for the golf course.

One folder caught his attention because it had no heading, nothing written on the tab. Inside it, there was a single page. It was folded in thirds as if it had been pulled straight from an envelope and shoved into the folder. It wasn't a legal document but instead a confession letter from a man named Wesley Pitts to Emmitt Layne. In the letter, Pitts confessed he had stolen money from Savannah Palms Golf Course, listing the amounts he had taken and the dates he had taken it. He further stated that he understood that Emmitt Layne would accept not to press charges as long as he never went near the golf course or contacted any member of the Layne family again. If he broke his word, Emmitt would use his confession to prosecute him.

As he replaced the page and put the folder back into the safe, a car could be heard coming up the driveway. The hair on the back of Sam's neck stood.

"Get out, Sam!" Charlotte yelled.

Sam peeked his head above the desk as the headlights shined through the front window into the foyer, lighting the room but then shutting off, along with the sound of the car's engine. Charlotte had disappeared into the kitchen. He followed her, but as he entered the kitchen, he remembered the notebook.

"Dammit," he muttered.

He hurried back into the office, grabbed the notebook and pushed the safe door shut. Voices could be heard on the porch. One was Brock's indistinguishable gruff tones as he complained about something. Sam couldn't make out his words, but soon after, a female voice answered.

"I wanted to go dancing," she said, her words slurred with each syllable drawn out.

Sam looked out into the foyer as the sound of Brock shoving the key into the front door's deadbolt hit him. He didn't have enough time to get through the foyer to the kitchen and out the back door without getting caught. The front door creaked open. Sam moved back into the office and ducked behind the desk. He pulled his elbows to his side, trying to make himself as small as he could.

"We can dance next time," Brock said. "In the meantime, you should—"

"What's wrong?" the female voice asked.

"I thought I, um, turned that light off."

Sam peered up at the lamp on the desk. He had forgotten to turn it off. His mind went blank, everything reduced to one single thought: If Brock saw him, he wouldn't be able to talk his way out. He glanced over his shoulder at the ladder, his muscles tensing; he had to move. He scrambled from behind the desk to the ladder. He put one foot on the bottom step and looked toward the balcony, but there was no place to hide up there. Only one option was left: He scurried behind the ladder, slipped into the closet and did his best to pull the door shut without making any noise.

Carey's voice echoed through his head. "It's a pretty obvious hiding spot." Sam moved toward the back of the closet, the slanted ceiling getting lower with each step.

"I know I turned it off," Brock said again. He was now standing in the office, somewhere near the door.

"You probably forgot," the woman said.

Brock didn't answer. Instead, his footsteps moved closer to the desk. Before he went around to the other side, he stopped, shuffled a few papers, then nothing. No noise at all. Sam pulled his phone from his pocket, silenced it, and typed a quick text to Linus.

"What's wrong?" the woman asked.

"Someone was in here," Brock said.

The closet around Sam seemed to shrink. He tapped Send on the three-word text to Linus and froze.

"Could it be that nosy neighbor you mentioned? What's her name?"

"Charlotte," Brock said, her name slicing through the air. "I told her to stay away tonight."

"I'm sure you're imagining things."

"Go to bed," Brock said in a monotone. "I'll be up in a minute."

"Don't be long." She giggled. "I may fall asleep if you make me wait."

Brock's footsteps moved to the other side of the desk. Sam followed the sound as Brock walked. The noise stopped, but the clicking sound of the lamp being turned off told Sam where Brock stood.

"Someone was here, and if I find out who it was... I'll kill anyone who messes with my shit."

Sam held his breath. Brock was no longer walking quietly. He was walking angrily.

"Or maybe they're still here," he said. His steps were louder. He moved slowly but stomped his feet, as if he wanted whoever was still in the office to know he knew they were there, hiding in the tiny closet.

"It's a pretty obvious hiding spot."

Chapter Thirty

Sam ducked his head and sat up. If anything, he could rush as soon as the door opened, catch Brock by surprise and knock him down before escaping through the kitchen. He could run into the woods next to the house and find Linus along the road. Brock would think it was a simple burglar and never know it was Sam.

He moved his free hand behind his back and felt for anything he could use as a weapon. His heart pounded in his ears, almost in rhythm with Brock's approaching footsteps. The tiny closet had grown darker, as if Brock was somehow blocking out any light that tried to squeeze through the cracks. Sam's hand grazed something solid. He reached for it.

The doorbell rang.

It was louder than he remembered, crossing the air like an arrow rushing toward its target. Brock's steps stopped.

"Honey, can you get that?" Brock yelled, his voice louder than the doorbell.

"I'm not decent," the woman said from the upstairs landing.

"You're never fucking decent," he mumbled.

Silence.

Sam imagined Brock staring at the closet door, annoyed that someone had dared to interrupt his little cat-and-mouse game. The doorbell rang again, but Brock didn't move. Sam's grip on his makeshift weapon tightened. It rang a third time and a fourth and a fifth. Whoever it was, they wanted to be let in right now.

Brock sighed. "Goddammit."

His footsteps started again, this time moving away from Sam. They moved toward Emmitt's desk, then from the desk to the office door. Sam crept to the closet door and put his hand on the round handle. Slowly, he turned it, listening for any sound that might give away his position. The door clicked. He paused and pushed it open a few inches, peering into the dark office.

"What the fuck do you want?" Brock asked the caller at the front door.

Sam stepped into the foyer, gluing himself to the back wall, as far from Brock as he could get. His movements were deliberate but silent, like a shadow inching across the floor.

"I don't give a shit what she said," Brock said as he looked back at the office door. Sam had already crossed behind him in the foyer, but froze as Brock turned, not allowing any movement to give him away.

"I'm only telling you what she said." The voice at the door belonged to Linus.

Instinctively, Sam tapped the phone in his pocket, but he continued to look toward the doorway leading into the dining room. He couldn't let Linus see him either. One glance toward Sam, and Brock would be alerted to his presence.

"Tell her she's not welcome here anymore." Brock's tone grew harsher.

Once inside the dining room, Sam increased the speed of his movements, still keeping as quiet as possible. He hurried into the kitchen and out the back door, being sure to push the door shut gently. He ran toward the woods at the north end of the house and turned the corner, pausing to get his breath as the chilly night air stung his throat.

Finally, he moved along the side of the house to the front corner next to the garage.

"You're going to leave now," Brock said.

At the corner of the house, Sam appeared. He walked toward Linus, still out of sight of Brock.

"We're not leaving until we talk to Madison," Linus said, trying to sound confident and not too shaky. "She's the one who ordered us here."

"We?" Brock asked as he stepped out of the doorway. He looked both ways, his eyes widening as Sam appeared, slightly out of breath from his quick dash around the house. Lines grew on Brock's face. It was as if the gears in his mind, which had been turning steadily with what he thought was going on, had ground to a halt.

"I can try texting her," Sam said, appearing calm despite the rapid beat of his heart.

Brock looked over his shoulder toward Emmitt's office. "The fuck did you come from?"

"I was in the car," Sam said. "I noticed you weren't letting Linus get inside, so I wanted to see what was going on."

Brock shook his head and the surprise from his face. He narrowed his eyes. "Both of you, leave right now, before I get angry." It was more of a command and not a suggestion.

Still catching his breath, Sam exchanged a glance with Linus. Sam knew he had found something that could put Brock firmly in his crosshairs, and Linus understood his task of saving Sam had been accomplished. Sam stepped off the porch, but Linus paused.

"If Madison does show up, would you be so kind as to take a message for us?"

Brock glared at them for a split second, then slammed the door.

"I don't think he was happy to see us," Linus said.

"He's never happy to see anyone. Thanks for rescuing me, by the way."

"How close was it?"

"Too close, but it was worth it." Sam pulled open the passenger door. "I need another favor."

"Two favors in one night? You're really pushing your luck."

They entered the car, both buckling their seat belts. Linus pushed the button to start his car and backed out of the driveway.

"Here's the thing," Sam said. "Every single person in this case is lying to me about their relationship with everyone else, and it's starting to piss me off."

"What do you mean?"

He pulled the small notebook from his pocket and handed it to Linus. Keeping his eyes mostly on the dark road ahead, Linus held it against the center of the steering wheel and shuffled through a few pages.

"What does all this mean?"

"It's all codes," Sam said, the word almost sticking in his throat. "Everything is written in code nowadays. Like when Dani texts me, she doesn't write out how are you, she puts three letters on the screen, hru. All small letters, no capitalization, and yet, without even thinking about it, I answer 'better now' with a smiley face."

"I've never seen you use an emoji in my life," Linus said.

"Not only that, but the way we keep score on the golf course, with plus and minus signs, and the numbers on the golf simulator screen." A laugh, almost more a huff of exasperation than amusement, escaped his lips. "Hell, even TNT at work. We joked that someone was justifying their new position by coming up with TNT, but they're doing what everyone else does. Creating codes to work through a project. It's exhausting."

"You sound like my grandpa," Linus said. "I play chess with him online. He's still back in Wyoming. When we play, I'll make a move, and the screen will say something like 'Re4+'."

"I don't know what that means," Sam said.

"Neither does he. That's the point. It's another one of those codes you're complaining about. I'll tell him it means Rook to e4, and the plus sign means I have his king in check. He complains about the codes the same way you are."

The receipt on Kristie's fridge flashed in Sam's brain. The odd total, the word Kings written underneath. Sam flipped through Brock's notebook again, looking at the letters.

"Everything is a code," Sam said. "Including Kings and those numbers." He smiled. "They mean something."

"What numbers? What do they mean?"

"I know where Kristie is."

Chapter Thirty-One

After seeing Linus off, Sam wasted no time hurrying to his own car. The Kings motel was a ten-minute ride from his house, north of Savannah, along a more rural stretch of land. He found the motel's entrance, drove in and parked between a large black truck and a green SUV.

He had quickly written down what he remembered from the receipt, his notes lying in the passenger seat beside him, the light from his phone hitting it. $51.77 for dinner for two and the tip of $9.61 made the total $61.38. He had never gone to a restaurant in his life where either the tip or the total wasn't a nice round number. This had to be on purpose.

The Kings had only one floor with fifty rooms, numbered from one to fifty. Looking down at the receipt, Peyton would have had control over two numbers: the tip and the total. Sixty-one was too high; it had to be room thirty-eight.

"Or it will be some random person who'll have no idea why I'm here," he mumbled to himself as he sat in the car while staring at the door to room thirty-eight.

He stepped out of the car, glancing around the lot. No one. Just a bunch of empty cars and quiet rooms with their curtains drawn.

He approached number thirty-eight and knocked on the door. Inside the room, there was sharp movement, as if someone had bolted from their bed. Footsteps grew louder and more deliberate as they approached the door. Sam backed away, allowing whoever was on the other side a clear view through the peephole of his smiling and non-threatening face.

"What do you want?" a male voice yelled from the other side of the door.

Sam glanced at the receipt and back at the door. He hadn't expected to hear a man's voice.

"Um, sorry to bother you," he said. "I was looking for someone. She left me a note saying she was here, but I must have misread it."

On the other side of the door, there was more movement, and the man's voice continued, although less loudly. He wasn't speaking to Sam, but to someone else in the room. Sam's pulse quickened. He shifted his weight from one foot to the other.

"Show me," the man said.

"Show you what?"

"The note."

Sam held his piece of paper in the air and moved it closer to the peephole. The man spoke again, but his voice was muffled as if he had turned around to speak to the other person in the room.

"What's your name?"

"Sam Norris."

The next response came from a woman. His heart skipped a beat, and a surge of adrenaline shot through him. He moved closer to the door, trying to catch any of the woman's words. The deadbolt lock clicked, the knob turned, and the door opened a few inches.

"Hi Kristie," Sam said. "Can we talk?"

Kristie Breckinridge held the door open. Behind her, a man stood near the bed. He looked to be in his sixties, his rugged face matching his voice. He was dressed in a dark green t-shirt tucked into a faded pair of blue jeans. He held a baseball bat in one hand and his phone in the other.

"Hurry inside," she said.

Sam moved past her as she peered into the parking lot for a few seconds longer. Then she shut the door, locked it and turned the deadbolt. The man near the bed stood with the bat on his shoulder as if he were on deck, ready to get his turn at bat.

"What are you doing here?" Sam asked.

"Were you followed?" Kristie asked.

"Followed? By who?"

"The police," the man said. "They think she's a murderer."

"No, they don't. They have someone else in custody." He turned to Kristie. "Although they do want to talk to you."

"It's only a matter of time before they realize Carey didn't do it," Kristie said, her chin trembling as she spoke. "We both know he's not capable of doing that to someone else. Once they do, they'll come after me."

Sam looked past her at the thick orange curtains hanging in the motel room's large window.

"Okay, yeah. I agree with you that he didn't do it," Sam said. "But that means someone else did."

"And it moves my name up your list at least one notch, doesn't it?"

"Logically, it has to."

Kristie's eyes dimmed, and she swallowed hard. Behind Sam, the sudden movement from the man was surprisingly swift, his grip tightening around the bat as he took a deliberate step forward. Sam's body tensed and he backed away, stumbling over the missing suitcase from her apartment.

"Dad. Stop." Kristie reached out, her fingers outstretched toward the man, halting him midstride.

"Dad?" Sam asked.

He stared at the man and closed his eyes, allowing his thoughts to go back to the descriptions he had heard from both Madison and Carey regarding the stranger at the back of the room.

"You were at the will reading," he said as he opened his eyes.

"What of it?" The man asked.

"You're her father, but you came to the will reading. Did you know Emmitt?"

"It's none of your business why I was there."

"Were you expecting money?"

The man stepped closer to Sam, his movements quicker than Sam had expected for his age. He dropped the bat from his shoulder to his side, ready to swing.

Sam backed away, his heel catching the edge of the suitcase, and this time he did more than stumble. He tried to plant his foot, but it rolled, and pain shot through his ankle. He went down hard, his shoulders hitting the ground first, his breath knocked out of him.

Kristie lunged between them. "Dad, I told you to stop."

She grabbed the bat with both hands and ripped it from his grip, then turned and tossed it onto the bed, offering a hand to Sam. He took it. She helped him to his feet. As he put weight on his left ankle, he cringed and leaned against the wall.

"His name is Wesley Pitts," she said.

Sam stood straight, the pain in his ankle pushing through, but it didn't matter. Wesley Pitts was a name he knew. He had seen it on a document in Emmitt's safe.

"He's my father and an ex-business partner of Emmitt's," Kristie said.

Sam turned to Kristie. "Your father? I thought Emmitt found you at a restaurant."

"He did because Dad told him where I worked."

"Can you blame me? I didn't want my daughter working at one of those places."

Sam remembered the rest of the note, including why Wesley had signed it. He wondered what Wesley would say.

"Why were you at the will reading?" Sam asked.

"I thought there was a chance he would leave me something."

"You stole from him," Sam said. "Why would he leave another penny to you in his will?"

"I thought he might take some pity on me. I'm older, down on my luck. I thought maybe he would want to help me out."

"I figured it was why he left me what he left me," Kristie said. "It was his way of helping Dad out without having to have his name said in front of the family."

"Why did you steal from Emmitt?" Sam asked.

"To help my mom, his ex-wife at the time, out of a jam with her new husband. When Emmitt found out, he was furious. He ended the relationship with Dad and kicked him out of Savannah."

"Why didn't you just ask him for the money?" Sam asked.

"It was no one's business why I needed it."

"He would have given it to you, especially if you were using it to help someone."

"One stubborn old man asking another stubborn old man for money to give to an ex?" Kristie said. "I'm not sure Emmitt would have been okay with it."

Wesley muttered something under his breath and looked away.

"If you're looking for someone to blame," she said. "Blame Maryanne. I think she's responsible for all that happened."

"Why do you say that?"

"Peyton didn't marry her because he loved her. He didn't even like her. She forced him to."

"How?" Sam asked.

"Maryanne blackmailed him. He only married her because she knew about his—"

She paused, her eyes shifting from Sam to her father.

"His what?" Sam asked.

"I hate talking about him like this. I don't think many knew what he was really going through. I tried to help him, but I couldn't."

"What was it?"

She took a seat on the bed, a sad smile on her face. "It's funny," she said. "All he wanted was a normal life. You know, owning his own successful business, the white picket fence, a couple of kids and a dog." She glanced from one man to the other as if she could see Peyton in his backyard, tossing the baseball around with a son while his wife, in her mind probably her, and his daughter lounged on the patio.

"What happened to that dream?" Sam asked. "What kept it from becoming a reality? From what I heard, he was successful and on his way."

Kristie shook her head. "He had a really bad gambling problem. I'm not talking about weekend poker with the boys or downloading the betting app to lose twenty dollars here and there. He had the kind of problem where he'd make a bet, swear it was the last one, then show up the next day with cash in hand to try to win back what he had lost the previous day."

Sam stayed quiet as she talked.

"He'd have a good week, and you could see it all over his face. He'd tip heavily, buy rounds for everyone, and assume the winnings would continue. Then he'd have a bad night, and he was a completely different person. Not violent, not even mean. It was more like depressed, as if he knew what he was doing was wrong, but he also knew he couldn't stop."

"What did he bet on?"

"Everything he could," she said. "We were out one night, and he told me the whole story. He talked about how everyone thinks it was an injury that ended his career, but it wasn't. His coach found him placing bets on his own team to lose."

"To lose?" Sam asked. "That's bad."

"Yeah, it is. Then, out of nowhere, he announced his shoulder was damaged beyond repair. It wasn't really hurt, but his coach gave him an easy way out. He couldn't tell Emmitt the truth. He started his agency, and it was doing well. He had even stopped gambling and worked hard to make his business thrive, but after a string of failures, he needed money. He had slowly watched as Brock and Dexter took every handout Emmitt offered and had heard Emmitt talk about how disappointed in them he was. In Emmitt's eyes, Peyton was different. He was the successful one. Emmitt was so proud of him, talking him up to everyone, telling people he would be his successor. Peyton was terrified that Emmitt would find out the truth and take everything away."

She walked over to the window, pulled the curtain a few inches aside and looked out. "Then, one night earlier this year, on one of his quick weekend trips to Vegas, he met Maryanne Preston. She knew everything he was going through, and she threatened to tell Emmitt unless he introduced her as his fiancée and quickly married her."

"And that's why no one knew," Sam said.

"Emmitt would have disowned him and probably given everything to Carey. Peyton offered to pay her to keep her quiet instead of marrying her, and she said the only way she would keep her mouth shut was marriage."

"Legally guaranteeing her half of what Peyton received in the will," Wesley said.

"And all of it if Peyton died," Sam said.

"I think she forced him to marry her and killed him for Emmitt's money," Kristie said with determination, as if she had been waiting to finally say those words out loud. "I think she found out who he was one night in Vegas, then took some time to learn more about him, and concocted the whole thing."

Sam had considered the possibility that Maryanne killed Peyton for the money, but he'd assumed they were a happy couple. This information certainly changed that angle. If it were true, it would explain a lot. But it still left Maryanne's death a mystery. He thought back to the note Beaumont showed him.

If you don't leave him alone, I will kill you.

The only way these words made sense was if someone knew about Maryanne and sent her this note to scare her away. As of now, that left only Kristie knowing their true history. Not only that, but if Peyton had gambling problems, where did the money come from that Cassandra had talked about? Evelyn had introduced herself to Peyton in Vegas as Maryanne, which meant she had already paid for the new identity. Where had those $27,000 come from?

"You really loved him, didn't you?" Sam finally asked.

"He was never a fling to me, but I would always be second place while she was around."

"Were you angry when you found out he married her?" Sam asked.

"Goddamn right I was."

"Angry enough to kill?"

Wesley reached for the bat and stood from where he was sitting. "Now you listen here—"

"Dad, it's fine." She wiped away a tear and allowed herself a second to calm down. "I didn't kill her."

Sam said nothing, watching Kristie as if she were waiting for him to deny it, to tell her he believed that she was innocent. He moved past her and the first bed, stopping near the front of the second bed.

"I can tell you don't believe me," Kristie said, turning to face him.

"It's the police you have to convince."

Silence held the room for a few seconds until Kristie let out a whimper. She took a seat on the bed and put her head in her hands.

"They have to find me first," she said.

Wesley pointed the barrel of the bat at Sam. "And you're not going to tell them anything."

Sam didn't move. "Kristie, if you didn't do it, talk to them. Tell them what you've told me. Tell them what you know."

"It's not happening," Wesley said. "I'm not losing my little girl."

Sam opened the door and stepped outside. Before closing it, he looked back. "Think about what I'm saying, okay? The police need to know everything to find out who did it. You may absolutely be a suspect, but if you didn't do it, you have nothing to worry about."

"I bet Carey felt the same way," she said.

Chapter Thirty-Two

Sam walked up the stairs of his porch, each step heavier than the last. The darkness and rain didn't help. He lived in a warm climate, but these late November, early December evenings had a chill in them that he didn't like. He had interacted with people at the plants who experienced snowstorms so bad that the plant would have to close because people couldn't get to work. Even on nights like this, he still had no interest in living in the snow.

"Blackmail is a damn good motive, and it's probably one of the oldest in the book," he muttered to himself, his voice drained of its usual energy. "Find the person being blackmailed, and you find the murderer."

Near the top of the stairs, he stopped and leaned against the railing. He turned his head to one side, one of his ears toward the living room window. The television was loud, louder than he would ever have it.

Another couple of steps, and the sound from the television was clearer. He recognized the man talking. It was *Outside the Lens*, a show he had hated for a while but had begun to pay more attention to. He wondered what episode it was, but he also knew his body demanded rest. The last thing he wanted was to walk into the house after a day like this and see his parents' faces on TV.

"The curtains are closed," he whispered.

A shiver ran over him. In all the time he had lived there, he'd rarely bothered with the curtains, even after dark, when privacy could be a concern. His house was near the beach. It had been built higher off the ground, allowing floodwater to flow underneath. He was also the last house on a dead-end road. His part of the road was rarely traveled, and anyone from the street looking through his window would only see the living room's ceiling.

But now, the sight of closed curtains increased the sense of dread already running through his body. He slid the key into the lock and turned it, easing the front door open with as little noise as possible.

"Kill anyone who messes with my shit..." had been Brock's words, and at the moment they bounced around Sam's head like a ball in a crazy pinball machine.

He pushed the door open a few more inches without stepping inside. Beaumont was only a phone call away. He pushed the door a little more, his heart pounding. A rush of blood in his ears drowned out the sound of the distant waves of the ocean crashing against the beach.

A little harder, still not stepping inside. A light rustling behind the curtains sent another ripple of fear through him. He reached for his phone while trying unsuccessfully to convince himself it had been the breeze from opening the door.

Once the gap was wide enough, he reached inside and flipped the light switch. The place stood stark like a lighthouse against the dark ocean. He burst through the door, hoping to scare his intruder, but instead of an intruder, he found Linus Hume at his dining room table. He had his laptop on with Brock's notebook and the simulator printouts from the night Maryanne was killed spread out in front of him.

Linus looked over the top of his laptop, orange dust from a bag of Cheetos scattered in his goatee.

"What are you doing?" he asked.

Sam breathed in and out a few times before speaking. "What in the everlasting hell are you doing here? You about gave me a goddamn heart attack."

"I wanted to see if I could make anything of these abbreviations in Brock's notebook."

Sam stood in the doorway a few seconds longer, letting some of the adrenaline drain from his body. His hands had stopped shaking, but his heart was still beating like the second hand of a sped-up clock. "You couldn't text me first? Tell me you'd be here?"

"I did," he said. "You didn't answer."

Sam shut the door behind him and flipped the lock. "Next time you break into my house, can you at least leave the TV off?" He grabbed the remote and muted it. "Especially that garbage."

"I didn't break in," Linus called after Sam, who had gone into the kitchen. "You gave me a key."

Sam opened the fridge and grabbed an already open bottle of water. He took the lid off and held it under the tap, filling it to the top, then took two long drinks and filled it again. As he walked past the stove, he yanked a towel hanging on the oven door and tossed it across the room at Linus's face.

"What's that for?"

"Wipe your beard. You look like a child."

Pulling a chair from the side of the table toward Linus, Sam took a seat. He glanced at the laptop screen.

"You're in TNT?" Sam turned the laptop to face him. More entries had been added with things they had learned over the past couple of days. "And you've been busy."

Linus shrugged. "I had time. I texted that Cassandra woman from the library today to see if she wanted to have dinner."

Sam's head snapped to him. "I didn't know you were interested."

"Me either," he said. "It was a spur of the moment thing."

"What'd she say?"

"She's working tonight, but I'm going to drive down Saturday and take her out."

"Glad to hear it. Maybe in the future you can break into her house instead of mine." Sam took the mouse and clicked through some of the entries. He opened Kristie's, noticing a few details, but not many, and pulled the laptop closer. He tapped Brock's notebook. "You figure out what any of those symbols in this thing mean?"

"Most of it looks like nothing." He hesitated, then turned back a few pages. "Except this," Linus said. "This number. It sounds familiar, and I don't know why."

Sam read down the page.

Code 341-BR: Target MM1 - Email Sent - Payment Received - 4.5 BTC ($87,058.305)

Linus's finger sat on the page above the 4.5 BTC line.

"That does sound familiar," Sam said. Leaning forward, he turned back to the first page. Across the top, someone had scribbled a web URL, but not the kind of URL he was used to. It started with http, but it was a random string of letters and numbers.

http://7f4k3x2y9on1n2b4

Below it, a numbered list had been written. Sam read every line out loud, pausing between each to consider what they meant.

1. Remember to Clear Logs

2. Always use VPN

3. Check BTC Fluctuation

4. Update encryption keys.

He had seen URLs like that in the past but couldn't remember where. Linus tilted the laptop back to him and typed the URL into a web browser. He pressed Enter but received only useless search results. Whatever it was, it didn't appear to be an active website. Sam turned to the next page in the notebook. At the top was a single line.

Code 117-AV: Target ZZ9 - Email Sent - Response Pending

The rest of the page was blank. On the next few pages, the style was similar. One simple line with some code, Sam didn't understand.

Code 256-LA: Target BDS - Email Sent - No Response - Nuke 'em

He flipped back to the page where Linus had pointed out the number that seemed familiar and read down it.

Code 341-BR: Target MM1 - Email Sent - Payment Received - 4.5 BTC ($87,058.305)

Response: 10/27 - asking how much

Response: 10/28 - agreeing to 4.5

Response: 10/28 - payment made

10/28: Restored System

10/30: 85% to K. X takes 15% ($13,058.75)

Note: 1/28 – Take down system. Demand more.

Throughout the next few pages, the format was the same. At the top of page three, another similar line.

Code 256-TZ: Target KK3 - Email Sent - No Response

At the top of page four, Sam read it twice, especially the last part.

Code 482-KQ: Target HH2 - Email Sent - Payment Refused. Nuke 'em.

"Nuke 'em?" Linus asked. "That's on a few more pages after. What could that mean?"

"It can't be good," Sam said.

Page five looked a lot like page two.

Code 509-LM: Target LL4 - Email Sent - Payment Received - 2.8 BTC ($55,746.348)

Response: 11/02 - asking how much

Response: 11/03 - demanded 2.5 BTC

Response: 11/03 - refused amount. 10% deleted.

Response: 11/03 - upped demand to 2.8 BTC.

Response: 11/04 - agreed to amount

Response: 11/04 - payment made

11/05: Restored System

11/05: 85% to X. K keeps 15% ($8,361.95)

Note: 2/12 – Take down system. Demand more.

Sam flipped through a few more pages. Each page was dedicated to what seemed to be an extortion that was either paid, used, or not answered. Whatever Brock was doing, he was probably K.

He flipped back to the first page and stared at the URL. He ran his finger down his laptop screen, examining the search results from Linus's search of the URL. The few that weren't useless referred to a web browser called

Ghost. According to the results, Ghost allowed users to access the dark web.

"Dark web," Sam said. "You ever been in there?"

"No way. I don't even like talking about it. How about you?"

"Nope."

Sam leaned back in his chair. He had seen a few documentaries on the dark web but hadn't yet gotten the courage to venture into it. He flipped to the second page and read each entry again.

"Brock isn't smart enough to pull off a scam like this," he muttered.

He reread the last few lines of the page and thought back to his conversation with Brock about a partner. He flipped to page two and reread the entries.

"Four point five BTC? Bitcoin?"

Another memory popped into his head. He glanced up at the TNT app, then back at the notebook. He remembered sitting with Carly, Linus and Scott in the conference room as Carly talked about TNT for the first time. All at once, he felt a heat rush through him. He inhaled sharply and stood, grabbing his phone to dial Scott.

"You remembered something," Linus said. "I know that look."

Sam listened to each ring, hoping Scott would answer, but what he finally got was his voicemail greeting. Sam didn't leave a message. Instead, he hung up and dialed Carly.

"What's wrong?" Carly said as soon as she answered the phone.

"Why does something have to be wrong?"

"It's dark out, and I have kids. Anytime someone calls me this late, something is wrong."

"Remember when Scott told us about how we got hacked? He said we paid them in Bitcoin." He put his phone on speaker and set it on the table, then, for Linus's benefit, he pointed at the BTC in the notebook. "We paid them Bitcoin so they would restore our systems?"

"I told them it was a bad idea because now they know we'll pay. It's only a matter of time before they come back for more."

Sam glanced down at the notebook. "In January," he said as Linus pointed to the 1/28 entry. "They're going to ask us for more money in January."

"How do you know?"

"We paid them exactly four and a half Bitcoin, didn't we?"

"Scott knew how to do that, so we tasked him to take care of it. Gil said as soon as we pay and regain control of the system, tear it down and rebuild everything. Passwords. Server names. Configuration files. Anything and everything we could think of. Whatever they injected into our system, we need to get it out. He's also installing new virus protection software and requiring everyone in the company to complete quarterly security training. I think he's looking into hiring an outside company to scan everything and make recommendations."

"I think I know who did it," Sam said. "But I need you to keep this conversation between us for now. At least for a day or two. I need to figure out what it means."

"Yeah, sure," Carly said. "As long as they don't hit us again in January."

"They'll be out of business by then," Sam promised.

He said goodbye and disconnected, pulled the laptop forward and clicked the link to download Ghost. He typed the URL into the browser and pressed Enter. The page took almost thirty seconds to finally reveal itself. At its center was a single yellow folder, positioned perfectly in the middle, both vertically and horizontally. As he moved the mouse over it, the cursor changed from a pointer to an arrow, signaling that interaction with the folder was possible.

"Don't click," Linus said.

"Yeah, I know."

The dark web was full of every virus you could think of. Sam glanced at the notebook. Had Brock set a trap for anyone who stole it from him and tried to access the page online?

Instead, Sam took a snapshot of his own computer's state, an image of its current settings and files. It was like a digital time capsule that would let him revert his laptop to this exact moment if he accidentally infected it with a virus.

"What are you doing?" Linus asked.

"I think it's time we play in the same environment as Brock."

Next, he initiated a virtual machine, a piece of software that created a simulated, separate computer within his actual laptop. It was like having a computer within a computer, allowing him to play in a sandbox environment isolated from his main system. They didn't touch. If his sandbox was infected, he could delete it and start over with a fresh copy.

He checked the virtual machine's settings, making sure he had done everything correctly, then took a deep breath and jumped in. He launched Ghost inside his new digital safe zone and moved back to the web page in the virtual machine, where the solitary yellow folder waited for him. This time, without any worry, he clicked it, revealing a list of folders and subfolders, each labeled to correspond with the pages in Brock's notebook.

Sam clicked the MM1 folder. It showed a single PDF file. He right-clicked it and then downloaded it. After that, he started a virus scan on the file. His antivirus software erupted into chaotic alerts, sounds blaring and pop-up windows filling the screen. They showed multiple warnings. Despite the software begging him to delete the file, close his laptop and throw it into the ocean, he kept going, confident the protective sandbox would keep his laptop safe.

One more click and an email popped up. It was from Morello's IT department, warning of a new virus with a link at the bottom for any random user to click and install something to keep them from getting sick.

It was like a digital vaccine. Click here, and you won't get sick. Except it was the opposite. Click here, and behind the scenes, a file was downloaded that infected your computer and every other computer connected to the network.

"This is what he sent to all the employees at Morello?"

"And it only took one person, someone who had no clue of the risk they were taking, to click on it and unleash chaos on our systems."

He exited the virtual machine, destroyed the sandbox and leaned back in his chair, releasing a heavy sigh as he rubbed his temples.

"What if Brock was the one Maryanne was blackmailing?" Sam asked out loud, partly for Linus's benefit but also for his own. "Is it possible X was Maryanne, and she knew what Brock was doing, taking fifteen percent of what he took in?"

He handed Linus the notebook and pulled the printouts from the golf simulator in front of him.

"Were you looking at these before I came home?" Sam asked him.

"I was wondering if there was anything here."

"You find anything?"

"Not that I saw," Linus said. There were seven printed pages, showing two players, Player One and Player Two. "I can't tell if someone else was with her, or if she was playing two balls."

Sam looked them over. He wasn't sure either. He had gone out to play two balls by himself more than once: one which he used to finesse his way to the green while powering his way down the fairway with the other, to see what kind of score he would get with both.

"These two players are very different," Sam observed.

"Maybe she was trying different strategies."

Sam glanced from Player One to Player Two. Which one was Maryanne? Was she both? He flipped to page two. It showed the results for the next five holes, with a similar pattern beginning to show between the two players.

Player One was in the middle of the fairway, not quite as long as Player Two, who was usually twenty yards farther and up the left side.

The scores were low, lower than he would have expected from Maryanne. He smiled, thinking about what it must have been like for Peyton and Maryanne to get to play together. Sam had wondered if he would ever be able to get Dani out there to play a round with him or at least ride on the cart.

He flipped through a couple more pages, observing the same pattern of shots. Even on the par three, Player Two was usually on the green. He wondered how Carey felt when he took Madison out and the two of them were able to play together, like a date on the golf course. He would make a point of texting Dani before he went to bed to see if she wanted to play sometime.

His eyes began to drift shut as he flipped to the next page. On the thirteenth hole, something caught his eye, something he hadn't been looking for.

"That's odd," he said.

"What's odd?" Linus asked, craning his neck to see what Sam was looking at.

Sam put a hand in the air. "Be quiet, give me a second."

Linus sat back down in his chair. Sam pulled TNT up and clicked on Juliet's name, reading through what he had written. Then he closed it and loaded the notes he had put in for Maryanne. Something was starting to form in his head.

"What are you remembering?" Linus asked.

Sam's mouth went dry. He put Juliet's yearbook photo on the table and set the picture of the necklace found near Maryanne's body next to it. He stood, his pulse picked up, and he put his hands on the table, looking straight down at the photos. He turned the picture of Juliet to its side.

"This whole time."

"This whole time, what?" Linus asked.

"I can't believe it."

He looked back at the printout of the golf holes, specifically the thirteenth hole, reading the description of each shot. He stepped back from the table, his heart thudding harder.

"If you don't leave him alone, I will kill you," Sam said, repeating the words from the note found among Maryanne's belongings. He looked at Linus. "I know what it means."

"Do you plan on sharing with the rest of the room?"

Sam wiped a bead of sweat from his forehead with the back of his hand and looked down at the two pictures one last time.

"I need to find the pants I wore to golf last week, then you and I are going to take a ride."

"This late?" Linus asked.

He gazed down at his evidence, each piece making no sense by itself, but together, he had the answer. His stomach tightened. He just needed one more thing to complete the puzzle. It would be the proof he would need. He grabbed Linus's keys from the table and tossed them at him.

"You're driving."

Chapter Thirty-Three

As Sam pulled his car into the Cedar Shoals Public Library parking lot, he glanced at the passenger seat. Linus had a cup holder with two Starbucks coffee cups filled to the brim in his lap. He hadn't said much along the way, not even when Sam had pulled off the highway to get the Starbucks. He had only asked Sam once why they were heading to Cedar Shoals, but Sam had declined to answer.

"Give me your phone," Sam said as he pulled his car near the door.

"Not until you tell me why we're here."

"I'm a good friend to you, right?" Sam asked.

"Most of the time," Linus said.

"That's right, I am. Give me your phone." He looked at the door, then back at Linus. "You didn't get your dinner with her tonight, but I'm going to give you an excuse to pop in and see her."

Linus's eyes narrowed as if he wanted to keep arguing, but Sam could see the joy hidden somewhere behind the confusion. "You're a real pain in my ass sometimes," he said as he put the coffee holder on the dashboard and handed Sam his phone.

"Great," Sam said. "I'll put that in my best man speech."

Sam fished both pictures out, set them on the center console, flipped on the overhead light, and snapped a photo of each. Then he opened

Linus's messages and sent a quick text to Bruce, asking him to find some documents, telling him he needed them by tomorrow night.

"I have a theory, and I'm hoping Uncle Bruce is as good as he claims," Sam said as he handed Linus his phone. "Take her a coffee, tell her you were in the area, and ask her if she'd ever seen either of these necklaces while Maryanne was staying with her."

"You're not staying?" Linus asked as he exited the car, coffee in hand.

"I have something else I need to check into, then I'll be back to get you."

Sam pulled away, watching Linus disappear through the doors. He headed out of the parking lot and onto a main road, following his GPS. At the next stoplight, he glanced at the photos he had put in the passenger seat. Then he turned his car into a small strip plaza and parked in front of a jewelry place between a nail salon and an ice cream store. The sign above the door read Cedar Shoals Jewelers, and the glowing neon sign in the window flashed Open. He killed the engine and went inside.

The store was small, a mom-and-pop place to service the jewelry needs of a small town. The scent of glass cleaner hit him as he approached a man in his fifties behind the counter.

"Evening," the man said. "What can I do for you?"

"I have kind of an odd question," Sam said as he set the photos on the glass and pushed them toward the man. "You ever seen either of these?"

The man leaned forward, taking his time as he studied each image. "I've been here almost five years now. I've seen a lot of jewelry in my time. I'm not sure I'll be able to remember every single one."

"If you've seen either of these, you'd remember both."

The man shook his head. "Not ringing a bell. And if I sold something like that heart," he said, tapping the photo, "I'd probably recall. Hearts are common, but with this one, the way the curves at the top of them are hooked, that's different. It's unique. I'd remember."

"I'm going to visit a few other shops around here. Do you think they'd remember?"

"No doubt in my mind," the man said.

Sam forced out a thank you and stepped into the evening air. He thought about Linus, wondering if he was getting anywhere with Cassandra. It would be a lot easier if she could answer the questions instead of him having to knock on doors, but he was pretty sure he knew what she would say.

Ten minutes later, he was in the next town, following his GPS down a narrow road lined with student housing for the local college on one side and fast food on the other. The second store was in a small plaza next to a Chinese restaurant. Sam pulled close to the door, but it was dark inside.

"Closed," he mumbled.

The third shop looked older. The sign was faded. The shop stood by itself, not attached to other shops on either side. A small "OPEN" sign was set in the window.

Sam went inside. An older man stepped out from the back, wiping his hands on a rag. He wore thick glasses.

"Evening," the man said. "Need a watch battery?"

Sam held up his wrist, showing the man he didn't wear a watch. "I'm interested in necklaces," he said as he set the sketches on the counter. "Specifically, these two."

The man leaned in, his eyes squishing together. Before he spoke, Sam saw something in his expression, something he hadn't seen from the jeweler at the first store.

"Well, I'll be damned," he said.

"You know one of them?" Sam asked.

"I know both of them."

Sam's pulse jumped. "Are you sure?"

"Oh yeah, it came in a long while ago." He took the picture of the necklace with the double Js and held it in the air. "I melted this one down, and I reworked it into that heart. Bit of a pain, though. I couldn't get those Js to form the top of the heart the way I wanted."

"Any way you can describe the person who brought it in?"

The man did not answer right away. Instead, he turned and moved slowly, disappearing into the back room of the building. From behind the door, it sounded like the man was moving shoeboxes around, grunting as he lifted each box. A few minutes later, he emerged from the back carrying a white box with numbers written on the side that Sam wasn't sure if they meant a time period or a group of order numbers.

"You keep records that go that far back?"

"Of course, I do," The man said with a snort. He set the box on the counter and removed the lid. "And I don't do it on computers, either. My oldest boy tried to switch me over to one of those things twenty-five years ago. He said it would make things easier. But then your power goes out, or you leave it in the car, and someone steals it. Or worse, the whole thing dies, and your whole business is down the drain. 'No, thanks,' I told him."

Sam smiled. He's had his own love-hate relationship with computers since he started earning a living with them. They pay the bills really well, but being completely off the grid sometimes seemed like an easier life.

The man continued, "He told me to keep living in the Stone Age and see where it gets me." He tilted his head and looked at Sam over the rim of his glasses. "I'll tell you where it got me, son. It got me a forty-four year business that put food on his plate every single night."

He pulled a stack of receipts held together by a rubber band, squinted and looked at it more closely. "No, too recent," he said.

Sam said nothing; the only sounds came from the wall clock ticking behind him. He glanced up at it, wondering again how Linus was doing.

The old man pulled another stack out, set it on the counter and removed the rubber band. He licked his thumb, then worked through them one by one, muttering dates as he set each one aside.

"It was summer. Hot as hell that week. The air conditioning was broken. I remember it as if it were yesterday."

"I can't even remember what I had for dinner yesterday," Sam said.

The man flipped past a few more, then stopped and backed up one. "There you are." He pulled it free and set it on the counter.

Sam took the receipt. It was a credit card payment, and a name was written on the top line with a matching signature at the bottom.

The man tapped it once. "That's who brought it in."

Chapter Thirty-Four

Sam stood over his ball on the thirteenth tee, looking down the fairway toward the sand trap where Juliet's remains had been found. The police had already cleared it, allowing people to play the hole again, but construction was still halted, and the ropes around the trap remained up, keeping people out until they finished their work.

The air was heavy. He took a breath and looked toward an overcast sky that promised rain at some point during the evening. It would have to be later, as Sam had special plans for this round of golf. Linus had gone first, hitting his shot into the left rough, as Sam had asked him to do. It wasn't something Linus usually did, hitting the ball out to the left, but Sam and Linus already knew their round wouldn't finish tonight. Their scores wouldn't matter.

Sam took a breath and swung his club, hitting the ball down the right side of the fairway. It landed and bounced twice before coming to a stop. They hopped on their cart and pulled up to the women's tees where Madison and Libby had been waiting.

"You gonna be okay with this?" Linus asked Sam.

"I think so," he said. "But keep an eye out."

Madison hit her ball out to the left, with Libby driving hers down the middle. They descended the steps from the tee box to their carts.

"Madison," Sam said. "Ride with me to my ball. Something's been bugging me for a few days, and I think we need to talk about it."

Madison slid her club into her bag and turned to Sam. She didn't question him, as if she knew they needed to talk. Linus hopped into Libby's cart holding the club he would use for his next shot.

"What are we doing?" Libby asked.

"We're driving to my ball," Linus said.

Madison took her seat next to Sam. "Is this golf talk, or, uh, the other thing?"

"It's not golf talk."

Sam drove the cart down the right side, away from Libby and Linus, who were driving toward Madison's ball on the left side of the fairway. He allowed the cart to slow near the woods, by the path leading to the bridge. This would be it, where the conversation would take place.

"Listen," Madison said, speaking before he could start. "I know you feel guilty about what happened, and I really am sorry. Tensions were high, and we're both missing someone. It was—"

"No," Sam said, interrupting her. "It's not that."

In South Plainfield, when it was time to get serious with Dani, the words had come easily. She was in the hospital, near death and handcuffed to a bed. His thoughts were only of her, making sure she was safe, able to go home free when she was ready to leave. In that case, Dani was innocent, but this case would be different.

Madison's mouth tightened. She shifted in the cart seat, her right hand holding the handle above her head tightly.

"If it's not about what happened the other night, then what is it?"

Sam reached into his back pocket and pulled out a picture. He opened it and handed it to her. The picture was of Juliet Summerfield and her boyfriend Joseph Weller. It was a copy of the one from the newspaper article Libby had shown them a few days earlier while sitting at Jenna Calloway's restaurant.

"What about it?" she asked, trying to sound nonchalant.

But Sam had seen the color drain from her face as she glanced at the picture then forward through the cart's front windshield.

"I need you to tell me what happened between the two of you on the night she died."

When she didn't answer, Sam tapped the accelerator hard enough to jerk the cart forward. Madison snapped her head toward him, her eyes wide.

"Madison, tell me what happened."

Madison reached for the Velcro on her glove, pulled it apart, then reapplied it, tightening it like a baseball player who's trying to kill time before the next pitch.

"Why are you asking me?"

"Because I believe you were there when it happened, possibly even caused it."

She let out a laugh, sharp and quick. "You're insane," she said. "Drive to your ball so we don't sit here holding up the people behind us."

"Madison, you're one of my closest friends. I know you better than most, and I know that every time we've talked about Juliet Summerfield, you've had something on your mind. You told me about how you and your dad came and played this hole. You knew about that path. You used to live on the other side of it. I've seen how you react to any of us talking about it. You can't even face me right now. I think you know what happened."

He put his hand on her chin and turned her head to face his. Her eyes had grown red and, though they were face to face, she still couldn't look into his.

"Tell me," Sam said, keeping his voice low.

"It was an accident," she said, her voice so low, her eyes finally meeting his, tears forming.

"Then tell me about it." He looked over his shoulder at Linus, who could not hear them. "I sent them the other way, so it's the two of us out here, me and you and no one else. I suspect you need to get this off your shoulders. I'm one of your best friends—please tell me."

Madison looked past him as if she were going to get up and run, but to his surprise, she stayed put in the seat, saying nothing.

"I'm not going to tell anyone," he said.

She wiped her eyes. "There was a guy," she whispered.

"Joe," he said as he lifted the photo.

"Juliet and I had known each other for a long time, but we were never super close. She went to a different school, and we would cross paths when we played volleyball against each other. I met Joe at a game. He was sitting in the stands watching me play. Cheering for me. After the game, I went over and chatted with him, gave him my number."

"Did you two go out?"

"For a while, and it was great. He was my first kiss, my first real love, and he treated me like I was the only person in his life. I ended up falling for him harder than I ever thought I would. Then, out of nowhere, he ghosted me. He stopped returning my calls and my texts; it was as if I didn't exist to him anymore. Three weeks later, I'm at a party."

She tightened her fingers around the handle over her head.

"I'm there enjoying myself, hanging with my friends, and he walks in, and he's with Juliet. They're holding hands, standing close to each other. It should have been me, but it was her."

"What happened the night she died?"

"I wanted to talk to her, but you know, do it somewhere where no one could hear us. It's so stupid looking back. It was a guy who never became anything but a blue-collar worker. He's still not married, but he has a couple of kids. I can't believe I ever liked him."

"That night, Madison. What happened?"

"I asked her to come over to the house to chat, then I asked her to walk with me. We were walking and talking, but not getting anywhere. On the walk, she told me how she had thought he was cute and asked him to hang out, and he agreed. It would have been okay, except it was while he and I were still together. How could she do that to me? She betrayed me, Sam, and I had thought maybe we could become friends. All I really wanted from her was an apology."

"You deserved it."

"I did," Madison said. "A guy treats me shitty, fine, I can deal with that, but she and I, even though we weren't close, we were always friendly. She knew enough about me to know how into him I was. We crossed the bridge, and I probably said something I shouldn't have. As we were stepping down off the bridge, she attacked me, pushed me, and I hit the ground hard. I got up and went after her, pushing her back. She tripped over a tree root and fell. Except, she didn't get up."

"What did you do?"

"I mean, I froze. I didn't know what to do. She wasn't moving, and I could see the blood pooling under her head."

"Why didn't you call anyone?"

"I was seventeen and scared, Sam." Madison lifted her head. "Besides, who would believe me?" Her voice cracked as she spoke. "You think the police would hear, 'We argued, and she fell, then she died,' and let me walk away? I saw her eyes. I saw what I did to her."

"They might have believed—"

"No," she said. "They wouldn't have."

"What about the sand trap?"

"I couldn't leave her there. They'd find her. They'd find out she was with me, and I'd be cooked. I needed time, so I dragged her out of the woods and took her to the trap. It was dark, and the course was closed. I knew no one would see me."

"And that's why you go left on this hole, isn't it? To avoid the sand trap?"

"I cringe every time someone hits their ball into it, knowing they could be walking on her." Her voice was rough, as if the words had scraped it raw. She swallowed hard and spoke again, this time more softly. "I feel terrible about it, Sam, I really do."

Sam's phone buzzed. He glanced down at it and pressed the cart's accelerator, propelling it forward. He turned the wheel to the left, taking them back toward the middle of the fairway.

"What are we doing?"

"We're done golfing for tonight," he said.

"I'm sorry," Madison said. Her voice caught. "I'm sorry, Sam. I should have called someone."

He kept his eyes forward.

"I was seventeen," she said. "I was stupid. I made it worse." Madison grabbed his arm, her hand shaking as she squeezed. "Please don't hate me."

"I don't hate you," he said.

Sam continued driving, cutting across the thirteenth fairway, his tires skidding in the damp grass. Madison let go of his arm and leaned forward, putting her hand on the dash but quickly pulling it back. Up ahead, the pavilion roof came into view. As he drove closer, the gathering of people milling about inside the pavilion became visible. The group included the three remaining Layne brothers, with Carey sitting at a picnic table, his hands cuffed in front of him.

"Carey," Madison yelled. She sat up in the seat, but then quickly turned to Sam. She pointed at Beaumont and a few other police officers standing outside the pavilion. "You're turning me in? You can't prove I did anything. I'll deny this conversation happened."

"Calm yourself," Sam said. "I have no plans of ruining your life over an accident that happened when you were seventeen. We have other business we need to handle."

Her body relaxed as she turned back to Carey, who had already noticed them.

"Maddy!" he yelled back.

"What do I do?" she asked Sam.

"Go sit next to Carey and say nothing unless I speak to you."

Chapter Thirty-Five

Beaumont stood near a picnic table with Carey sitting in front of him, his handcuffed hands resting on the table. Linus stood in the back near the pavilion's posts. Libby had driven next to him but stayed in the cart, and Scott was now in the seat next to her. Linus had done what Sam asked, telling Beaumont to bring Carey while alerting Scott that he should also be there.

He pulled the cart to a stop, and Madison jumped out. For a split second, it looked as if she would run, but she seemed to think better of it and went to Carey's side, her golf spikes tapping the cement as she hurried to him.

"Maddy," Carey said as he tried to stand.

She threw herself on the bench next to him. After a quick kiss, she closed her hands around his cuffed ones. "Are you okay?"

"Happy to be out of that jail, even if it's for a brief field trip to my golf course." Carey looked around the room. "Do you know what's going on?"

Madison glanced at Sam. "I don't, Sam brought me over here but wouldn't tell me why."

Allen Bryce Foster came to stand next to Carey. Brock had chosen a picnic table on one end of the pavilion while Dexter sat at the other, as far from his brother as he could get.

Sam tapped the small notebook he had been carrying in his pocket all afternoon.

Several officers had positioned themselves on all sides of the pavilion, including Jacobs, who kept most of his attention on Carey. Others stood near Brock and Dexter.

Behind Sam, one of Savannah Palms' grounds-crew members had climbed on a tractor and started mowing the seventeenth fairway while another had a blower to clear the leaves off the sixteenth green.

Beaumont met Sam at the edge of the pavilion. Before Sam could step onto the cement floor, Beaumont stopped him by a rusty charcoal grill used to cook burgers and hot dogs during league outings.

"We're still waiting on two more," he said to Sam. "They didn't want to come voluntarily, so we had to use force. They should be here within minutes."

Sam nodded; he had noted Kristie's and Wesley's absence.

"For the record, I don't like this." Beaumont regarded the group. "This isn't how we normally conduct an arrest."

"He likes the drama," Linus said as he joined the pair. He asked Sam, "Should I get the laptop set up?"

"Yep." Sam addressed Beaumont. "I know you don't like this, but I can't sleep, and I'm tired of seeing Carey sitting in a jail cell for something he didn't do."

"You better hope for your sake you're right, or you're going to make plenty of enemies today, and I'm going to be at the top of that list."

"I'm certainly going to make enemies today," Sam said.

Linus had moved to the center of the pavilion, everyone staring his way as he pulled his laptop from his bag and connected it to the projector. The only light came from the two lamps, one on each side of the pavilion, as the sun traveled on its way below the horizon for the evening.

At one end of the pavilion, a chair scraped against the cement. Heads turned toward Brock as he stood and tapped the table. "Excuse me, but what are we doing here?" He pointed at Linus. "And what the fuck is he doing?"

"I told you to stop talking and sit down," Beaumont said.

"This is bullshit, man. Unless you have a legal reason to keep me here, I'm leaving."

Beaumont turned to Sam. "Do we have a legal reason?"

"We sure do."

Beaumont pointed at Officer Jacobs. "Take Mr. Layne into custody. Person of interest in a double homicide investigation."

"I knew it," Dexter said from across the pavilion.

Allen shot to his feet, his legal pad held high in the air. "On what basis? Person of interest isn't—"

"Sit down, Counselor," Beaumont said. "You'll get your turn to speak."

"I didn't do shit," Brock said as he pushed his chair back and took a step.

Jacobs put one hand on Brock's shoulder, a strong hand, and held him in place. With his other hand, he pulled one of Brock's arms behind his back, hard enough to stop Brock from struggling.

"Give me the other hand," Jacobs said. "Or I'll get the Taser out." Brock swung his other arm behind his back, allowing Jacobs to snap handcuffs on him. "Now you'll sit down, and you'll shut up unless you are spoken to," Jacobs said as he forced Brock back into the small metal chair.

"You son of a bitch." Dexter stood and took a few steps toward Brock. "You killed them both. I knew it was—"

"Him, too," Sam said.

A couple of officers near Dexter didn't wait for Beaumont to agree. They grabbed him, put handcuffs on him and sat him back next to Emily, who said nothing. She only stared at her husband, her mouth open.

"Doesn't matter to me," Dexter said. "I didn't kill anyone. I'll be taking legal action against all of you. Allen, take notes on what you're seeing."

Allen pulled his phone from his bag, set it on a stand, opened the video recorder, and pressed the record button.

"You okay with that?" Beaumont asked Sam.

"Only if you are."

Beaumont didn't blink. "Go ahead and roll it, Counselor. This will fend off anyone who claims we did anything wrong. It also gives us a nice, clean transcript of who said what that we can use during the trial."

"Trials," Sam said, correcting him.

Beaumont frowned at Sam.

Throughout this exchange, Sam kept an eye on Carey, curious about his reaction to his brothers being put in handcuffs. Carey always had a good poker face, but at that moment, he stared at Brock as if he were ready to attack his older brother. Madison sat next to him, her hand on his, possibly the only thing keeping Carey from following through with whatever was going through his head.

Beaumont's radio crackled. He tilted his ear to his shoulder and listened for a few seconds.

"That should be the rest of our little party," he said.

Linus finished his setup, opened TNT and showed it on the screen. As he did, the hum of two golf carts could be heard coming over the hill. The first held Kristie Breckinridge and a male officer Sam didn't recognize. The second cart held Wesley Pitts next to another officer. Both carts came to rest near the pavilion. As Wesley stood, Sam noticed he was wearing handcuffs. He also had a black eye, and his jaw was swollen.

"What happened to him?" Beaumont asked.

"He got a little rowdy when we tried to pick him up," one of the officers said. "I told him he was under arrest for harboring a suspect."

Allen stood and spun his phone around, being sure to record everything he could.

"You hit him?" Beaumont asked the officer, loudly enough for the camera to pick up.

"No, sir. He refused to come along, so we had to use force. It was during this point where his face hit the ground a little too hard."

"Who's the old guy?" Brock yelled from across the pavilion.

Carey looked at Sam. "I think that's the guy from the will reading."

"We'll get to that soon enough," Sam said.

He stepped into the light of the projector, looking like a singer on stage, the lights in his eyes. The moths that had been flying around the lamps had migrated to the bigger light source. Linus swatted a few of them away.

"Tonight, we're going to wrap up a few things, but we're not going to start with murder. We're going to start with money," Sam told the group, which fell silent immediately to hear what he had to say.

Linus flipped away from TNT to the first page of his presentation. It showed cartoon dollar bills falling from the sky.

"Throughout the last couple of weeks, I've talked to all of you one-on-one, asked you what you saw at the will reading. One of the questions I asked was who left the room that night. Not a single person said Carey left the room at any point. Everyone else who is here now left that room at least once, which means any one of you, except Carey, could have put something in Peyton's food."

Carey shifted in his chair, the cuffs rattling as he lifted his hands. His eyes moved from face to face around the pavilion, then landed hard on Sam.

"He had nothing to do with Peyton's death," Sam told Beaumont. "The fact that any of you could even think Carey murdered his brother while knowing he never left the room still blows my mind."

Beaumont's eyes narrowed. "We caught him standing—"

"I know how you caught him. I was there. But I don't care. As I've told you over and over, he had nothing to do with it."

"Get to the point, Norris," Beaumont said. "Or I'm shutting this down."

Sam turned to the crowd. "The funny thing, I didn't really care what happened in the last moments of Peyton's life. I wasn't going to solve a murder by trying to reconstruct the will reading. You were all there. You all left the room at least once, and any of you could have done it. The question I had was *why*."

As Sam finished his sentence, Linus went to the next page in his presentation. It was a giant question mark. He looked up and blinked at the screen, wondering if Linus had opened the wrong presentation.

"I figured you'd go here next," Linus said. "Based on the last time we did this."

"Nice touch," Sam said, smiling at his friend. He addressed the group again. "What I really wanted to know was why someone would do this." Sam turned to Allen. "And, of course, the answer for almost all of you is money."

"Why did you look at me when you said that?" Allen asked.

"Oh, please. You were bleeding that family dry. Peyton was going to cut you off. Carey was going to cut you off. It didn't matter who received the bulk of the inheritance, you were out on the street the next day. Lucky for you, Peyton died, and this threw the whole plan into a tizzy. You walked through the kitchen as you left. You could have easily put something in his food to cause the allergic reaction."

Allen turned the camera to face Sam. "Be careful what you say, son. You could find yourself on the other side of a libel charge."

"Calm down, Counselor," Sam said, addressing him the same way Beaumont had. "I already know you didn't kill Peyton." He turned to face Kristie. "But then there's you."

Kristie lifted her chin as if Sam had walked over and slapped her across the face. Her eyes flicked to Wesley, then back to Sam.

"Me?" she asked.

"You were angry at Peyton."

Kristie blinked. "Why would I—?"

Emily didn't wait for Sam to respond. "Oh, please," she said as she crossed her arms. "You were sleeping with him."

"What? No. That isn't—"

"You don't have to deny it, sweetie," Emily said. "The way you two looked at each other, it was obvious."

"No wonder the old man kept you around," Brock said. "Were you screwing him too?"

Wesley spoke up. "You shut your mouth or—"

"Did you make him pay for drinks, or did he pay you in other ways?"

Wesley rose to his feet, his handcuffs clinking. "Say another word," he growled.

Emily spoke again, more softly. "We did see you two arguing at the will reading while Maryanne was in the bathroom."

"I didn't do it," Kristie said, tears forming in her eyes. "I loved him."

"And when you found out he was married, you were pissed," Sam said.

"Now, you hold on," Wesley said. "I can tell you for a fact she didn't do it."

"Why?" Sam asked. "Because it was you who did it?" Wesley's mouth snapped shut, and the color drained from his face. "You stole money from the course."

"You stole from us?" Brock asked.

"He did," Sam said. "It was a few months after Emmitt bought the course. And Emmitt told you if he ever saw you again, he'd press charges."

"Okay, great," Wesley said. "Sounds like a motive to kill Emmitt. Last time I checked, I couldn't poison someone by giving them cancer."

"No," Sam said, shaking his head slowly. "That's a motive to kill Peyton. I saw your agreement in the safe. I also saw your signature on it. Once

Peyton took over, he would have access to that safe and that same piece of paper. What if he, or more likely Maryanne, wanted that money back? That's why you were at the will reading. You wanted to know who you needed to be afraid of next."

Sam held three fingers in the air, ticking off each finger as he spoke. "You had the motive. You had the means. You had the opportunity."

"What opportunity?"

"Simple," Sam said as he looked at Kristie. "Your daughter ran the bar and restaurant."

Carey twisted on the bench, his eyes moving from Wesley to Kristie while a ripple moved through the rest of the group.

"Daughter?" Carey asked.

Brock laughed out loud, breaking the silence, as Dexter's mouth fell open.

"Yeah," Sam said. "Kristie's father used to be partners with Emmitt in this golf course, but he stole money, got caught and was asked to leave. No charges to be pressed. Instead, a lifelong threat that maybe, at some point, it could happen."

"I didn't kill anyone," Wesley said.

"No, you didn't," Sam said. He looked at Kristie. "Neither of you killed Peyton."

Behind him, Brock stirred in his chair. "Hey, come on. What the fuck are we doing here? Why are you wasting our time with this grand performance? Are you going to go one by one, ruling us all out until you point at someone and make your accusation? If so, hurry up. It's getting tiresome."

Sam turned and walked along the pavilion, crossing through the glare of the projector and stopping at the table across from Brock. He reached into his pocket and pulled out the small black notebook, slapping it on the table.

Brock's eyes snapped to the notebook. His face reddened as he looked past Sam. "Arrest him," he yelled to Beaumont. "He broke into my house and stole my property."

"I didn't break into anything," Sam said. "Charlotte let me in, and she gave me the code to the safe."

"That's a bullshit loophole," Brock said.

Sam lifted the notebook between two fingers and angled it toward Brock as if he were going to give it back. Brock leaned forward, but with his hands behind his back, he couldn't take it. Sam shifted his stance and set it into Beaumont's open palm instead.

"You can't use anything you took from the safe against me in court. That's an Illegal search and seizure. I know my rights. You need a warrant," Brock spat.

Beaumont looked at Allen, then down at his phone, making sure the camera caught his face. "You just claimed this notebook out loud in front of a room full of witnesses. And it's on video. Thanks for that, Counselor." He took the phone from the table and handed it to one of the officers. "Keep recording and send me the video before you give him that phone back."

"Yes, sir," the officer said.

Beaumont turned back to Brock. "We'll argue about warrants in court. Right now, I'll be keeping this as evidence instead of giving it back to you so you can destroy it."

"This is bullshit," Brock said.

"What's so important about that notebook?" Emily asked Dexter. He said nothing.

"Great question," Sam said. He made a motion toward Linus, who flipped to the next page of his presentation. On the screen were the contents of the second page of the notebook.

"What does it mean?" Beaumont asked.

"Would you like to tell us?" Sam asked Dexter, but Dexter kept quiet. Sam spun around to Brock. "How about you?"

Brock glanced at Allen, then back at the screen. "Figure it out for yourself."

"I guess it's a good thing I already did," Sam said with a smirk. "Hey, Scott, you want to contribute?"

Scott flinched as if Sam had touched him with a hot poker. He stood, his knee clipping the cart. The bottle of soda he had been drinking from slipped from his hand and hit the cement, coming to rest under Allen's feet. "Me? What can I do?"

"That final week we were all in South Plainfield, you had to come in on a Sunday and work. Tell the room why."

"Uh, someone in the company clicked a link they shouldn't have, and we were hacked."

Brock's cuffed hands bumped against the table as he shifted in the chair.

Scott continued, "All of our files were locked. I was asked to take care of it."

Sam pointed at the projector screen. "First line, it says MM1," He looked down at Brock. "Morello Manufacturing. Did the hackers demand money?"

"They did," Scott said.

"And did we pay?"

"Four and a half bitcoin." He looked at the screen, recognition on his face. He pointed to it. "Down to the penny, it's that exact amount that's up there on the screen."

"You were scamming people?" Emily asked Brock.

"He wasn't the only one." Sam had come to a stop before Dexter. "Brock was taking eighty-five percent, but that X up there, that's you. It's funny, for a long time, I didn't think you knew how to even use a computer. I thought you were, if you'll pardon me for saying it, a bit of an idiot. But over time, I'm finding out these little tidbits here and there, and then you go and mention the Perlin algorithm to me. No one who only dabbles knows what that is. You're a serious coder, and you wrote the code. You gave it to Brock, and he managed the business while you sat in your basement doing who knows what."

"Talk about your passive income," Scott mumbled from the back of the pavilion.

"Good luck proving it," Dexter said, glaring at Brock.

"Doesn't mean I killed Peyton!" Brock protested.

"Peyton knew about it, though, didn't he?" Sam asked. He had no proof of this, but he threw it out as a bluff anyway.

"He didn't know what Dexter and I were doing. We had no reason to kill him. Neither of us."

Heads turned to Dexter as soon as Brock mentioned his name. Sam smiled at him.

"Leave my name out of your mouth, Brock," Dexter yelled. He added to Sam, "I wasn't involved with him and had nothing to do with it. I don't care what Brock wrote in his notebook; I had nothing to do with Peyton's murder."

"I know," Sam said.

"You know?" Dexter asked.

"Of course, I do, because I know who did do it."

"Jesus Christ," Carey mumbled. "You really are drawing this out."

Sam made another quick signal to Linus, who flipped his presentation to a picture of the different tree nuts that Peyton would have been allergic to. "Y'all thought he died from one of these."

"He did," Emily said. "We saw him choke, then Maryanne hit him with the EpiPen, but it didn't help, and he died."

"You saw her inject him with an EpiPen, but that EpiPen had been tampered with. It didn't contain the epinephrine that would have saved his life."

The air in the pavilion seemed to have been sucked out at Sam's words.

"What was in it?" Emily asked.

One of the officers pulled the jug of rat poison from a golf cart and set it on an empty picnic table.

"That," Sam said.

Carey lifted his wrists off the table while Madison's grip moved up to his forearm. She gazed at the jug. Brock and Dexter glanced at each other while Kristie put her hands on her dad's shoulders. Beaumont stood near the edge of the cement, his eyes locked on Sam.

"Okay, so which one of them killed Mr. Layne?" Beaumont finally asked, a tinge of annoyance in his words.

"None of them," Sam said.

Chapter Thirty-Six

"It *was* Maryanne who killed him," Kristie said. "I knew it."

All eyes were focused on Sam, who now stood on the edge of the pavilion.

"Maryanne Preston-Layne was not who you think she was," he finally said.

A low murmur traveled over the pavilion. The wood of the picnic tables creaked as people shifted and leaned forward. Handcuffs rattled from each side. Carey glanced at Madison, who looked as shocked as everyone, and even Allen seemed surprised, which shouldn't have surprised Sam, but it did. It was only Kristie who stayed neutral, as if she had been waiting for this information to come out.

"Who was she?" Emily asked.

"Her real name was Evelyn Delaney. She was the half-sister of Juliet Summerfield." Sam pointed to his right without looking back. "And Juliet Summerfield was the young woman whose remains were dug up from that sand trap a week ago."

Sam paused, allowing everyone to catch their breath and calm down.

"Evelyn Delaney, or Eve as she was known by her acquaintances, grew up in a rough home. Her mother died young, and her alcoholic father remarried quickly, which angered Evelyn. She left home after high school but visited her father sometimes, and when Juliet was born, Eve didn't exactly take to her younger sister."

"Why?" Emily asked.

"From what I was able to work out. Juliet was the golden child. It was as if once Eve's mother was gone, her father stopped caring for her. It was all about his new baby, Juliet, with his new wife. When Juliet disappeared at seventeen, Eve was visiting, but she soon left."

"Are you saying Maryanne killed her younger sister and buried her body?" Carey asked.

Sam's eyes flashed to Madison, then back to Carey. "I'm saying I had considered it as a possibility, yes."

More stirring from the crowd.

"Then Eve went to Vegas, got herself involved in some of the underground poker that was going on. She went to jail, then got out. Then she bumped into a man she later learned was Peyton Layne."

"Peyton never went to Vegas," Allen said.

"He did, Allen," Kristie said sadly. "He went there a lot."

Sam continued, "You all thought Peyton was the smart businessman, the perfect son that everyone here had been misled to think he was, but like the rest of you, he had issues. Unfortunately for him, it was gambling. He did a lot, and when Evelyn Delaney bumped into him, she already learned who he was. She had done her research, and when she found out he was the oldest son in a rich family whose father had cancer, she pounced."

"How awful," Libby mumbled from her golf cart.

"It gets worse. Over time, she threw out little hints to both Peyton and Emmitt, eventually convincing Emmitt to change his will, giving Peyton everything. She was smart and knew how to be subtle with Emmitt, knew exactly what she had to say to get him to turn against his sons. It was a skill that served her well during her previous criminal endeavors. Once the new will was finished, she told Peyton, 'Marry me, or I'll tell everyone what I know about you.'"

"I knew there was something about her I didn't like," Emily said.

"If he had told her to go pound sand," Sam said, "she would have exposed him, and Emmitt would have cut him out of the will. Carey would have most likely gotten the golf course, and Brock and Dexter would have been looked on a little more favorably by Emmitt, especially if he'd heard what Peyton really was."

"And she's the one who poisoned him, right?" Kristie asked. "You have to have proof now, or you wouldn't have dragged us out here."

"I have plenty of proof for everything I'm saying tonight, and if Maryanne did kill Peyton, that begs the question, who killed her and why?"

For most of you, money would be the reason for murder, but for some, it would be revenge. But there is one person sitting here in this little pavilion on a quiet Tuesday night for whom both money and revenge were the incentives for a horrible murder."

Sam let the silence sit for a few seconds. This time, no one dared look around, it seemed, perhaps for fear of what they might see.

Sam moved toward Carey, but walked past him, stopping in front of Madison.

"And that person was you," he said.

Chapter Thirty-Seven

The words tasted sour in his mouth. He hadn't wanted to say them, not against his friend—but after everything he had learned, he had cause to wonder if she really was his friend. He curled his fingers and held them by his side to keep them from shaking.

"You met her in that golf simulator room, played sixteen holes with her, then you beat her to death with a golf club."

For a split second, the entire golf course had gone quiet. The mowing had stopped. The leaf blower had been turned off. No one in the pavilion said a word. It was Carey who broke the silence as he jerked against his cuffs, the metal scraping the tabletop. He pushed his chair back and lunged to his feet, tipping the chair over. A police officer held him in place.

"What are you talking about?" Carey asked.

Sam ignored him. He only looked at Madison. It didn't matter what anyone else was doing right now. He didn't care about the surprise that was most likely on Libby's face. The two women had been riding together for years, yet Libby had never suspected what Madison was capable of.

The previous night on the car ride home, Sam had told Linus. He also hadn't believed it, and even when Sam began showing the proof, it still took some convincing.

Sam didn't even look at Carey. He knew he was delivering a hurt that he wished he could spare his best friend of so many years. But it had to be done.

"Madison," Sam said.

For a second, she didn't blink. Her mouth opened as if she had been punched in the gut by her friend; she stared at Sam as if he were speaking a language she didn't understand.

"No," she finally said. "It wasn't me."

Sam didn't move. He stood there, his eyes glued to her.

Madison's jaw tightened. "You're wrong."

"Gimme thirteen," Sam told Linus.

Linus shifted his presentation to show the thirteenth hole from the printout on the night Maryanne was killed.

"Player One and Player Two," Sam said. "Maryanne is Player One. You're Player Two. Look at that ball flight from the tee. Way out to the left, like you did tonight. Like you do every single night when I play with you. Even on the simulator, you kept your strategy intact."

"Lots of people go left," Carey said. "That proves nothing."

His lips pursed, Sam looked sad for his friend. His name would be cleared, but he would lose something big in the process. He had already lost so much the last few weeks.

"When Madison York was young, she knew Juliet Summerfield," Sam began. All ears were cocked toward him now as his audience sat, tired but fascinated by the twist. He addressed Madison. "You were friends, right? Not great friends, but you knew each other because you played volleyball on opposing high school teams. Am I right? That's what you told me as we drove over here."

Madison's eyes were suddenly cold as she stared, realizing he had tricked her. He had never intended to keep her secret.

"You and her, in love with the same guy, but in the end, Joe picked Juliet. Not you."

Without needing a signal, Linus flipped the show to the next slide, showing a close-up of the necklace around Juliet's neck in the picture from the convenience store.

"There it is, right there," Sam said, turning and pointing. "J and J, Juliet and Joe. He chose her, and you got angry."

"He has it wrong," she said to Carey, then to Beaumont. "I was there. I was the person she was going to see that night, but he's twisting it. He's making it sound like I'm a monster, but it was an accident, I swear. That's all it was."

"Go ahead, then," Sam said. "Tell them what happened."

The tears were still in her eyes, but the look behind them was different. He wondered if it was the same look Juliet had seen that night.

"It was an accident," she said. "I was seventeen. I didn't wake up that day and decide to hurt someone. We got into a fight, and she fell. She hit her head and didn't wake up. I didn't know what to do. I swear." She pleaded with Carey. "I didn't want to fight. I wanted to talk, that's all. But things got heated, and she pushed me. I...I was upset. I shoved her back." Madison's voice cracked. "She hit her head."

The pavilion fell quiet, and Madison lowered her head to the table as she cried. Sam didn't buy it. He continued.

"Years later, someone reentered Madison's life, someone she had never expected to see again."

Linus flipped to the next slide. A large picture of Maryanne Preston filled the screen. It wasn't a picture anyone had seen; instead, Cassandra had given it to Linus the night Sam dropped him off with two cups of coffee and a question.

"You knew her as Eve," Sam said as Madison lifted her head slightly and looked at the screen. "You didn't know she was grifting Peyton, and she didn't know you were dating Carey. But there you were, a chance meeting at the golf course. Eventually, she showed you something, didn't she? A letter in a plastic bag?"

At the mention of the letter, Madison's crying stopped mid-breath. She lifted her head from the table, the color draining from her face.

"You have it?" Sam asked Beaumont.

Beaumont reached inside his jacket and pulled out the letter, in a plastic evidence bag, holding it high enough for everyone to see the letters that had been cut from the magazines and newspaper articles to form the words.

"*If you don't leave him alone, I will kill you.*"

Sam let the words hang in the air before continuing. "It was thought by the police that Maryanne had received this from someone she was blackmailing, but that's not what it was. It was Madison who created this seventeen years ago and left it to Juliet at her house. Maryanne was there when the letter slipped in; she read it and followed Madison. I suspect Juliet was on her way home, and the two girls met, then went into the woods. Maryanne must have followed and seen the whole *accident,* if it was even an accident."

Again, Carey pushed against the officer's grip, but the two hands on his shoulders held him in place. "Maddy," he said. "Tell me he's lying."

Madison said nothing. She didn't look at Carey.

"Why are you doing this?" Carey asked Sam.

"Don't blame me for any of this," Sam said, his eyes never leaving Madison. "She demanded money from you back then, didn't she? Some large amount? She knew where you lived, in that big house through the woods that you told me about, and she knew your family had money. She was probably happy her half-sister was gone, if anything, so she took that money and disappeared. You thought that was it. You'd never have to see her again. But then, out of nowhere, she was back in your life, worming her way into the family you had already wormed your way into.

"At some point, she demanded money again. She showed you the letter that she had kept after all these years, the proof she needed to start demanding money. According to a former roommate, Eve had a couple of windfalls while they lived together. I believe one of those windfalls was you paying her. How much was it? I bet the first time you paid her, it was exactly $27,000. Am I right?"

Sam wondered if Madison would answer him, but she stayed silent.

"She used that cash to change her identity. It gave her a new name, a new Social Security number, driver's license. Pretty much everything she needed to become Maryanne Preston. As she learned about you, she also learned you had gotten yourself inside the Layne family. She learned about Peyton and thought she'd found herself a winning lottery ticket in him, but then, she kept demanding money from you at the same time. You weren't happy about that. Then Emmitt died, and you saw your opportunity. Take out Maryanne right there, in front of everyone. You didn't know Peyton would receive the bulk of the estate, giving motives to everyone else in the room, but you wanted this to happen with his family around. They would all blame each other, and no one would look your way."

"What made *you* look her way?" Emily asked Sam.

"I wasn't, not until that dinner party you put together. While Brock and Dexter were arguing, Brock asked a very important question. Why did she care so much? Why did she care what would happen with the golf course? Was it because she cared about Carey?" He looked down at Madison. "No, you never cared about Carey. I'm not sure if you ever cared about any of us. It was because you needed him to have the golf course so you could protect what you buried underneath that sand trap."

"It's not true," Carey yelled.

Sam ignored him and kept at Madison: "When you left the room to allow Carey to cope with the results of the will reading, while you called your mom, you made a quick stop to the kitchen, found Maryanne's bright orange drink, scraped pieces from a fruit and nut bar into it. You knew she had the same allergies as Peyton."

Sam walked toward the center of the room toward Linus. He reached into Linus's bag and pulled out a green wrapper.

"You remember giving me this?"

Madison's eyes flicked to the wrapper in Sam's hand. Her face tightened, but she stayed silent.

"What is that?" Carey asked.

Sam handed the wrapper to Beaumont. "It's the wrapper from the fruit-and-nut bar you gave me last week after league. Remember, the kitchen was closed, and I was starving." He told Beaumont. "I assume you can match this to what was found in Maryanne's drink?"

Beaumont handed the wrapper to another officer. "Get this tested."

"You had it all planned," Sam continued. "You had replaced the EpiPen in her purse with the one you tampered with, the one you put the rat poison into. She would drink the spritz, have a reaction, then inject herself. It would kill her. You would be free of everything." Sam looked at Carey as he spoke these words, attempting to get him to understand what Madison had done. "The problem was, Peyton drank from her glass first. He had the reaction, and she hit him with the EpiPen, killing him."

"Madison?" Carey said. "You didn't?"

"She did," Sam said firmly. "And when Maryanne didn't die that night, she came up with a backup plan. Meet her, talk to her about the blackmail, ask her to stop since she had ended up with most of your father's inheritance."

Sam didn't wait for Linus to click the mouse this time; he leaned down and pressed the right arrow key on the laptop's keyboard. The next slide showed a list of transactions from an offshore bank account they had traced to Madison's business. Uncle Bruce had come through. According to what they were looking at, once a month, large amounts of money had been transferred from that account.

"Every month, you sent her cash, a percentage of your profits."

"From the looks of it," Beaumont said, stepping into the pavilion for the first time. "It was a very large percentage."

Sam said, "I'm guessing late in your round of golf, Maryanne finally told you she wouldn't be stopping anything. She had her money to live on with Peyton gone, but you would continue to pay. Your cash would be her fun money. She didn't even need it. She just wanted to keep messing with you. I bet she even said that to you, didn't she?"

He stood in front of her and bent down, staring into her eyes across the table.

"You got angry, and you beat her to death."

Chapter Thirty-Eight

"Carey was there by himself that night. He was always there by himself on Tuesdays after they closed. After you killed her, you left, found a phone and called the police, anonymously reporting that there was a dead body at the golf course and that they needed to get there."

Sam had never learned if or how she had made the call from the police, but it was the only missing piece he had, and it had to fit, so he ran with it.

"The police would find him in the building, already know the history from interviewing people after Peyton died and immediately arrest him. Did you frame him on purpose, or was that a happy accident?"

Madison finally looked up. Her face had changed, contorted into something Sam had never seen before. Her nostrils flared. Her face was red, and she was sweating.

"That's a great story," she said. Her voice shook. "But all you have is a fruit-and-nut wrapper that anyone can buy anywhere, a letter you can't prove I wrote and a bunch of transactions my very successful business made as I moved my money around." She pointed at Kristie. "What about her?"

"Me?" Kristie asked. "I didn't do anything."

"I'm not the only one who left the room at the will reading, and you've already shown that she wanted revenge against Peyton and Maryanne." She raised both hands, one pointing toward Brock and another toward Dexter. "And these two idiots are committing federal crimes. Peyton and Maryanne could have easily found out and threatened them. You've got nothing on me. You yourself even said Maryanne could have killed Peyton."

"I'm sure when the good detective over there compares your fingerprints to the unknowns on the letter, he'll find they match."

"Good luck proving it had anything to do with the murder."

"Go to Maryanne's transactions," he said to Linus, hoping Uncle Bruce had come through a second time.

He smiled as a list of Maryanne's transactions filled the screen; the amounts and dates of the money going into her account matched exactly what had come out of Madison's, including the very first transaction, an even twenty-seven thousand dollars.

"No wonder you were broke and I was buying your dinner every week. She was bleeding you dry."

"Another coincidence," Madison said. "She lent me money. I was paying her back. You have nothing concrete. This is all speculation."

"Next slide," Sam said.

Linus switched to the next slide. It showed the two drawings he had made of the necklaces, one from Libby's picture and the other from what Beaumont had shown him.

"Recognize that?" Sam asked.

"Two photos of two necklaces? I've never seen either of those necklaces before in my life."

"It's not two necklaces, Madison. It's the same necklace. I know it, and you know it. You ripped that Double J necklace off Juliet's dead body before you buried her, then you went away to college in a small town about two hours south of here. You took that necklace to a jewelry store near your college. You asked the man there to melt down the Js and turn them into that heart." Sam pointed to the photo of the necklace on the right.

She shrugged. "Prove it."

Linus switched to the next slide. Sam didn't even have to turn around to look at the screen. Madison's expression said it all.

"That's the receipt, and that's your signature at the bottom. That necklace didn't come off Maryanne as she was killed. It came off you as you beat her to death."

Beaumont walked toward Madison. "Miss York, please put your hands behind your back." He put handcuffs on her. "You have the right to remain silent."

Madison's shoulders fell as Beaumont clicked the handcuffs shut. Her voice came out thin, quiet, as if she were begging.

"You promised," she said. "You said you wouldn't tell anyone."

"I said I'd excuse the one you claimed was an accident, but you took that necklace from her, melted it down and wore it like a trophy, like a hunter who hangs the heads of his kills on his walls so he can always be reminded of what he'd done? I'll never excuse that."

"It's not true," Carey said. He turned to Madison. "How can it be true?"

"He's lying. He's not telling you the whole truth, baby. I swear. He made up everything to cover up the fact that he kissed me after dinner last Friday. He feels guilty about it. He's afraid I'll tell his little girlfriend, and she'll break up with him."

Carey went rigid, his face blank as if his brain needed a few seconds to comprehend, then the anger hit. "You kissed her?" he yelled.

He rushed at Sam, but Beaumont grabbed Carey by his collar and yanked him back. Carey's legs gave out, and he hit the cement. Beaumont quickly took the handcuffs off Carey and rolled him over.

"You're being let off the hook, Mr. Layne. You're not a suspect anymore, so calm the hell down." He motioned to Brock and Dexter and told Jacobs, "Bring those two along. I have some questions for them too."

Jacobs and two other officers led Brock and Dexter toward the path with Allen following behind them. Sam shook his head at the thought of the Layne family still needing Allen and Allen still taking their money.

Beaumont walked Madison past Sam and Carey. She brushed against Sam's shoulder, saying nothing, keeping her eyes on the concrete.

Carey slammed his fist against the picnic table hard enough to rattle it. Sam flinched. Heat crawled up his neck, but he kept his mouth shut.

Another officer grabbed Carey's arm. "Come on, Mr. Layne. Let's get you downtown and formally released."

Emily also followed, looking bedraggled, leaving only Sam, Scott, Libby and Linus in the pavilion. The lamps hummed, and the whine of the golf carts' engines grew quieter as they disappeared over the hill.

"You okay?" Libby asked Sam.

He nodded.

"When did you know?"

"At the dinner party, when Brock asked her why it mattered so much. I tried everything I could to push it out of my head. But then, last night, it found its way back in while I was looking at the printouts from the round of golf the second person played with Maryanne the night she was killed. You and I have played with Madison at least a hundred times. That person got around the course the same way she does, especially thirteen."

"I'm sorry," Libby said.

"Me too," he whispered.

Linus moved next to him. "What are you going to do next?"

"I don't know. I feel so guilty about that kiss, and I have to tell Dani about it before she finds out from someone else."

"You said she kissed you. How are you guilty of anything?"

Sam took a breath. "Because for a brief second, I enjoyed it, and I didn't immediately stop."

We met Libby Price in this book. She is a reporter for The River Street Register.

She followed this story through the couple weeks it happened. Check out her articles here.

www.jerryevanoff.com/RiverStreetRegister

Ready for Book 3? It will be released on November 10th, 2026.

Depending on the date you're reading this, you can either preorder it or order it here:

www.jerryevanoff.com

Do you enjoy Science Fiction?

I also have a science fiction series about a guy who travels through time, you know, your typical Marty McFly type of guy who does something in the past that mucks up the future. There are currently two books in the series.

It's a mix of Back to the Future and Lost

If it sounds like something that could be for you, check out my website, www.jerryevanoff.com for more information.

You can also get a free novella called Origins by signing up at my website.

Go to **www.jerryevanoff.com.**

Thank you so much to everyone who helped me write this book, including my mom and dad, my sister, my friends and the rest of the people around me.

Thanks to my writer's group as always for telling me when I'm doing something wrong and complimenting me when I'm doing something right.

Thanks to 100Covers for doing my cover, Ellie Pilcher for helping with marketing and my amazing editor: CB Moore.

Jerry Evanoff decided a few years after his 40th birthday that he wanted to write. After writing about Big Brother (yep, the TV show) for many years and thinking up scenarios where he was the hero in everyday life situations (like thwarting a bank robbery or saving a kitten), he decided to write a series about something he wished he could do.

Travel through Time

He sat down at his keyboard, and almost three years later, he had his masterpiece, a story about a guy (in no way based on Jerry) who traveled through time, mucked up the future and had to fix it by not sleeping with his mother...and probably doing other stuff too.

But then, after watching way too many episodes of Perry Mason, a show that came out 20 years before Jerry's birth, he felt like he needed to write books where people died, and an amateur sleuth (in no way based on Jerry), solved the case and got the girl.

Jerry here: Okay. I need to stop for a moment. I feel like I'm writing a terrible match.com profile, but for some reason, I'm writing it in the third person. From here on out, I'm doing this in the first person. Here we go...

In my other life, I'm a full-time web developer. I kinda teeter that line between complete and utter nerd and sports-loving non-nerd. If I'm not outside golfing (which is pretty much the only time I go outside...seriously, going outside to take my garbage to the street is a chore), I'm probably at my computer checking my fantasy football scores, eating chicken quesadillas and watching Perry Mason, MST3K, or Rifftrax.

I decided to write one day while I was reading the I Am Number Four Series. A major character was killed off, and I said out loud: "I can write better than that!"

Whether or not I did is a question I will go ahead and answer myself: Probably not, but according to my mom, I'm a genius.

Although I think legally she has to say that.

www.ingramcontent.com/pod-product-compliance
Lightning Source LLC
LaVergne TN
LVHW020708110826
845149LV00012B/2165

9798995749417